GN HERNAND
0003000055265
Is this how you see me?
Hernandez, Jaime,
ATCHISON
2019-05-21

WITHDRAWN

W9-AHR-239

IS THIS HOW YOU SEE ME?

JAIME HERNANDEZ

FANTAGRAPHICS BOOKS

FANTAGRAPHICS BOOKS INC.
7563 Lake City Way NE
Seattle, Washington, 98115

Editor and Associate Publisher: Eric Reynolds
Book Design: Jacob Covey
Production: Paul Baresh
Publisher: Gary Groth

Is This How You See Me? is copyright © 2019 Jaime Hernandez. This
edition is copyright © 2019 Fantagraphics Books Inc. Permission to
reproduce content must be obtained from the author or publisher.
Is This How You See Me? was originally serialized in *Love and Rockets:
New Stories* numbers 7 and 8, as well as *Love and Rockets: Vol. IV*
numbers 1 through 5. All rights reserved.

ISBN 978-1-68396-182-6
Library of Congress Control Number: 2018949546

First printing: March 2019
Printed in China

CONTENTS

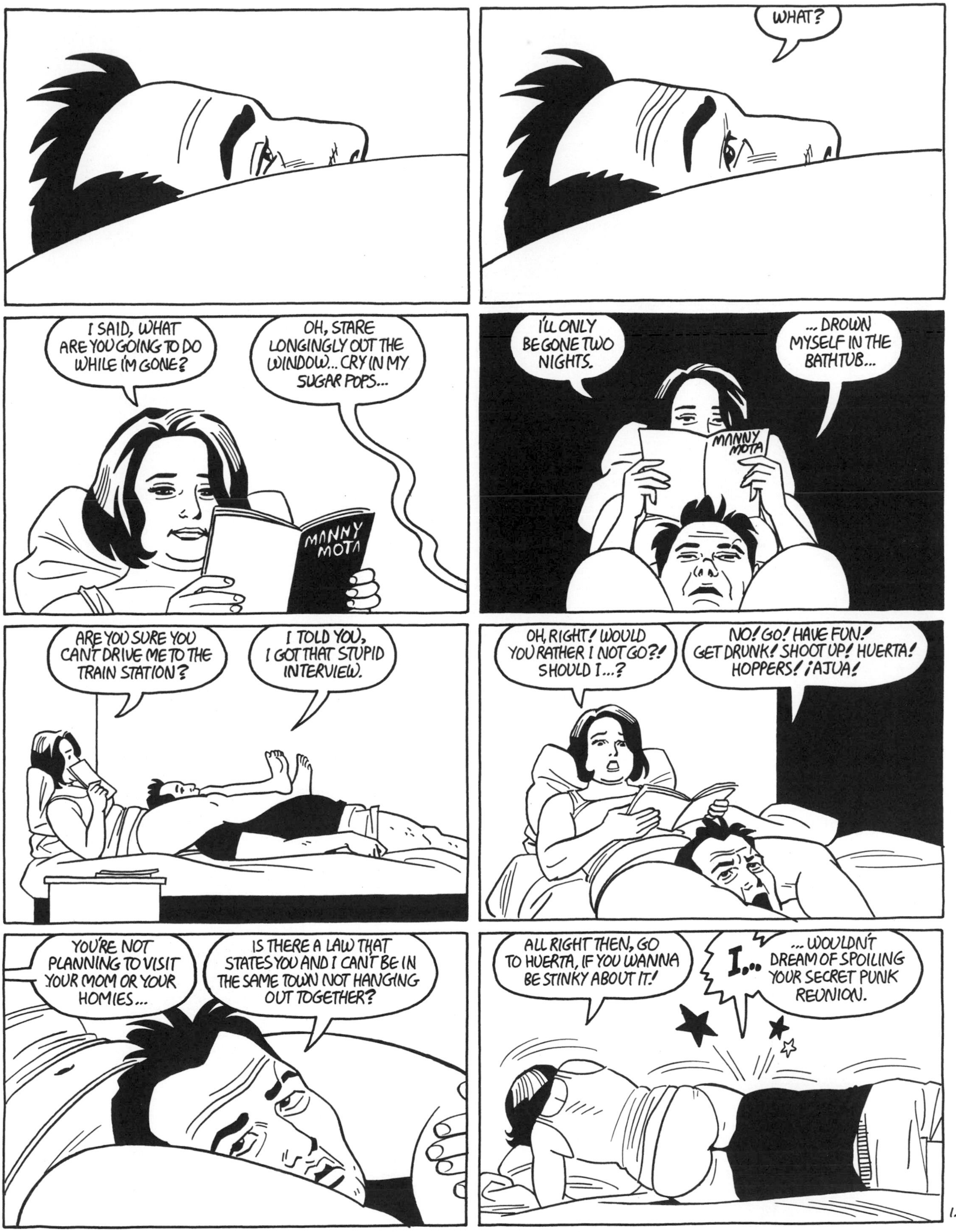
WHAT?
I SAID, WHAT ARE YOU GOING TO DO WHILE I'M GONE?
OH, STARE LONGINGLY OUT THE WINDOW... CRY IN MY SUGAR POPS...
MANNY MOTA
I'LL ONLY BE GONE TWO NIGHTS.
... DROWN MYSELF IN THE BATHTUB...
MANNY MOTA
ARE YOU SURE YOU CAN'T DRIVE ME TO THE TRAIN STATION?
I TOLD YOU, I GOT THAT STUPID INTERVIEW.
OH, RIGHT! WOULD YOU RATHER I NOT GO?! SHOULD I...?
NO! GO! HAVE FUN! GET DRUNK! SHOOT UP! HUERTA! HOPPERS! ¡AJUA!
YOU'RE NOT PLANNING TO VISIT YOUR MOM OR YOUR HOMIES...
IS THERE A LAW THAT STATES YOU AND I CAN'T BE IN THE SAME TOWN NOT HANGING OUT TOGETHER?
ALL RIGHT THEN, GO TO HUERTA, IF YOU WANNA BE STINKY ABOUT IT!
I...
... WOULDN'T DREAM OF SPOILING YOUR SECRET PUNK REUNION.
1.

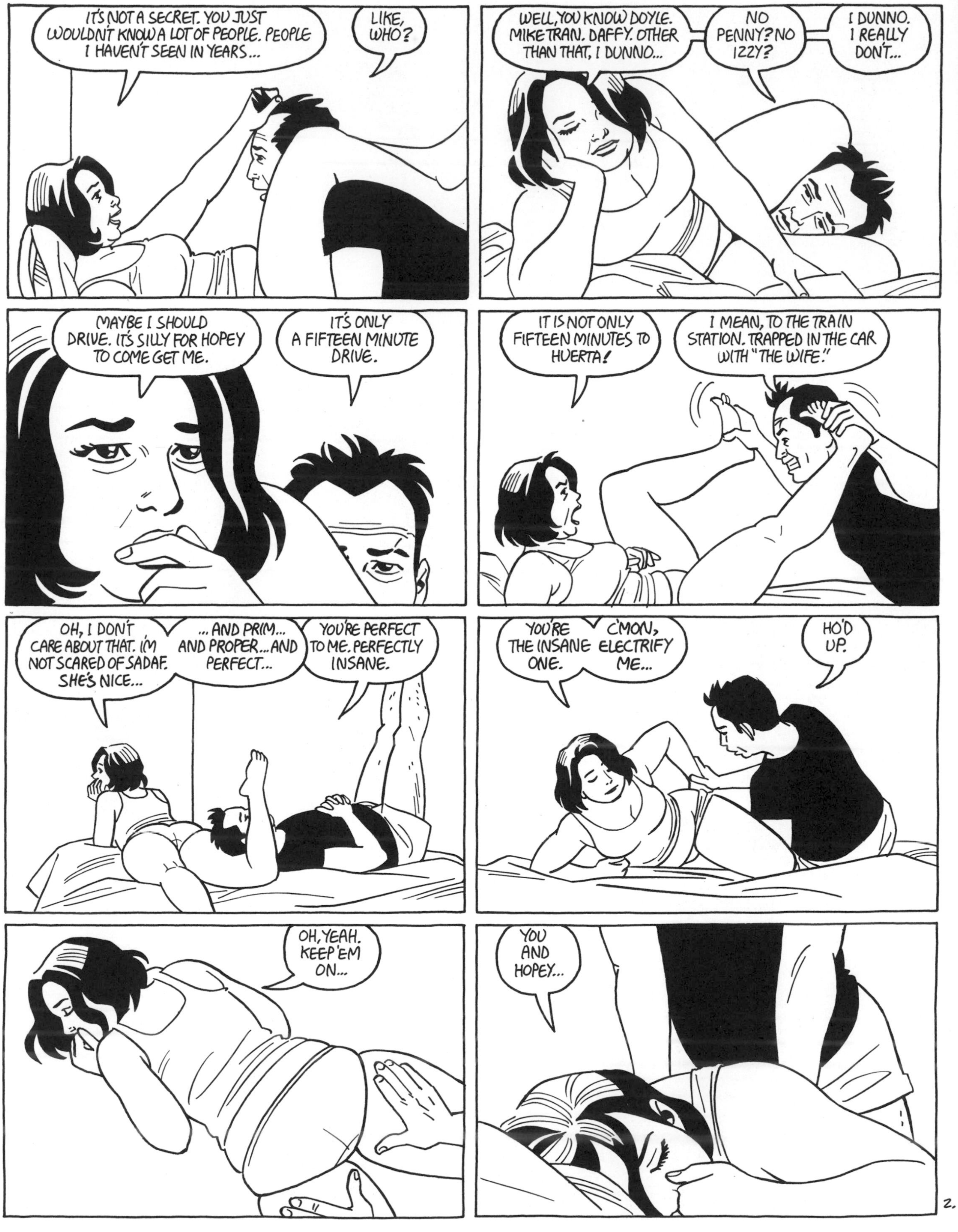

IT'S NOT A SECRET. YOU JUST WOULDN'T KNOW A LOT OF PEOPLE. PEOPLE I HAVEN'T SEEN IN YEARS...
LIKE, WHO?
WELL, YOU KNOW DOYLE. MIKE TRAN. DAFFY. OTHER THAN THAT, I DUNNO...
NO PENNY? NO IZZY?
I DUNNO. I REALLY DON'T...
MAYBE I SHOULD DRIVE. IT'S SILLY FOR HOPEY TO COME GET ME.
IT'S ONLY A FIFTEEN MINUTE DRIVE.
IT IS NOT ONLY FIFTEEN MINUTES TO HUERTA!
I MEAN, TO THE TRAIN STATION. TRAPPED IN THE CAR WITH "THE WIFE."
OH, I DON'T CARE ABOUT THAT. I'M NOT SCARED OF SADAF. SHE'S NICE...
...AND PRIM... AND PROPER... AND PERFECT...
YOU'RE PERFECT TO ME. PERFECTLY INSANE.
YOU'RE THE INSANE ONE.
C'MON, ELECTRIFY ME...
HO'D UP.
OH, YEAH. KEEP 'EM ON...
YOU AND HOPEY...
2.

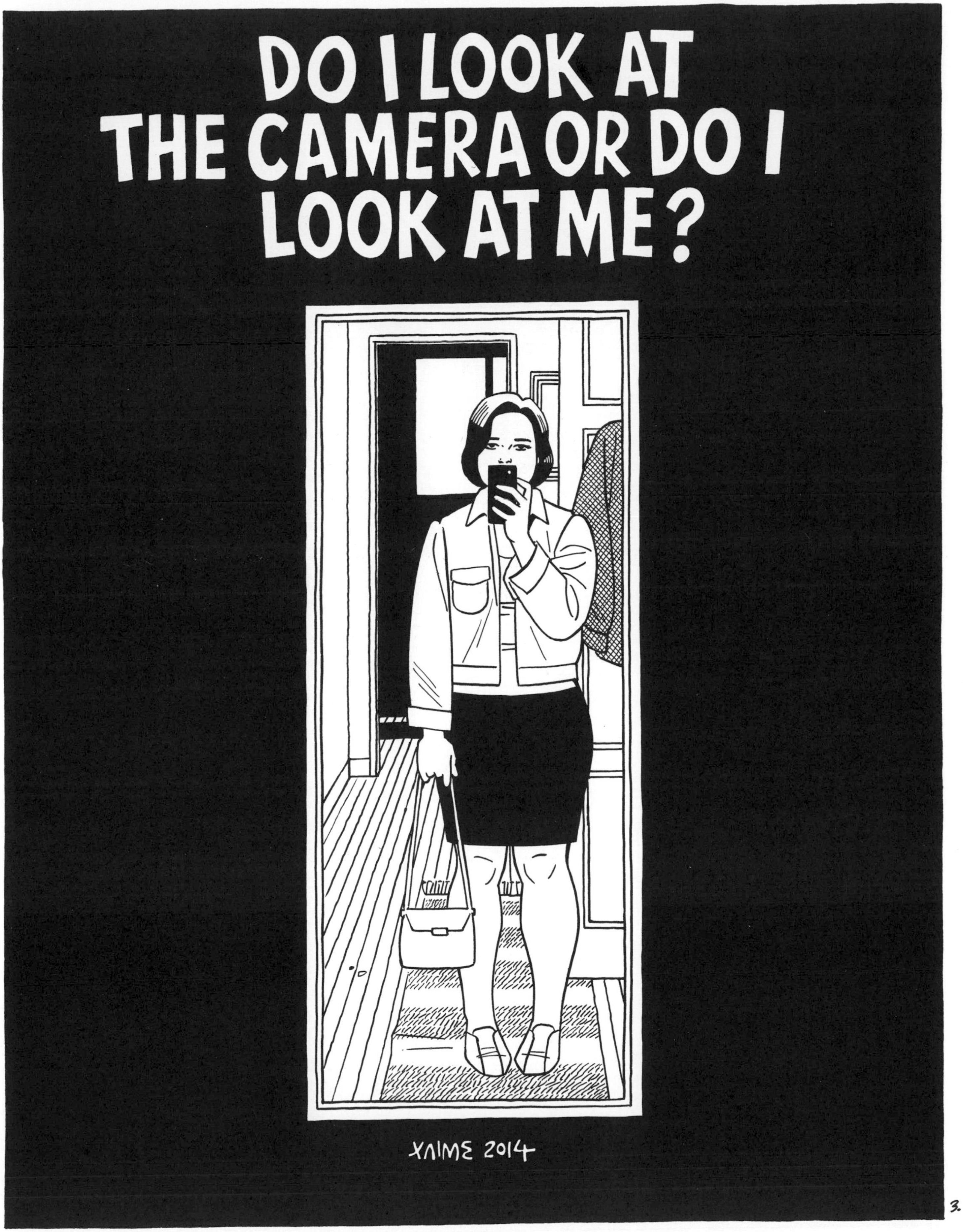
DO I LOOK AT THE CAMERA OR DO I LOOK AT ME?
XAIME 2014
3.

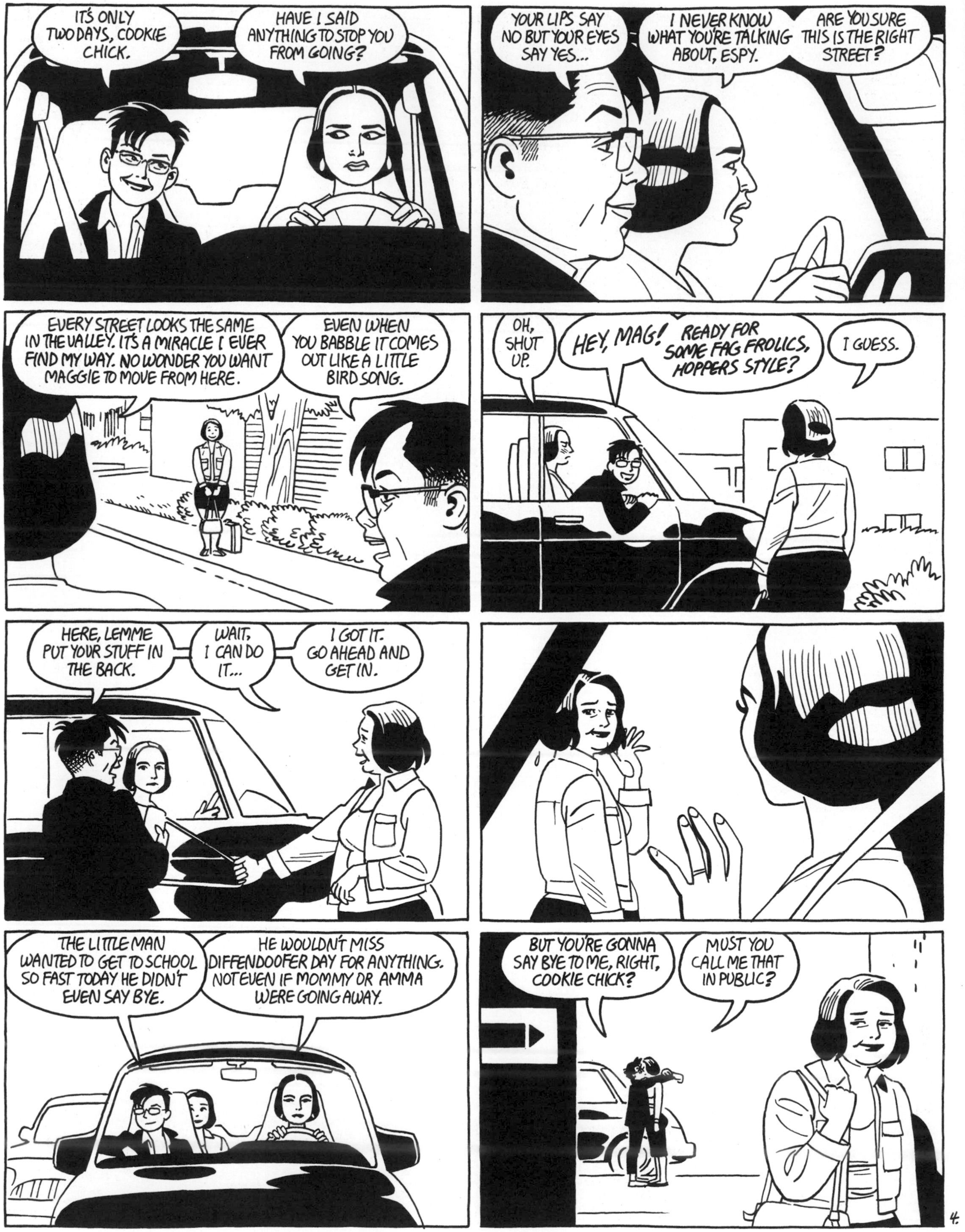
IT'S ONLY TWO DAYS, COOKIE CHICK.
HAVE I SAID ANYTHING TO STOP YOU FROM GOING?
YOUR LIPS SAY NO BUT YOUR EYES SAY YES...
I NEVER KNOW WHAT YOU'RE TALKING ABOUT, ESPY.
ARE YOU SURE THIS IS THE RIGHT STREET?
EVERY STREET LOOKS THE SAME IN THE VALLEY. IT'S A MIRACLE I EVER FIND MY WAY. NO WONDER YOU WANT MAGGIE TO MOVE FROM HERE.
EVEN WHEN YOU BABBLE IT COMES OUT LIKE A LITTLE BIRD SONG.
OH, SHUT UP.
HEY, MAG!
READY FOR SOME FAG FROLICS, HOPPERS STYLE?
I GUESS.
HERE, LEMME PUT YOUR STUFF IN THE BACK.
WAIT, I CAN DO IT...
I GOT IT. GO AHEAD AND GET IN.
THE LITTLE MAN WANTED TO GET TO SCHOOL SO FAST TODAY HE DIDN'T EVEN SAY BYE.
HE WOULDN'T MISS DIFFENDOOFER DAY FOR ANYTHING. NOT EVEN IF MOMMY OR AMMA WERE GOING AWAY.
BUT YOU'RE GONNA SAY BYE TO ME, RIGHT, COOKIE CHICK?
MUST YOU CALL ME THAT IN PUBLIC?
4.

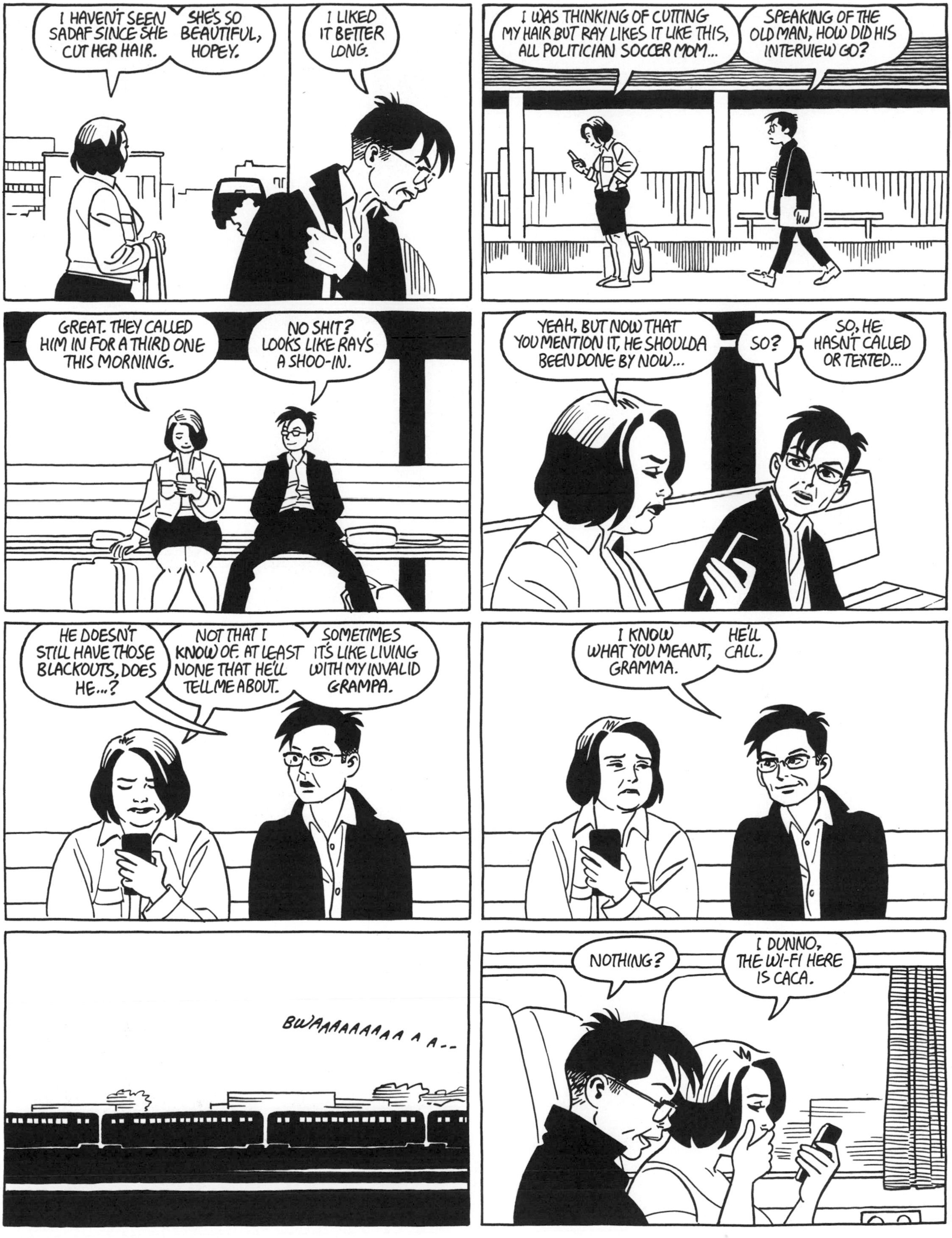
I HAVEN'T SEEN SADAF SINCE SHE CUT HER HAIR.
SHE'S SO BEAUTIFUL, HOPEY.
I LIKED IT BETTER LONG.
I WAS THINKING OF CUTTING MY HAIR BUT RAY LIKES IT LIKE THIS, ALL POLITICIAN SOCCER MOM...
SPEAKING OF THE OLD MAN, HOW DID HIS INTERVIEW GO?
GREAT. THEY CALLED HIM IN FOR A THIRD ONE THIS MORNING.
NO SHIT? LOOKS LIKE RAY'S A SHOO-IN.
YEAH, BUT NOW THAT YOU MENTION IT, HE SHOULDA BEEN DONE BY NOW...
SO?
SO, HE HASN'T CALLED OR TEXTED...
HE DOESN'T STILL HAVE THOSE BLACKOUTS, DOES HE...?
NOT THAT I KNOW OF. AT LEAST NONE THAT HE'LL TELL ME ABOUT.
SOMETIMES IT'S LIKE LIVING WITH MY INVALID GRAMPA.
I KNOW WHAT YOU MEANT, GRAMMA.
HE'LL CALL.
BWAAAAAAAAA A A...
NOTHING?
I DUNNO, THE WI-FI HERE IS CACA.

5.

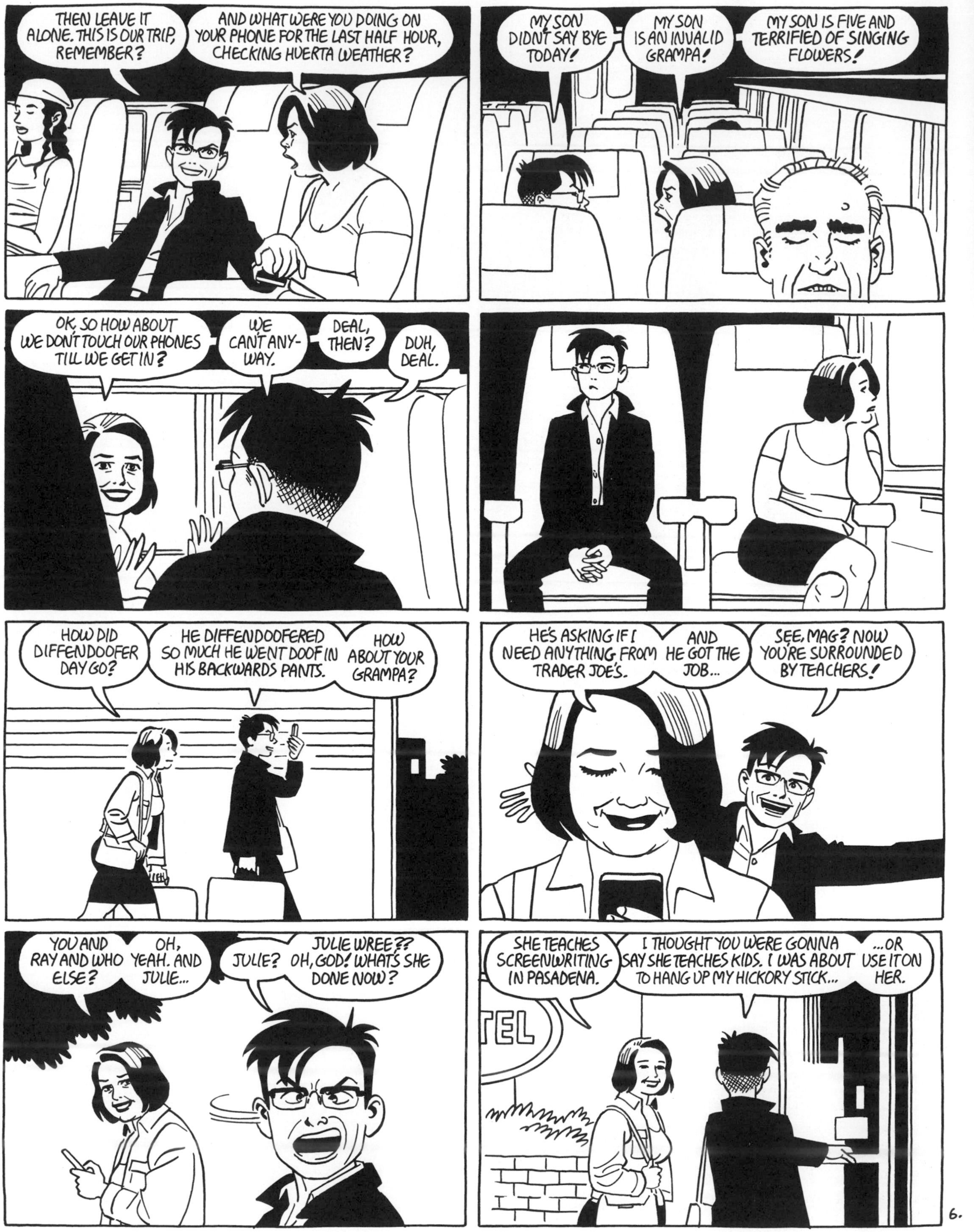

THEN LEAVE IT ALONE. THIS IS OUR TRIP, REMEMBER?
AND WHAT WERE YOU DOING ON YOUR PHONE FOR THE LAST HALF HOUR, CHECKING HUERTA WEATHER?
MY SON DIDN'T SAY BYE TODAY!
MY SON IS AN INVALID GRAMPA!
MY SON IS FIVE AND TERRIFIED OF SINGING FLOWERS!
OK, SO HOW ABOUT WE DON'T TOUCH OUR PHONES TILL WE GET IN?
WE CAN'T ANY-WAY.
DEAL, THEN?
DUH, DEAL.
HOW DID DIFFENDOOFER DAY GO?
HE DIFFENDOOFERED SO MUCH HE WENT DOOF IN HIS BACKWARDS PANTS.
HOW ABOUT YOUR GRAMPA?
HE'S ASKING IF I NEED ANYTHING FROM TRADER JOE'S.
AND HE GOT THE JOB...
SEE, MAG? NOW YOU'RE SURROUNDED BY TEACHERS!
YOU AND RAY AND WHO ELSE?
OH, YEAH. AND JULIE...
JULIE?
JULIE WREE?? OH, GOD! WHAT'S SHE DONE NOW?
SHE TEACHES SCREENWRITING IN PASADENA.
I THOUGHT YOU WERE GONNA SAY SHE TEACHES KIDS. I WAS ABOUT TO HANG UP MY HICKORY STICK...
...OR USE IT ON HER.
TEL
6.

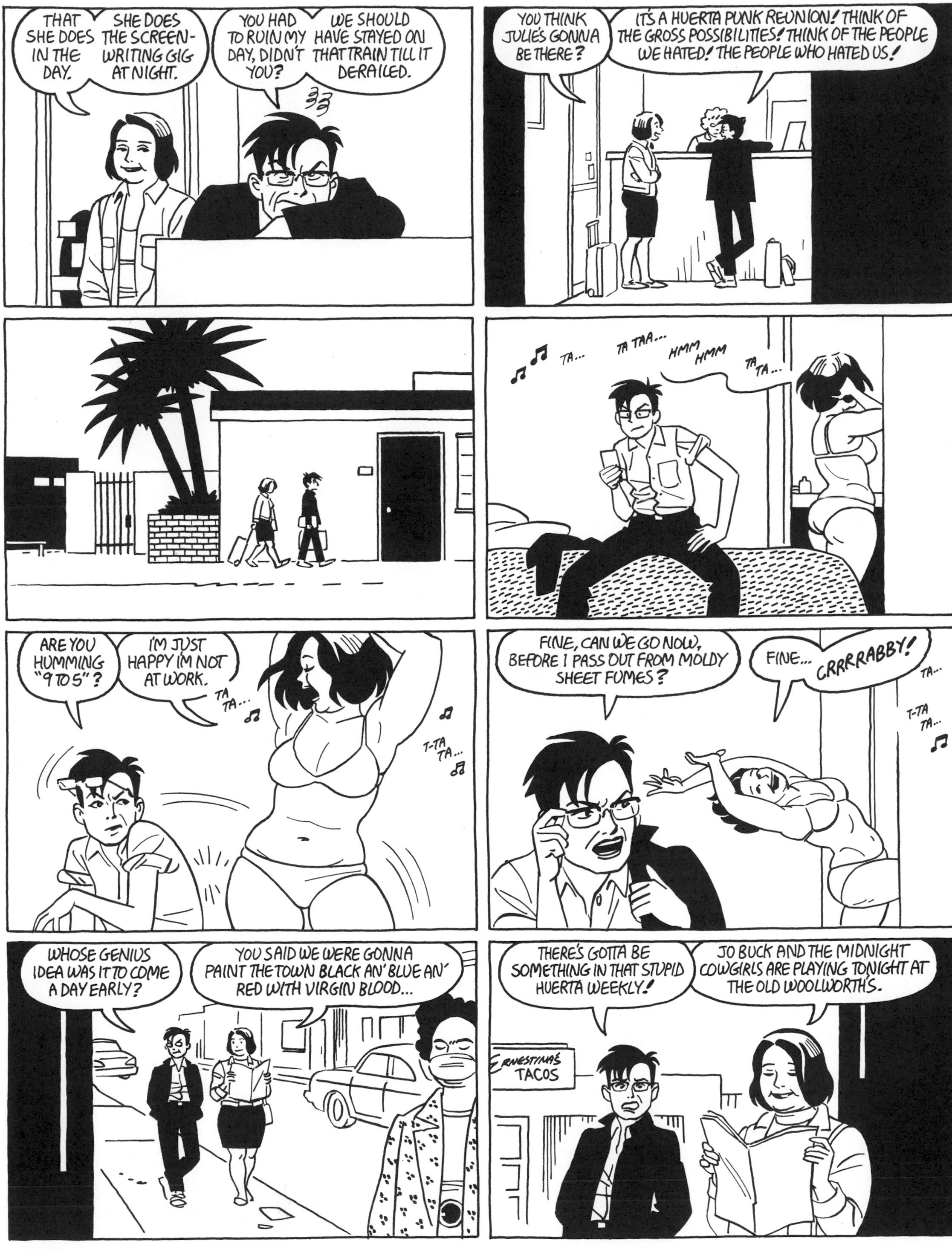
THAT SHE DOES IN THE DAY.
SHE DOES THE SCREEN-WRITING GIG AT NIGHT.
YOU HAD TO RUIN MY DAY, DIDN'T YOU?
WE SHOULD HAVE STAYED ON THAT TRAIN TILL IT DERAILED.
YOU THINK JULIE'S GONNA BE THERE?
IT'S A HUERTA PUNK REUNION! THINK OF THE GROSS POSSIBILITIES! THINK OF THE PEOPLE WE HATED! THE PEOPLE WHO HATED US!
TA... TA TAA... HMM HMM TA TA...
ARE YOU HUMMING "9 TO 5"?
I'M JUST HAPPY I'M NOT AT WORK.
TA TA...
T-TA TA...
FINE, CAN WE GO NOW, BEFORE I PASS OUT FROM MOLDY SHEET FUMES?
FINE... CRRRRABBY!
TA... T-TA TA...
WHOSE GENIUS IDEA WAS IT TO COME A DAY EARLY?
YOU SAID WE WERE GONNA PAINT THE TOWN BLACK AN' BLUE AN' RED WITH VIRGIN BLOOD...
THERE'S GOTTA BE SOMETHING IN THAT STUPID HUERTA WEEKLY!
JO BUCK AND THE MIDNIGHT COWGIRLS ARE PLAYING TONIGHT AT THE OLD WOOLWORTH'S.
ERNESTINA'S TACOS
7

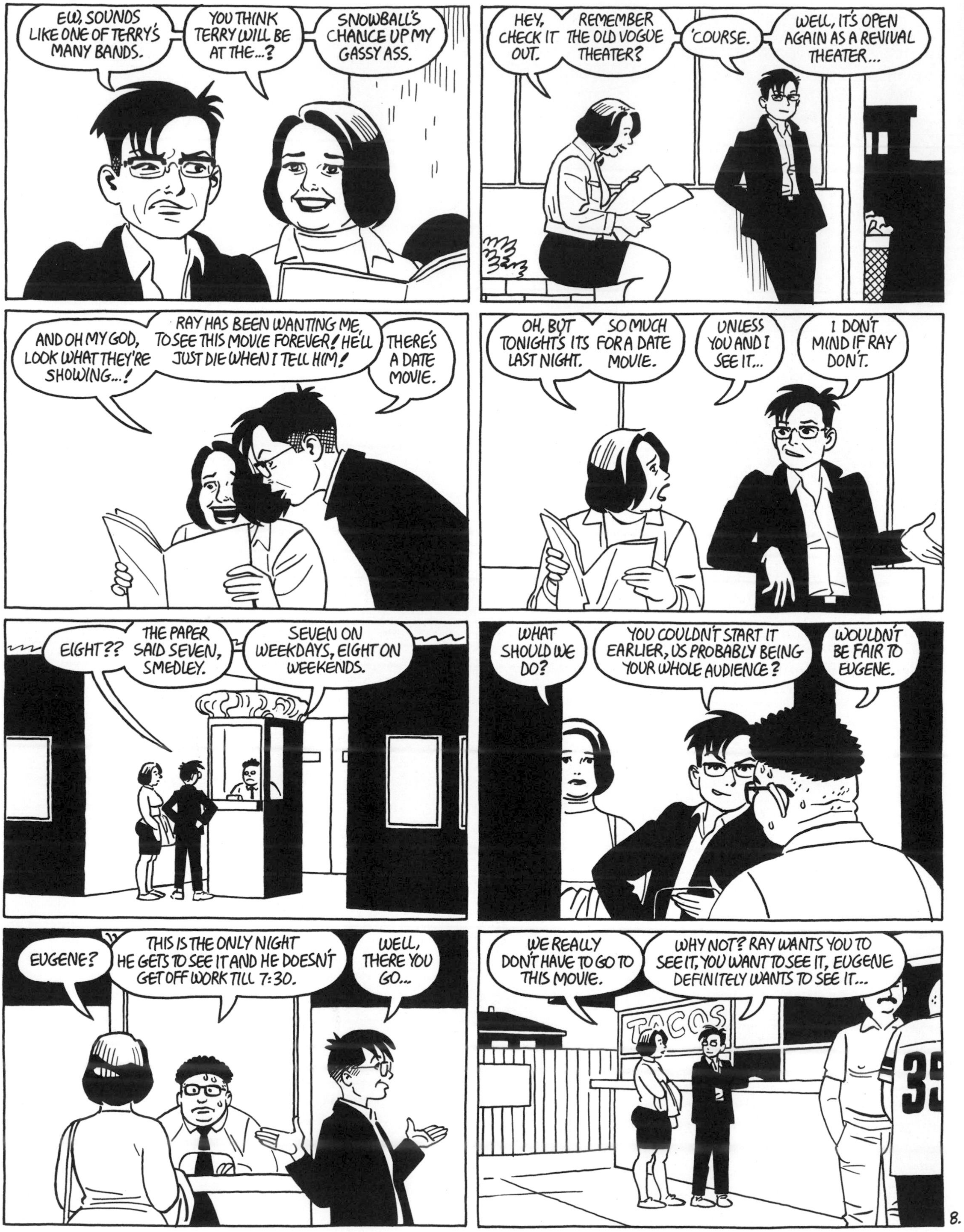
EW, SOUNDS LIKE ONE OF TERRY'S MANY BANDS.
YOU THINK TERRY WILL BE AT THE...?
SNOWBALL'S CHANCE UP MY GASSY ASS.
HEY, CHECK IT OUT.
REMEMBER THE OLD VOGUE THEATER?
'COURSE.
WELL, IT'S OPEN AGAIN AS A REVIVAL THEATER...
AND OH MY GOD, LOOK WHAT THEY'RE SHOWING...!
RAY HAS BEEN WANTING ME, TO SEE THIS MOVIE FOREVER! HE'LL JUST DIE WHEN I TELL HIM!
THERE'S A DATE MOVIE.
OH, BUT TONIGHT'S ITS LAST NIGHT.
SO MUCH FOR A DATE MOVIE.
UNLESS YOU AND I SEE IT...
I DON'T MIND IF RAY DON'T.
EIGHT??
THE PAPER SAID SEVEN, SMEDLEY.
SEVEN ON WEEKDAYS, EIGHT ON WEEKENDS.
WHAT SHOULD WE DO?
YOU COULDN'T START IT EARLIER, US PROBABLY BEING YOUR WHOLE AUDIENCE?
WOULDN'T BE FAIR TO EUGENE.
EUGENE?
THIS IS THE ONLY NIGHT HE GETS TO SEE IT AND HE DOESN'T GET OFF WORK TILL 7:30.
WELL, THERE YOU GO...
WE REALLY DON'T HAVE TO GO TO THIS MOVIE.
WHY NOT? RAY WANTS YOU TO SEE IT, YOU WANT TO SEE IT, EUGENE DEFINITELY WANTS TO SEE IT...
TACOS
35
8.

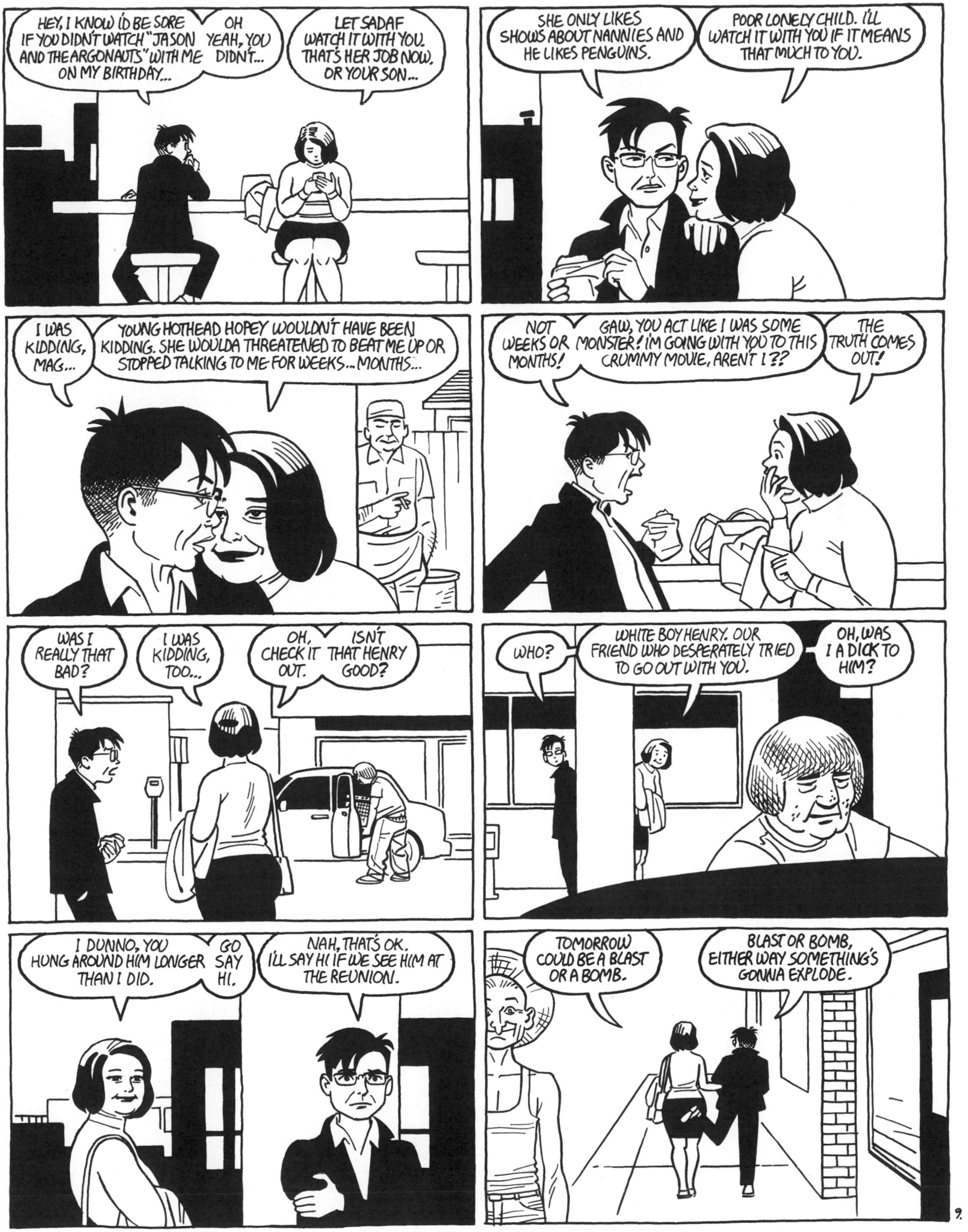
HEY, I KNOW I'D BE SORE IF YOU DIDN'T WATCH "JASON AND THE ARGONAUTS" WITH ME ON MY BIRTHDAY...
OH YEAH, YOU DIDN'T...
LET SADAF WATCH IT WITH YOU. THAT'S HER JOB NOW. OR YOUR SON...
SHE ONLY LIKES SHOWS ABOUT NANNIES AND HE LIKES PENGUINS.
POOR LONELY CHILD. I'LL WATCH IT WITH YOU IF IT MEANS THAT MUCH TO YOU.
I WAS KIDDING, MAG...
YOUNG HOTHEAD HOPEY WOULDN'T HAVE BEEN KIDDING. SHE WOULDA THREATENED TO BEAT ME UP OR STOPPED TALKING TO ME FOR WEEKS... MONTHS...
NOT WEEKS OR MONTHS!
GAW, YOU ACT LIKE I WAS SOME MONSTER! I'M GOING WITH YOU TO THIS CRUMMY MOVIE, AREN'T I??
THE TRUTH COMES OUT!
WAS I REALLY THAT BAD?
I WAS KIDDING, TOO...
OH, CHECK IT OUT.
ISN'T THAT HENRY GOOD?
WHO?
WHITE BOY HENRY. OUR FRIEND WHO DESPERATELY TRIED TO GO OUT WITH YOU.
OH, WAS I A DICK TO HIM?
I DUNNO, YOU HUNG AROUND HIM LONGER THAN I DID.
GO SAY HI.
NAH, THAT'S OK. I'LL SAY HI IF WE SEE HIM AT THE REUNION.
TOMORROW COULD BE A BLAST OR A BOMB.
BLAST OR BOMB, EITHER WAY SOMETHING'S GONNA EXPLODE.
9.

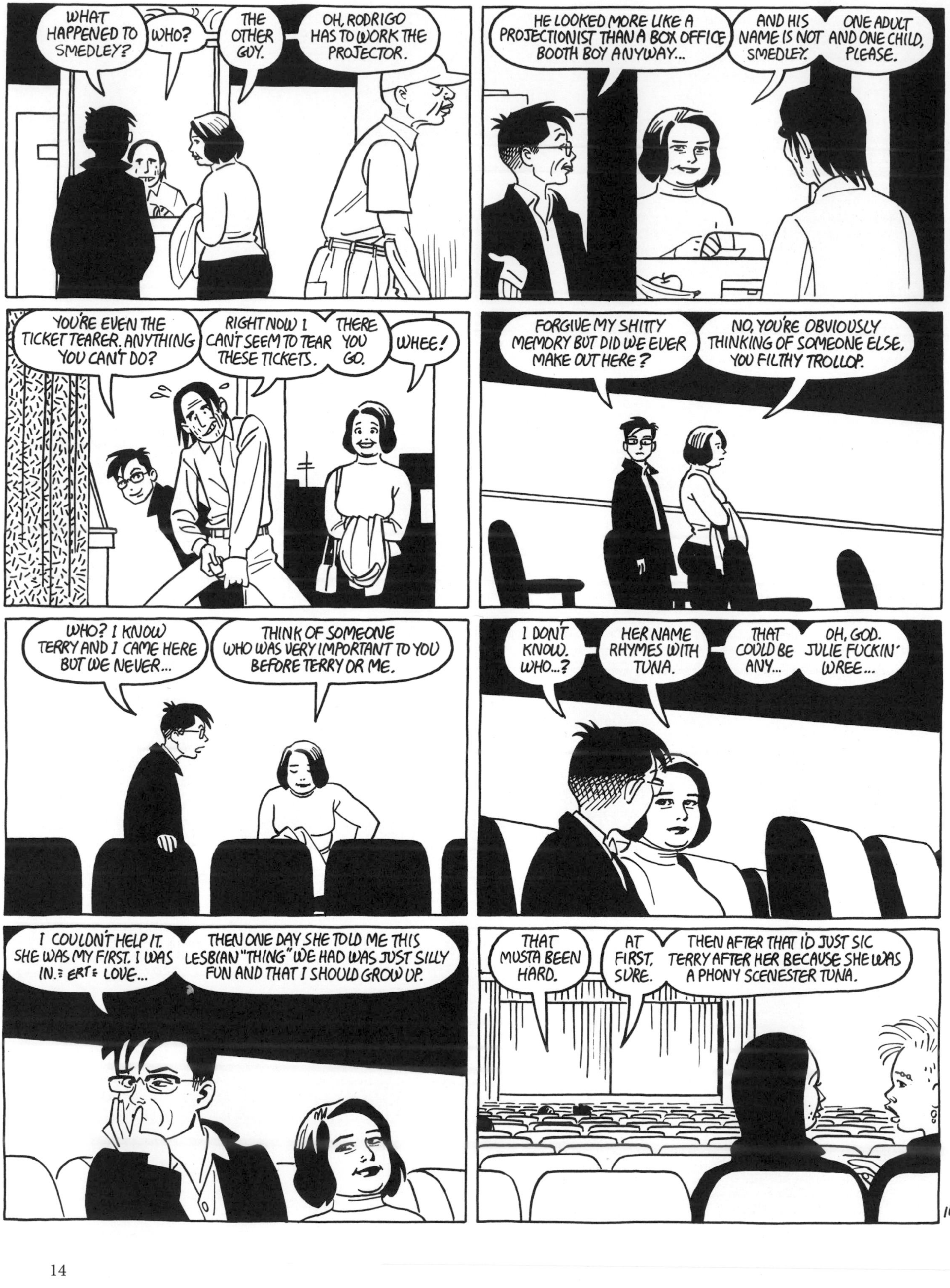
WHAT HAPPENED TO SMEDLEY?
WHO?
THE OTHER GUY.
OH, RODRIGO HAS TO WORK THE PROJECTOR.
HE LOOKED MORE LIKE A PROJECTIONIST THAN A BOX OFFICE BOOTH BOY ANYWAY...
AND HIS NAME IS NOT SMEDLEY.
ONE ADULT AND ONE CHILD, PLEASE.
YOU'RE EVEN THE TICKET TEARER. ANYTHING YOU CAN'T DO?
RIGHT NOW I CAN'T SEEM TO TEAR THESE TICKETS.
THERE YOU GO.
WHEE!
FORGIVE MY SHITTY MEMORY BUT DID WE EVER MAKE OUT HERE?
NO, YOU'RE OBVIOUSLY THINKING OF SOMEONE ELSE, YOU FILTHY TROLLOP.
WHO? I KNOW TERRY AND I CAME HERE BUT WE NEVER...
THINK OF SOMEONE WHO WAS VERY IMPORTANT TO YOU BEFORE TERRY OR ME.
I DON'T KNOW. WHO...?
HER NAME RHYMES WITH TUNA.
THAT COULD BE ANY...
OH, GOD. JULIE FUCKIN' WREE...
I COULDN'T HELP IT. SHE WAS MY FIRST. I WAS IN. ≡ERT≡ LOVE...
THEN ONE DAY SHE TOLD ME THIS LESBIAN "THING" WE HAD WAS JUST SILLY FUN AND THAT I SHOULD GROW UP.
THAT MUSTA BEEN HARD.
AT FIRST, SURE.
THEN AFTER THAT I'D JUST SIC TERRY AFTER HER BECAUSE SHE WAS A PHONY SCENESTER TUNA.

10.

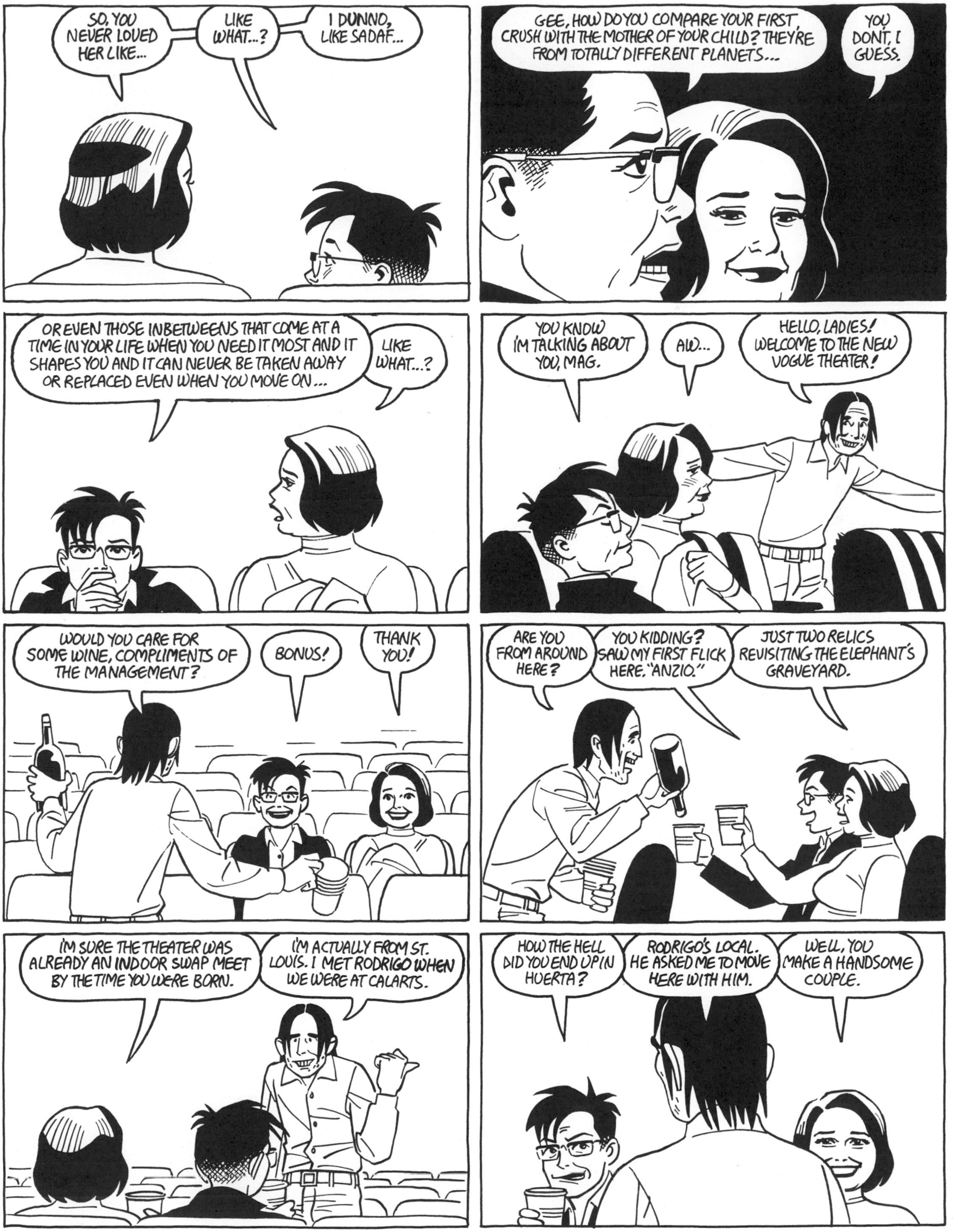
SO, YOU NEVER LOVED HER LIKE...
LIKE WHAT...?
I DUNNO, LIKE SADAF...
GEE, HOW DO YOU COMPARE YOUR FIRST, CRUSH WITH THE MOTHER OF YOUR CHILD? THEY'RE FROM TOTALLY DIFFERENT PLANETS...
YOU DONT, I GUESS.
OR EVEN THOSE INBETWEENS THAT COME AT A TIME IN YOUR LIFE WHEN YOU NEED IT MOST AND IT SHAPES YOU AND IT CAN NEVER BE TAKEN AWAY OR REPLACED EVEN WHEN YOU MOVE ON...
LIKE WHAT...?
YOU KNOW I'M TALKING ABOUT YOU, MAG.
AW...
HELLO, LADIES! WELCOME TO THE NEW VOGUE THEATER!
WOULD YOU CARE FOR SOME WINE, COMPLIMENTS OF THE MANAGEMENT?
BONUS!
THANK YOU!
ARE YOU FROM AROUND HERE?
YOU KIDDING? SAW MY FIRST FLICK HERE. "ANZIO."
JUST TWO RELICS REVISITING THE ELEPHANT'S GRAVEYARD.
I'M SURE THE THEATER WAS ALREADY AN INDOOR SWAP MEET BY THE TIME YOU WERE BORN.
I'M ACTUALLY FROM ST. LOUIS. I MET RODRIGO WHEN WE WERE AT CALARTS.
HOW THE HELL DID YOU END UP IN HUERTA?
RODRIGO'S LOCAL. HE ASKED ME TO MOVE HERE WITH HIM.
WELL, YOU MAKE A HANDSOME COUPLE.
11.

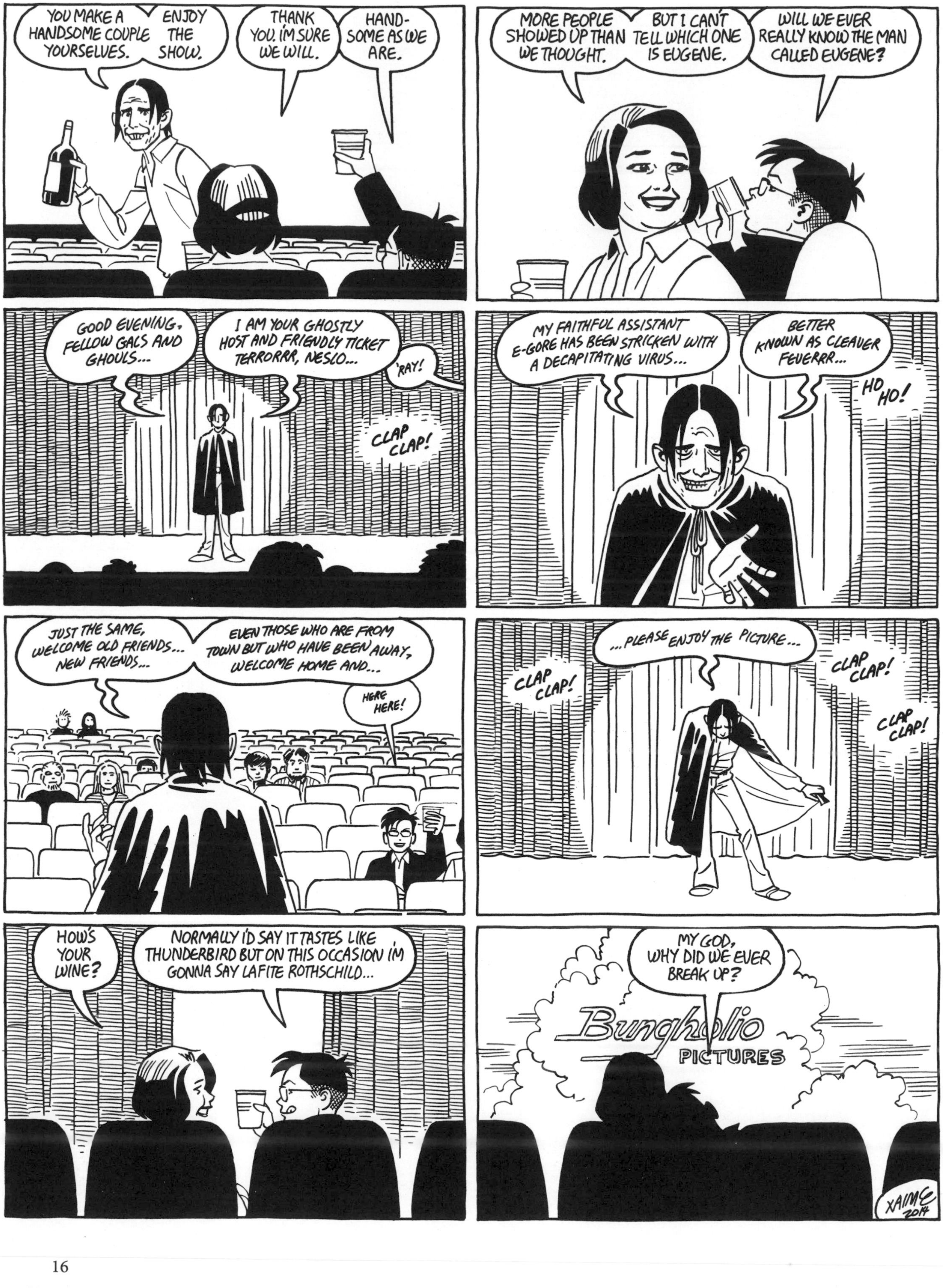
YOU MAKE A HANDSOME COUPLE YOURSELVES.
ENJOY THE SHOW.
THANK YOU. I'M SURE WE WILL.
HAND-SOME AS WE ARE.
MORE PEOPLE SHOWED UP THAN WE THOUGHT.
BUT I CAN'T TELL WHICH ONE IS EUGENE.
WILL WE EVER REALLY KNOW THE MAN CALLED EUGENE?
GOOD EVENING. FELLOW GALS AND GHOULS...
I AM YOUR GHOSTLY HOST AND FRIENDLY TICKET TERRORRR, NESCO...
'RAY!
CLAP CLAP!
MY FAITHFUL ASSISTANT E-GORE HAS BEEN STRICKEN WITH A DECAPITATING VIRUS...
BETTER KNOWN AS CLEAVER FEVERRR...
HO HO!
JUST THE SAME, WELCOME OLD FRIENDS... NEW FRIENDS...
EVEN THOSE WHO ARE FROM TOWN BUT WHO HAVE BEEN AWAY, WELCOME HOME AND...
HERE HERE!
...PLEASE ENJOY THE PICTURE...
CLAP CLAP!
CLAP CLAP!
CLAP CLAP!
HOW'S YOUR WINE?
NORMALLY I'D SAY IT TASTES LIKE THUNDERBIRD BUT ON THIS OCCASION I'M GONNA SAY LAFITE ROTHSCHILD...
MY GOD, WHY DID WE EVER BREAK UP?
Bungholio
PICTURES
XAIME 2014
12.

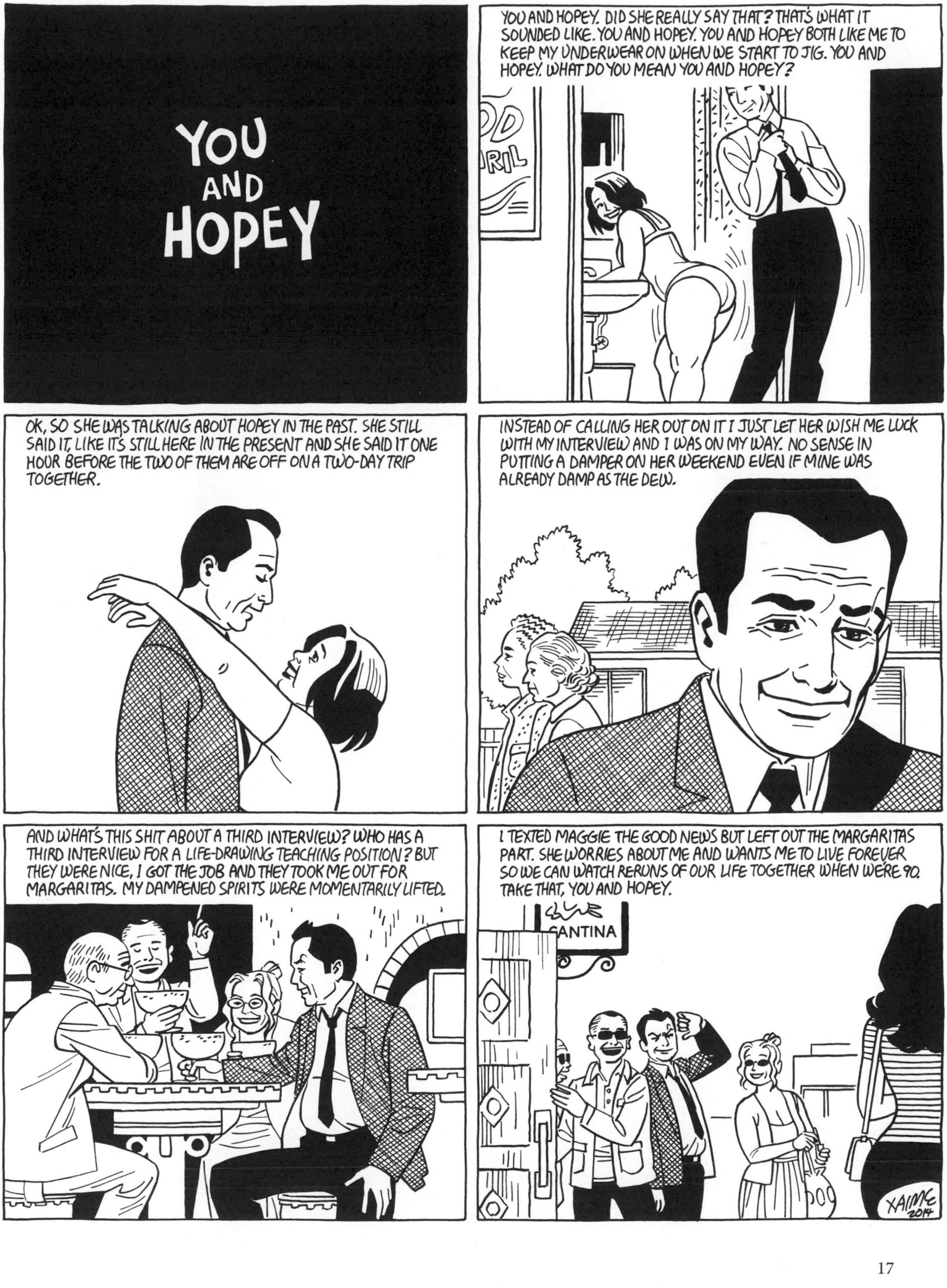
YOU AND HOPEY
YOU AND HOPEY. DID SHE REALLY SAY THAT? THAT'S WHAT IT SOUNDED LIKE. YOU AND HOPEY. YOU AND HOPEY BOTH LIKE ME TO KEEP MY UNDERWEAR ON WHEN WE START TO JIG. YOU AND HOPEY. WHAT DO YOU MEAN YOU AND HOPEY?
OK, SO SHE WAS TALKING ABOUT HOPEY IN THE PAST. SHE STILL SAID IT, LIKE IT'S STILL HERE IN THE PRESENT AND SHE SAID IT ONE HOUR BEFORE THE TWO OF THEM ARE OFF ON A TWO-DAY TRIP TOGETHER.
INSTEAD OF CALLING HER OUT ON IT I JUST LET HER WISH ME LUCK WITH MY INTERVIEW AND I WAS ON MY WAY. NO SENSE IN PUTTING A DAMPER ON HER WEEKEND EVEN IF MINE WAS ALREADY DAMP AS THE DEW.
AND WHAT'S THIS SHIT ABOUT A THIRD INTERVIEW? WHO HAS A THIRD INTERVIEW FOR A LIFE-DRAWING TEACHING POSITION? BUT THEY WERE NICE, I GOT THE JOB AND THEY TOOK ME OUT FOR MARGARITAS. MY DAMPENED SPIRITS WERE MOMENTARILY LIFTED.
I TEXTED MAGGIE THE GOOD NEWS BUT LEFT OUT THE MARGARITAS PART. SHE WORRIES ABOUT ME AND WANTS ME TO LIVE FOREVER SO WE CAN WATCH RERUNS OF OUR LIFE TOGETHER WHEN WE'RE 90. TAKE THAT, YOU AND HOPEY.
CANTINA
XAIME 2014

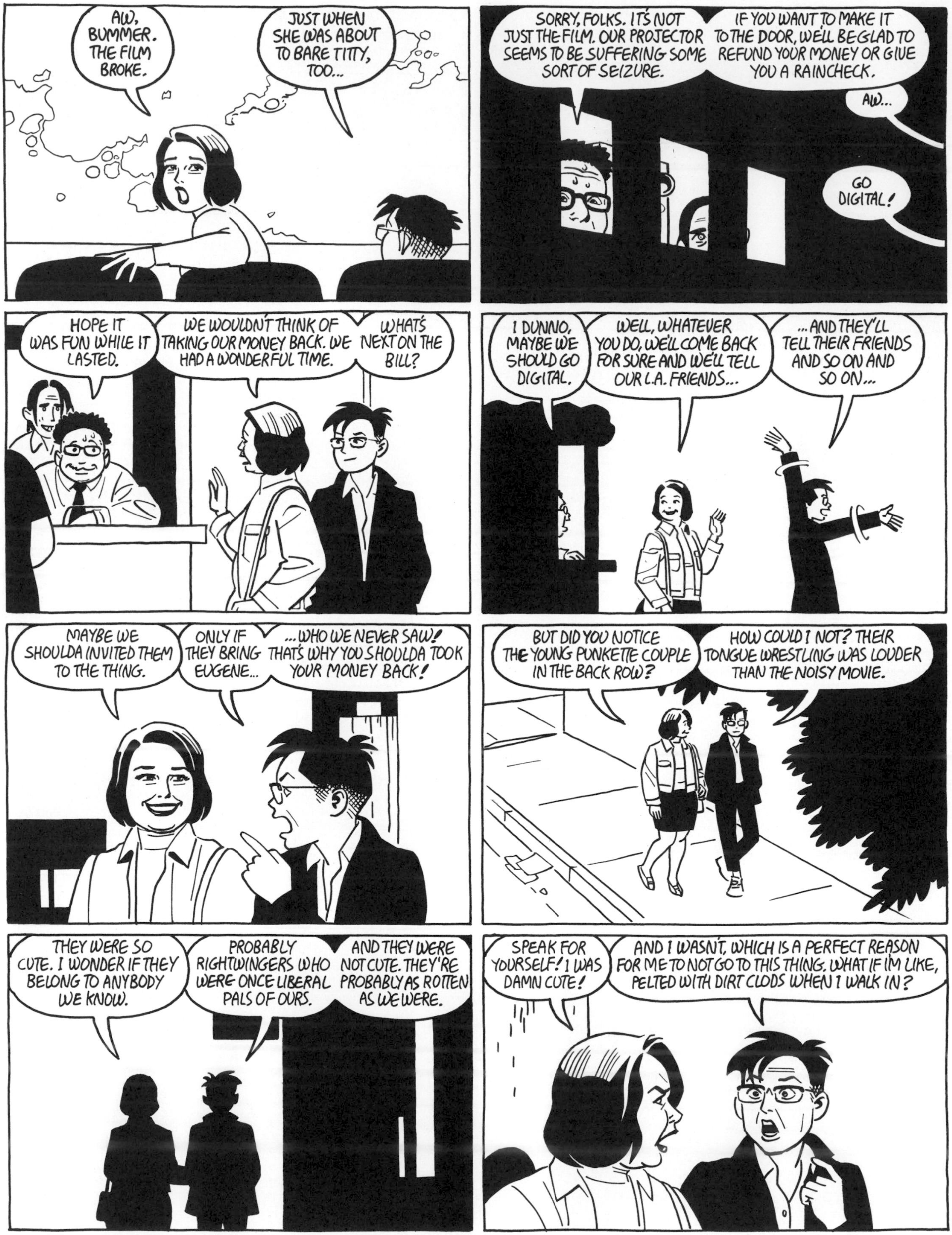
AW, BUMMER. THE FILM BROKE.
JUST WHEN SHE WAS ABOUT TO BARE TITTY, TOO...
SORRY, FOLKS. IT'S NOT JUST THE FILM. OUR PROJECTOR SEEMS TO BE SUFFERING SOME SORT OF SEIZURE.
IF YOU WANT TO MAKE IT TO THE DOOR, WE'LL BE GLAD TO REFUND YOUR MONEY OR GIVE YOU A RAINCHECK.
AW...
GO DIGITAL!
HOPE IT WAS FUN WHILE IT LASTED.
WE WOULDN'T THINK OF TAKING OUR MONEY BACK. WE HAD A WONDERFUL TIME.
WHAT'S NEXT ON THE BILL?
I DUNNO, MAYBE WE SHOULD GO DIGITAL.
WELL, WHATEVER YOU DO, WE'LL COME BACK FOR SURE AND WE'LL TELL OUR L.A. FRIENDS...
...AND THEY'LL TELL THEIR FRIENDS AND SO ON AND SO ON...
MAYBE WE SHOULDA INVITED THEM TO THE THING.
ONLY IF THEY BRING EUGENE...
...WHO WE NEVER SAW! THAT'S WHY YOU SHOULDA TOOK YOUR MONEY BACK!
BUT DID YOU NOTICE THE YOUNG PUNKETTE COUPLE IN THE BACK ROW?
HOW COULD I NOT? THEIR TONGUE WRESTLING WAS LOUDER THAN THE NOISY MOVIE.
THEY WERE SO CUTE. I WONDER IF THEY BELONG TO ANYBODY WE KNOW.
PROBABLY RIGHTWINGERS WHO WERE ONCE LIBERAL PALS OF OURS.
AND THEY WERE NOT CUTE. THEY'RE PROBABLY AS ROTTEN AS WE WERE.
SPEAK FOR YOURSELF! I WAS DAMN CUTE!
AND I WASN'T, WHICH IS A PERFECT REASON FOR ME TO NOT GO TO THIS THING. WHAT IF I'M LIKE, PELTED WITH DIRT CLODS WHEN I WALK IN?
1.

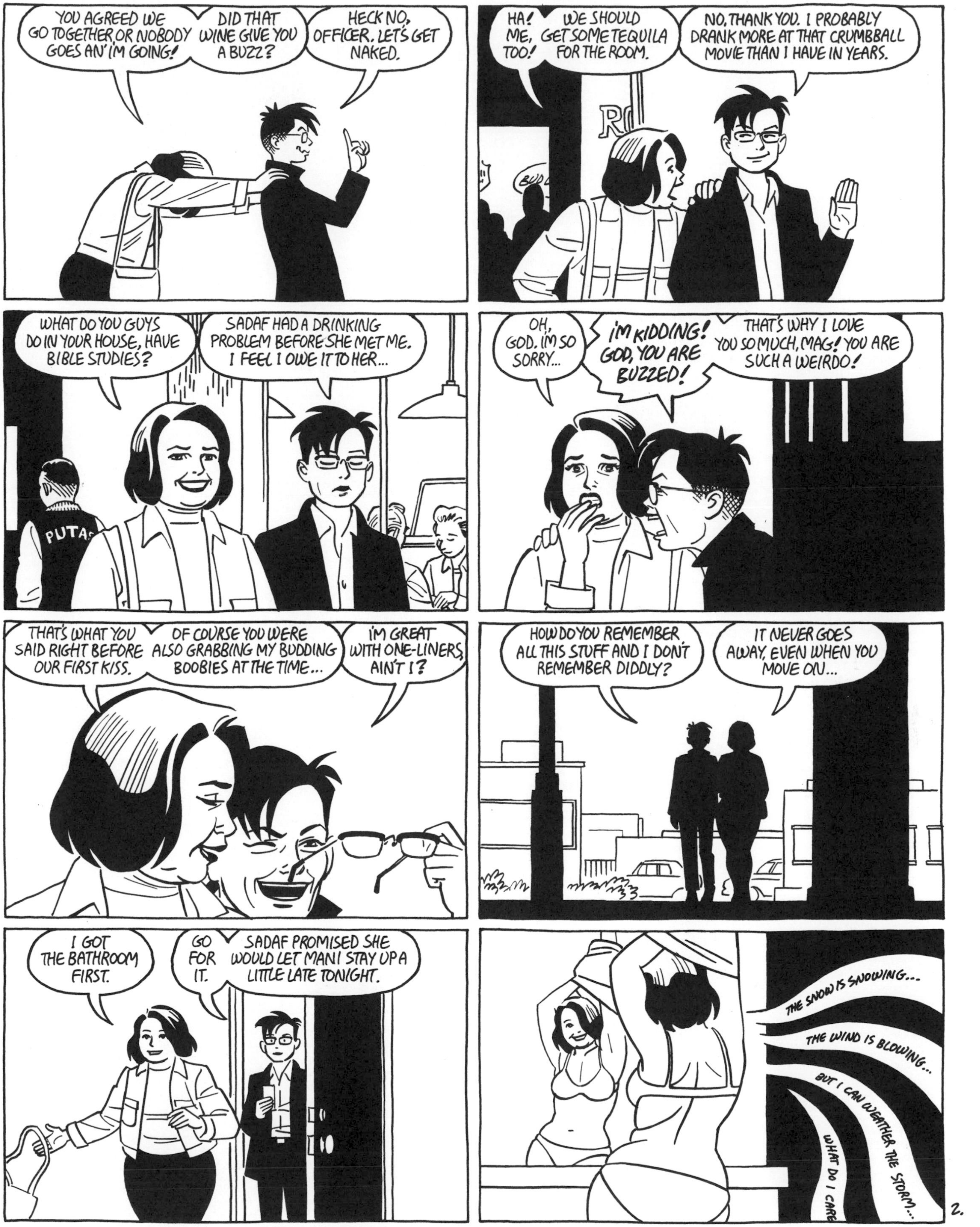
YOU AGREED WE GO TOGETHER OR NOBODY GOES AN' I'M GOING!
DID THAT WINE GIVE YOU A BUZZ?
HECK NO, OFFICER. LET'S GET NAKED.
HA! ME, TOO!
WE SHOULD GET SOME TEQUILA FOR THE ROOM.
NO, THANK YOU. I PROBABLY DRANK MORE AT THAT CRUMBBALL MOVIE THAN I HAVE IN YEARS.
WHAT DO YOU GUYS DO IN YOUR HOUSE, HAVE BIBLE STUDIES?
SADAF HAD A DRINKING PROBLEM BEFORE SHE MET ME. I FEEL I OWE IT TO HER...
OH, GOD. I'M SO SORRY...
I'M KIDDING! GOD, YOU ARE BUZZED!
THAT'S WHY I LOVE YOU SO MUCH, MAG! YOU ARE SUCH A WEIRDO!
THAT'S WHAT YOU SAID RIGHT BEFORE OUR FIRST KISS.
OF COURSE YOU WERE ALSO GRABBING MY BUDDING BOOBIES AT THE TIME...
I'M GREAT WITH ONE-LINERS, AIN'T I?
HOW DO YOU REMEMBER ALL THIS STUFF AND I DON'T REMEMBER DIDDLY?
IT NEVER GOES AWAY, EVEN WHEN YOU MOVE ON...
I GOT THE BATHROOM FIRST.
GO FOR IT.
SADAF PROMISED SHE WOULD LET MANI STAY UP A LITTLE LATE TONIGHT.
THE SNOW IS SNOWING...
THE WIND IS BLOWING...
BUT I CAN WEATHER THE STORM...
WHAT DO I CARE
2.

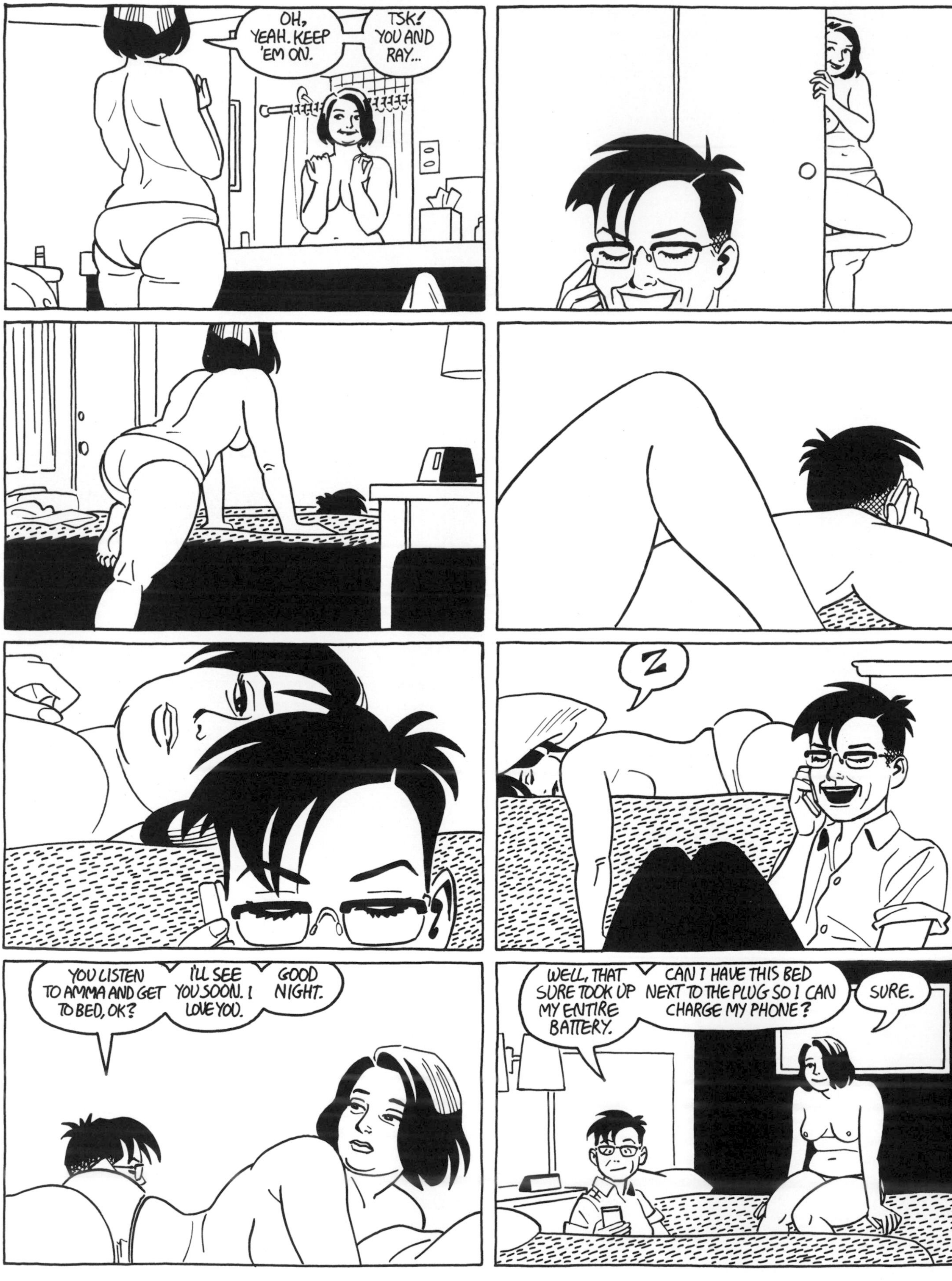
OH, YEAH. KEEP 'EM ON.
TSK! YOU AND RAY...
Z
YOU LISTEN TO AMMA AND GET TO BED, OK?
I'LL SEE YOU SOON. I LOVE YOU.
GOOD NIGHT.
WELL, THAT SURE TOOK UP MY ENTIRE BATTERY.
CAN I HAVE THIS BED NEXT TO THE PLUG SO I CAN CHARGE MY PHONE?
SURE.
3.

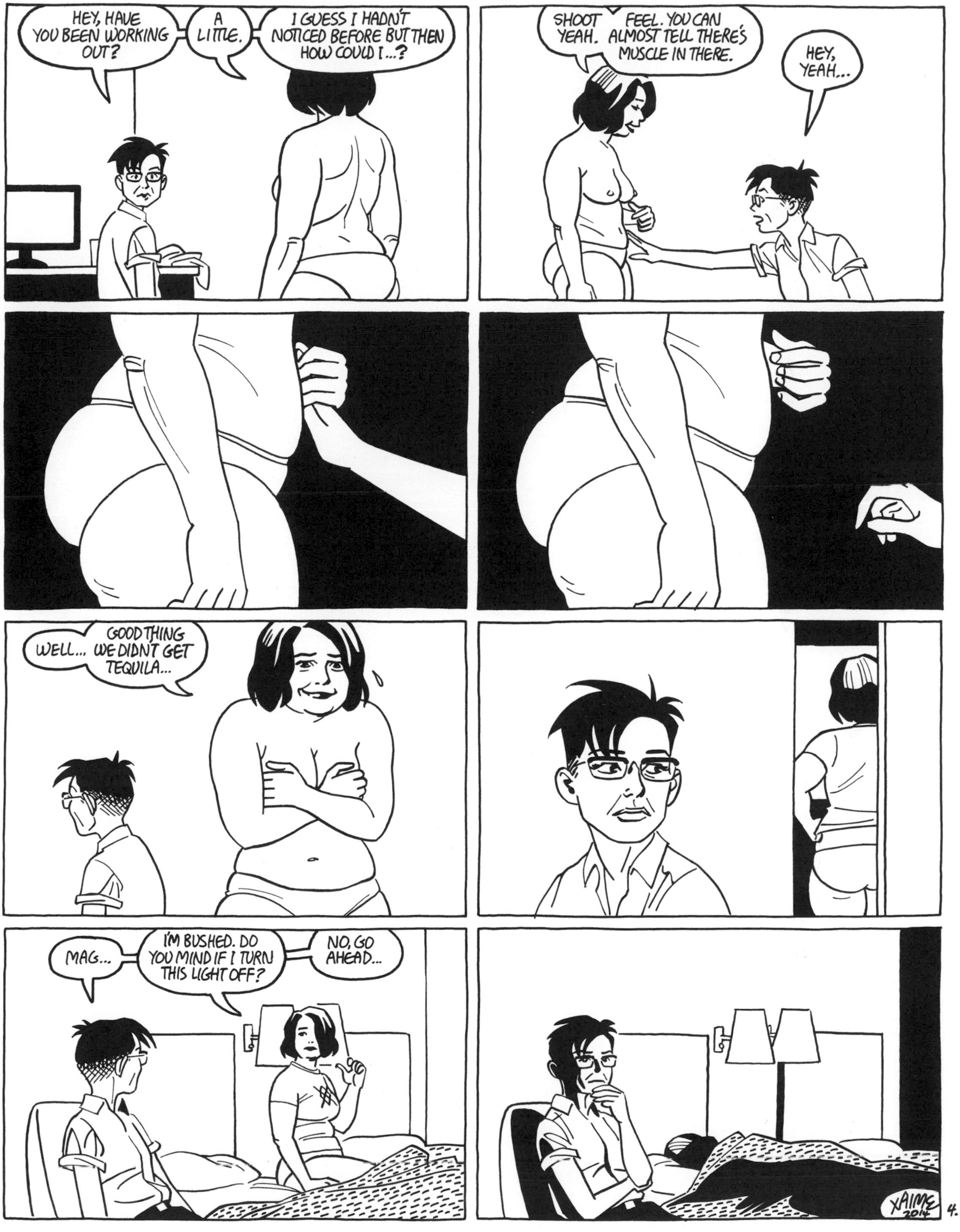
HEY, HAVE YOU BEEN WORKING OUT?
A LITTLE.
I GUESS I HADN'T NOTICED BEFORE BUT THEN HOW COULD I...?
SHOOT YEAH.
FEEL. YOU CAN ALMOST TELL THERE'S MUSCLE IN THERE.
HEY, YEAH...
WELL...
GOOD THING WE DIDN'T GET TEQUILA...
MAG...
I'M BUSHED. DO YOU MIND IF I TURN THIS LIGHT OFF?
NO, GO AHEAD...
XAIME 2014
4.

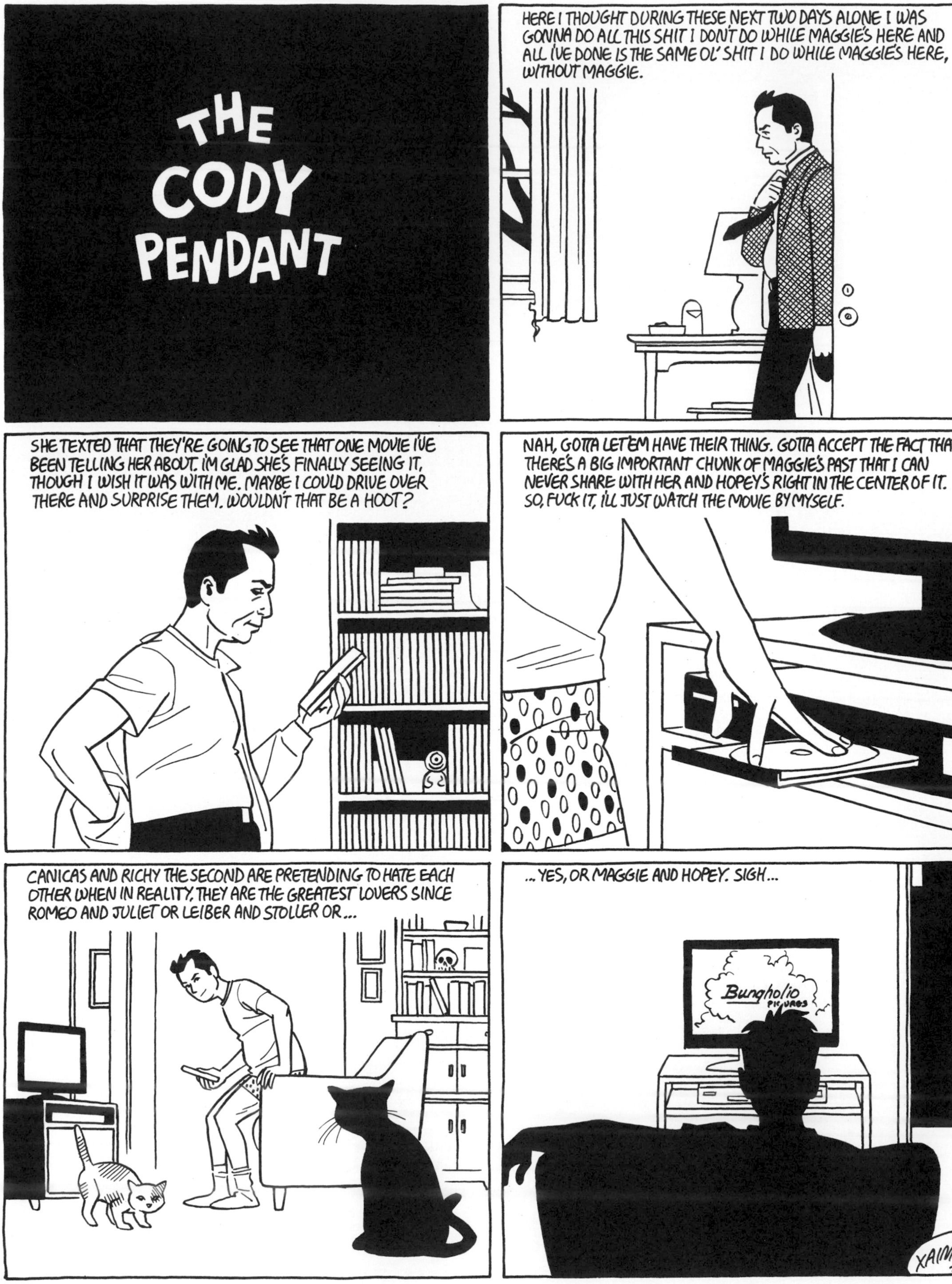
THE CODY PENDANT
HERE I THOUGHT DURING THESE NEXT TWO DAYS ALONE I WAS GONNA DO ALL THIS SHIT I DON'T DO WHILE MAGGIE'S HERE AND ALL I'VE DONE IS THE SAME OL' SHIT I DO WHILE MAGGIE'S HERE, WITHOUT MAGGIE.
SHE TEXTED THAT THEY'RE GOING TO SEE THAT ONE MOVIE I'VE BEEN TELLING HER ABOUT. I'M GLAD SHE'S FINALLY SEEING IT, THOUGH I WISH IT WAS WITH ME. MAYBE I COULD DRIVE OVER THERE AND SURPRISE THEM. WOULDN'T THAT BE A HOOT?
NAH, GOTTA LET'EM HAVE THEIR THING. GOTTA ACCEPT THE FACT THAT THERE'S A BIG IMPORTANT CHUNK OF MAGGIE'S PAST THAT I CAN NEVER SHARE WITH HER AND HOPEY'S RIGHT IN THE CENTER OF IT. SO, FUCK IT, I'LL JUST WATCH THE MOVIE BY MYSELF.
CANICAS AND RICHY THE SECOND ARE PRETENDING TO HATE EACH OTHER WHEN IN REALITY, THEY ARE THE GREATEST LOVERS SINCE ROMEO AND JULIET OR LEIBER AND STOLLER OR...
...YES, OR MAGGIE AND HOPEY. SIGH...
Bungholio PICTURES
XAIME 2014

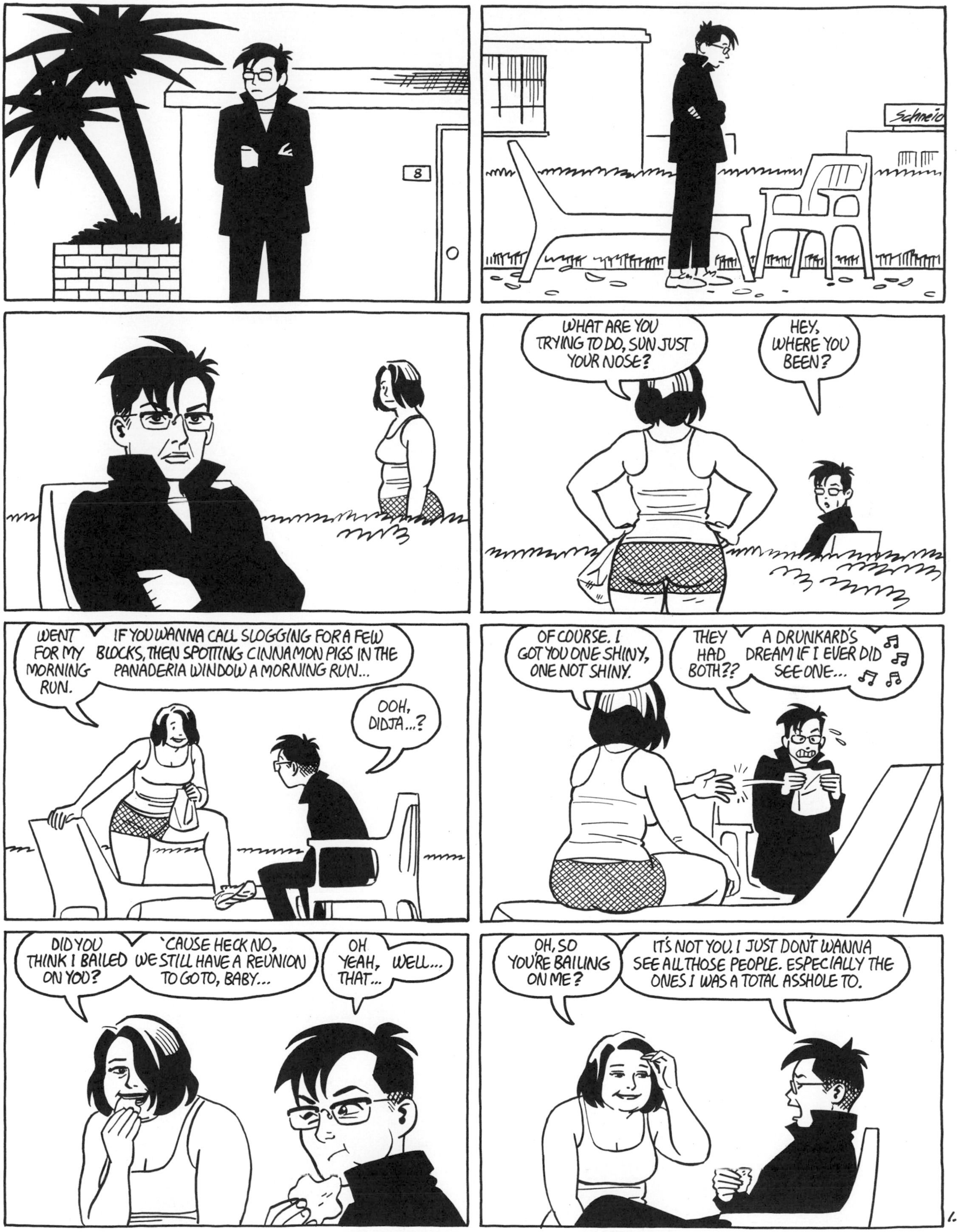

8
Schneid
WHAT ARE YOU TRYING TO DO, SUN JUST YOUR NOSE?
HEY, WHERE YOU BEEN?
WENT FOR MY MORNING RUN.
IF YOU WANNA CALL SLOGGING FOR A FEW BLOCKS, THEN SPOTTING CINNAMON PIGS IN THE PANADERIA WINDOW A MORNING RUN...
OOH, DIDJA...?
OF COURSE. I GOT YOU ONE SHINY, ONE NOT SHINY.
THEY HAD BOTH??
A DRUNKARD'S DREAM IF I EVER DID SEE ONE...
DID YOU THINK I BAILED ON YOU?
`CAUSE HECK NO, WE STILL HAVE A REUNION TO GO TO, BABY...
OH YEAH, THAT...
WELL...
OH, SO YOU'RE BAILING ON ME?
IT'S NOT YOU. I JUST DON'T WANNA SEE ALL THOSE PEOPLE. ESPECIALLY THE ONES I WAS A TOTAL ASSHOLE TO.
1.

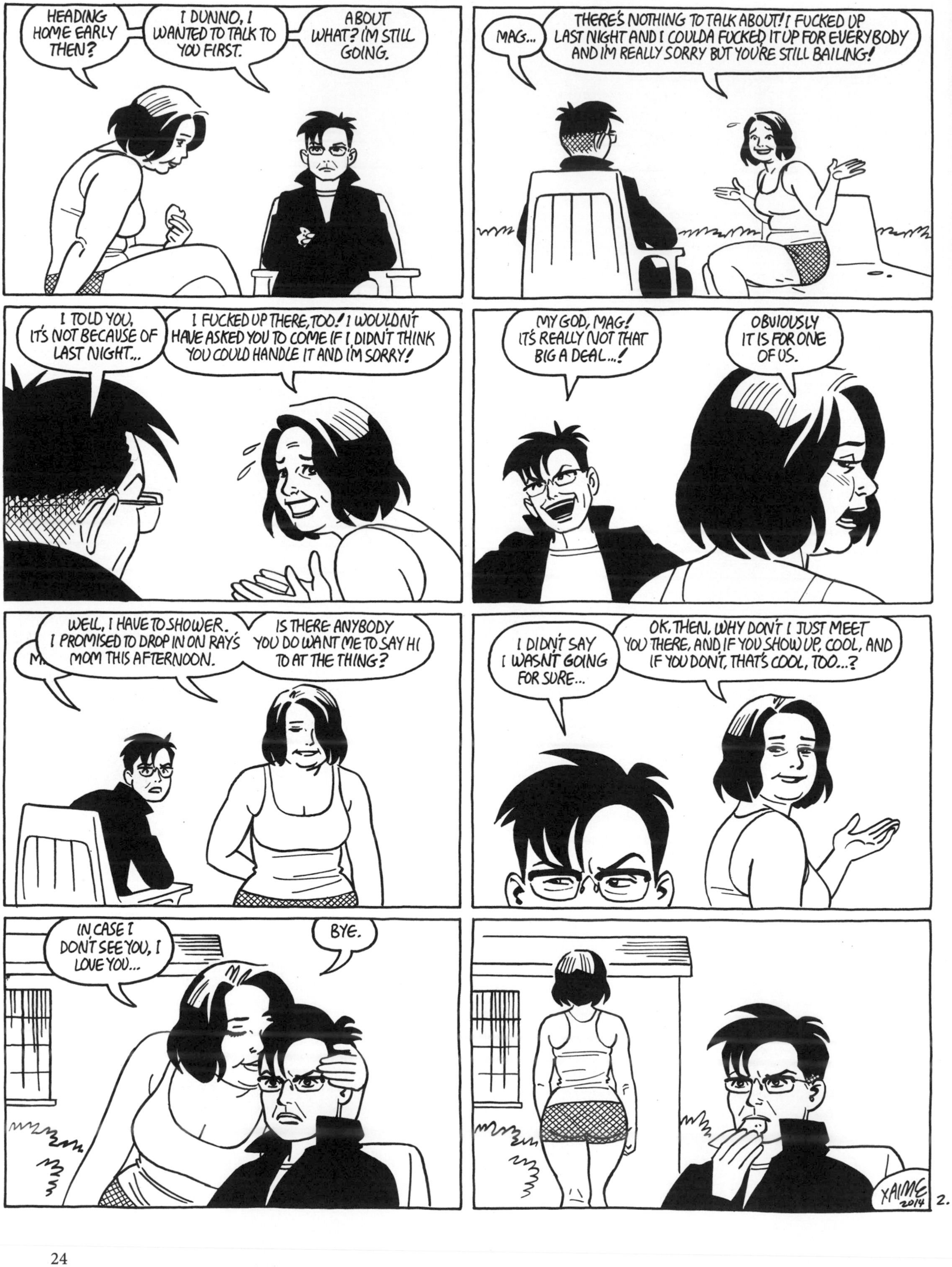
HEADING HOME EARLY THEN?
I DUNNO, I WANTED TO TALK TO YOU FIRST.
ABOUT WHAT? I'M STILL GOING.
MAG...
THERE'S NOTHING TO TALK ABOUT! I FUCKED UP LAST NIGHT AND I COULDA FUCKED IT UP FOR EVERYBODY AND I'M REALLY SORRY BUT YOU'RE STILL BAILING!
I TOLD YOU, IT'S NOT BECAUSE OF LAST NIGHT...
I FUCKED UP THERE, TOO! I WOULDN'T HAVE ASKED YOU TO COME IF I DIDN'T THINK YOU COULD HANDLE IT AND I'M SORRY!
MY GOD, MAG! IT'S REALLY NOT THAT BIG A DEAL...!
OBVIOUSLY IT IS FOR ONE OF US.
WELL, I HAVE TO SHOWER. I PROMISED TO DROP IN ON RAY'S MOM THIS AFTERNOON.
IS THERE ANYBODY YOU DO WANT ME TO SAY HI TO AT THE THING?
I DIDN'T SAY I WASN'T GOING FOR SURE...
OK, THEN, WHY DON'T I JUST MEET YOU THERE, AND IF YOU SHOW UP, COOL, AND IF YOU DON'T, THAT'S COOL, TOO...?
IN CASE I DON'T SEE YOU, I LOVE YOU...
BYE.
XAIME 2014
2.

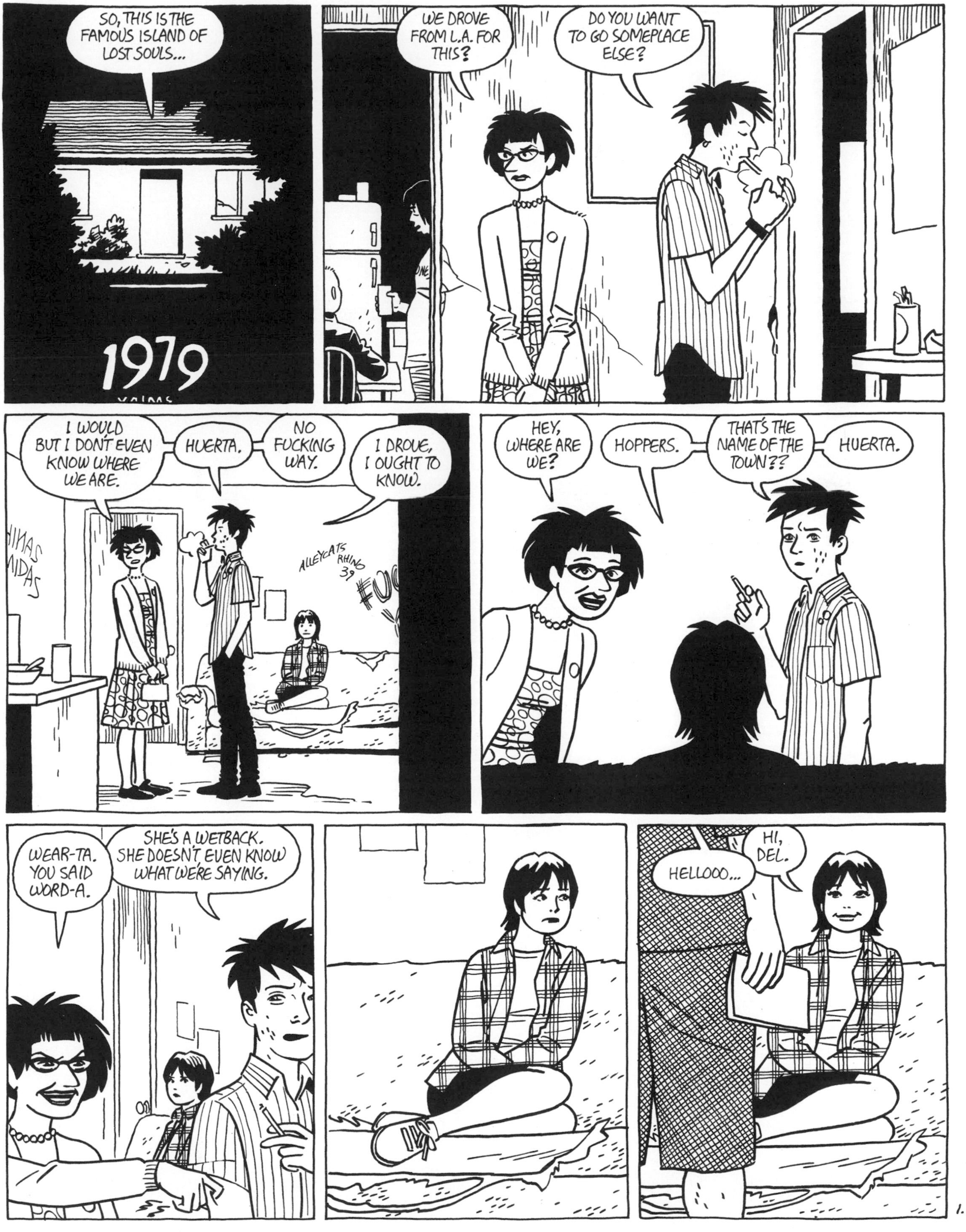
SO, THIS IS THE FAMOUS ISLAND OF LOST SOULS...
1979
WE DROVE FROM L.A. FOR THIS?
DO YOU WANT TO GO SOMEPLACE ELSE?
I WOULD BUT I DON'T EVEN KNOW WHERE WE ARE.
HUERTA.
NO FUCKING WAY.
I DROVE, I OUGHT TO KNOW.
ALLEYCATS RHINO 39
HEY, WHERE ARE WE?
HOPPERS.
THAT'S THE NAME OF THE TOWN??
HUERTA.
WEAR-TA. YOU SAID WORD-A.
SHE'S A WETBACK. SHE DOESN'T EVEN KNOW WHAT WE'RE SAYING.
HELLOOO...
HI, DEL.

1.

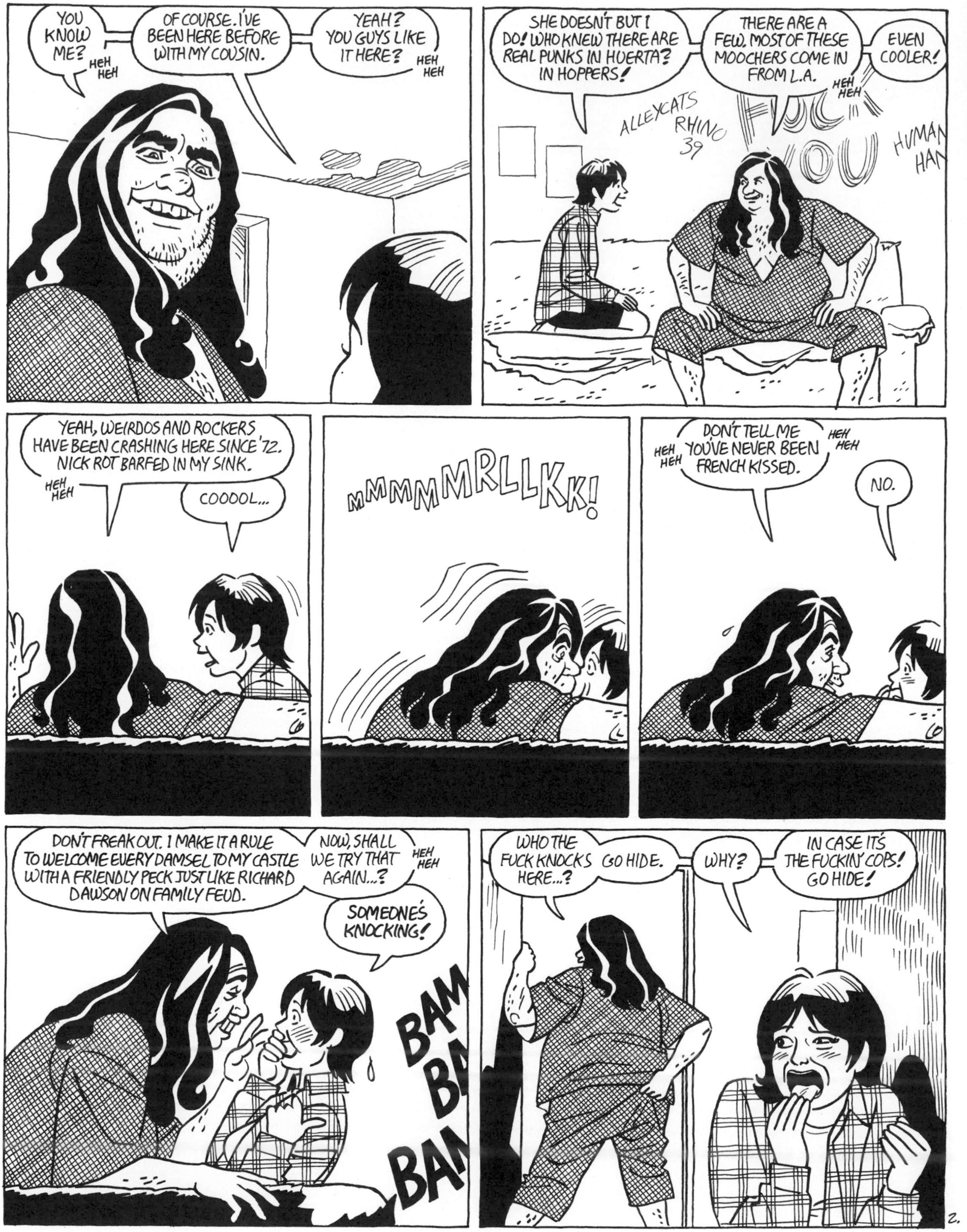
YOU KNOW ME?
HEH HEH
OF COURSE. I'VE BEEN HERE BEFORE WITH MY COUSIN.
YEAH? YOU GUYS LIKE IT HERE?
HEH HEH
SHE DOESN'T BUT I DO! WHO KNEW THERE ARE REAL PUNKS IN HUERTA? IN HOPPERS!
THERE ARE A FEW. MOST OF THESE MOOCHERS COME IN FROM L.A.
HEH HEH
EVEN COOLER!
ALLEYCATS
RHINO 39
YEAH, WEIRDOS AND ROCKERS HAVE BEEN CRASHING HERE SINCE '72. NICK ROT BARFED IN MY SINK.
HEH HEH
COOOOL...
MMMMMMRLLKK!
HEH HEH
DON'T TELL ME YOU'VE NEVER BEEN FRENCH KISSED.
HEH HEH
NO.
DON'T FREAK OUT. I MAKE IT A RULE TO WELCOME EVERY DAMSEL TO MY CASTLE WITH A FRIENDLY PECK JUST LIKE RICHARD DAWSON ON FAMILY FEUD.
NOW, SHALL WE TRY THAT AGAIN...?
HEH HEH
SOMEONE'S KNOCKING!
WHO THE FUCK KNOCKS HERE...?
GO HIDE.
WHY?
IN CASE IT'S THE FUCKIN' COPS! GO HIDE!
2.

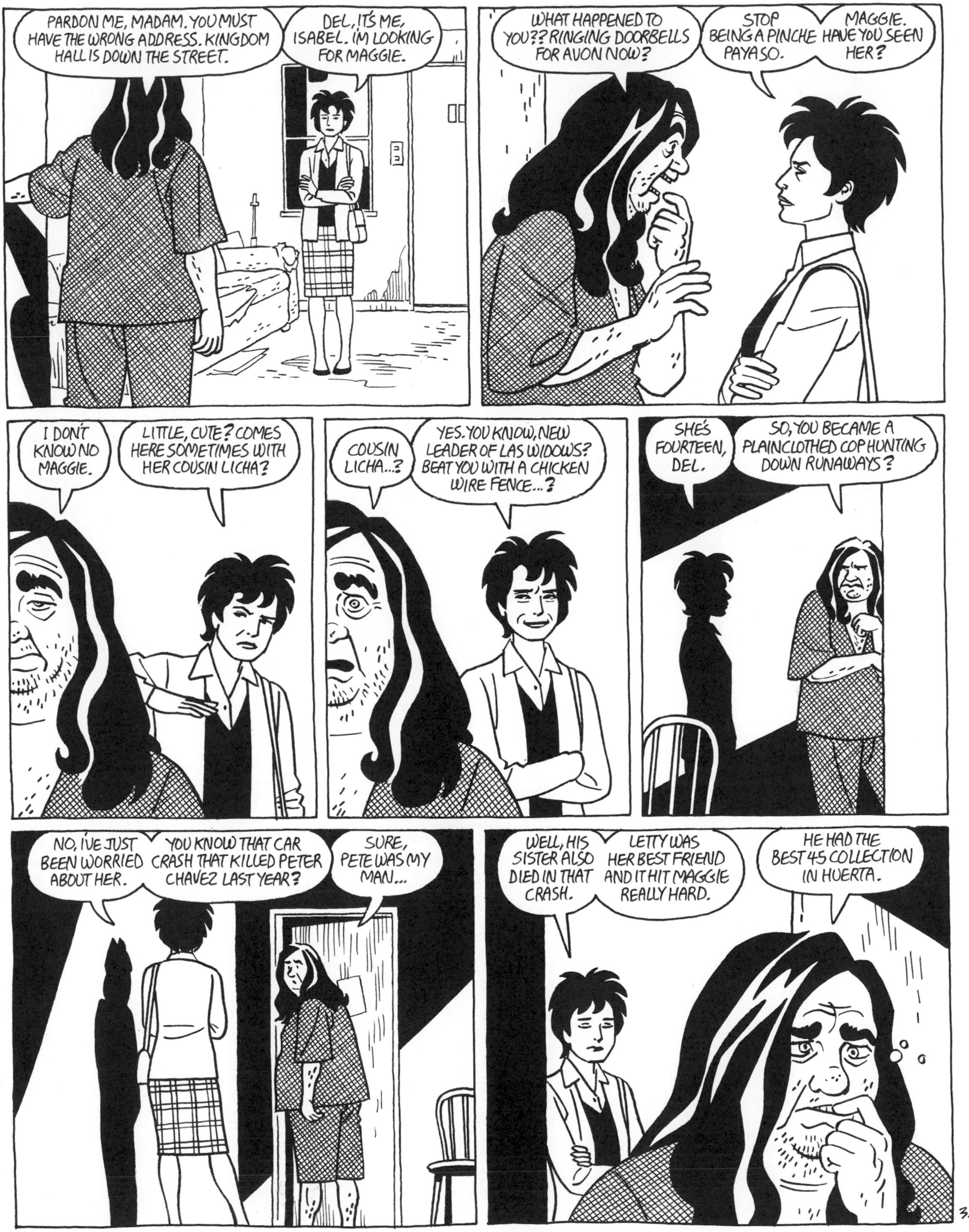

PARDON ME, MADAM. YOU MUST HAVE THE WRONG ADDRESS. KINGDOM HALL IS DOWN THE STREET.
DEL, IT'S ME, ISABEL. I'M LOOKING FOR MAGGIE.
WHAT HAPPENED TO YOU?? RINGING DOORBELLS FOR AVON NOW?
STOP BEING A PINCHE PAYASO.
MAGGIE. HAVE YOU SEEN HER?
I DON'T KNOW NO MAGGIE.
LITTLE, CUTE? COMES HERE SOMETIMES WITH HER COUSIN LICHA?
COUSIN LICHA...?
YES. YOU KNOW, NEW LEADER OF LAS WIDOWS? BEAT YOU WITH A CHICKEN WIRE FENCE...?
SHE'S FOURTEEN, DEL.
SO, YOU BECAME A PLAINCLOTHED COP HUNTING DOWN RUNAWAYS?
NO, I'VE JUST BEEN WORRIED ABOUT HER.
YOU KNOW THAT CAR CRASH THAT KILLED PETER CHAVEZ LAST YEAR?
SURE, PETE WAS MY MAN...
WELL, HIS SISTER ALSO DIED IN THAT CRASH.
LETTY WAS HER BEST FRIEND AND IT HIT MAGGIE REALLY HARD.
HE HAD THE BEST 45 COLLECTION IN HUERTA.
3.

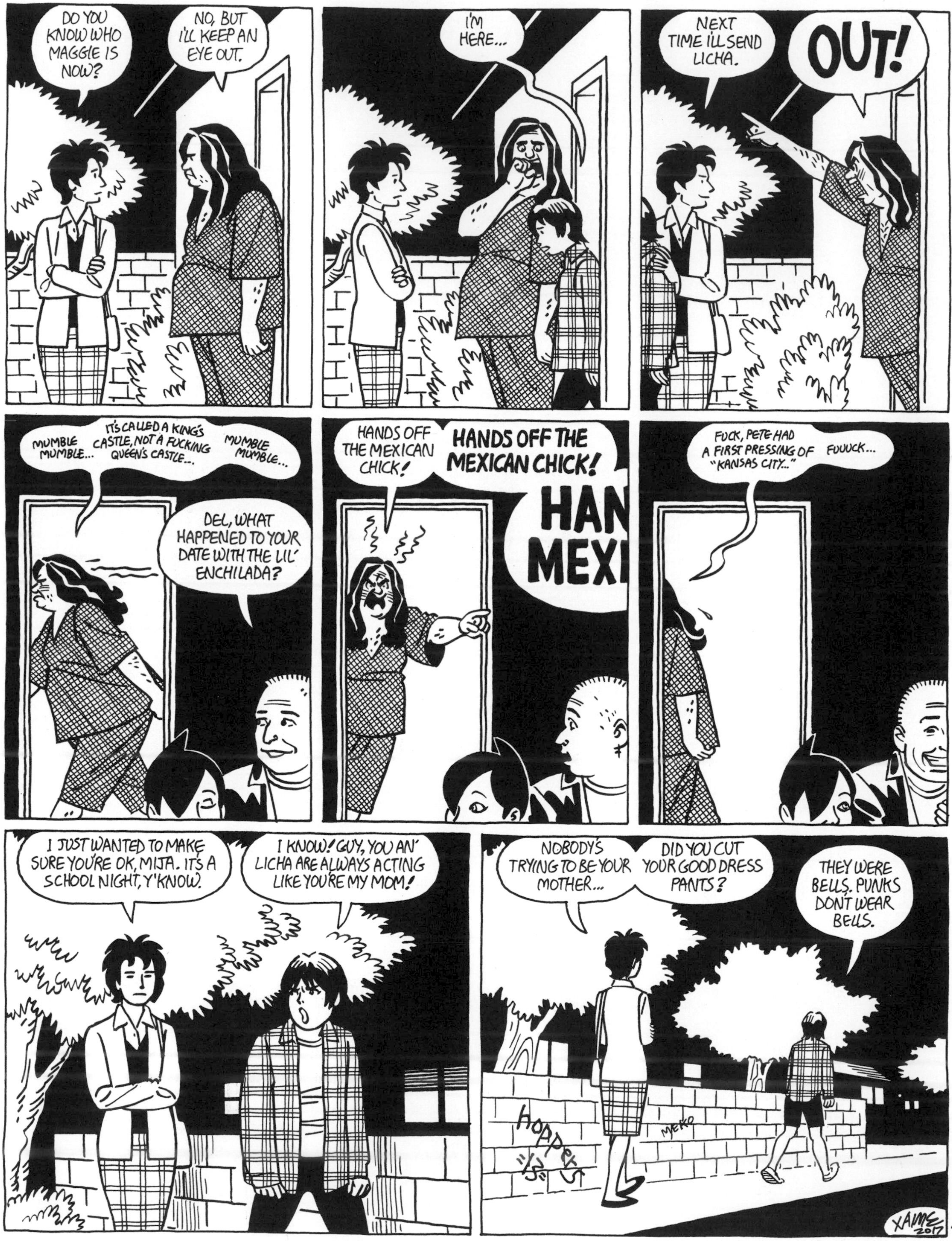

DO YOU KNOW WHO MAGGIE IS NOW?
NO, BUT I'LL KEEP AN EYE OUT.
I'M HERE...
NEXT TIME I'LL SEND LICHA.
OUT!
MUMBLE MUMBLE...
IT'S CALLED A KING'S CASTLE, NOT A FUCKING QUEEN'S CASTLE...
MUMBLE MUMBLE...
DEL, WHAT HAPPENED TO YOUR DATE WITH THE LIL' ENCHILADA?
HANDS OFF THE MEXICAN CHICK!
HANDS OFF THE MEXICAN CHICK!
HAN MEXI
FUCK, PETE HAD A FIRST PRESSING OF "KANSAS CITY..."
FUUUCK...
I JUST WANTED TO MAKE SURE YOU'RE OK, MIJA. IT'S A SCHOOL NIGHT, Y'KNOW.
I KNOW! GUY, YOU AN' LICHA ARE ALWAYS ACTING LIKE YOU'RE MY MOM!
NOBODY'S TRYING TO BE YOUR MOTHER...
DID YOU CUT YOUR GOOD DRESS PANTS?
THEY WERE BELLS. PUNKS DON'T WEAR BELLS.
HOPPERS 13
XAIME 2017
4.

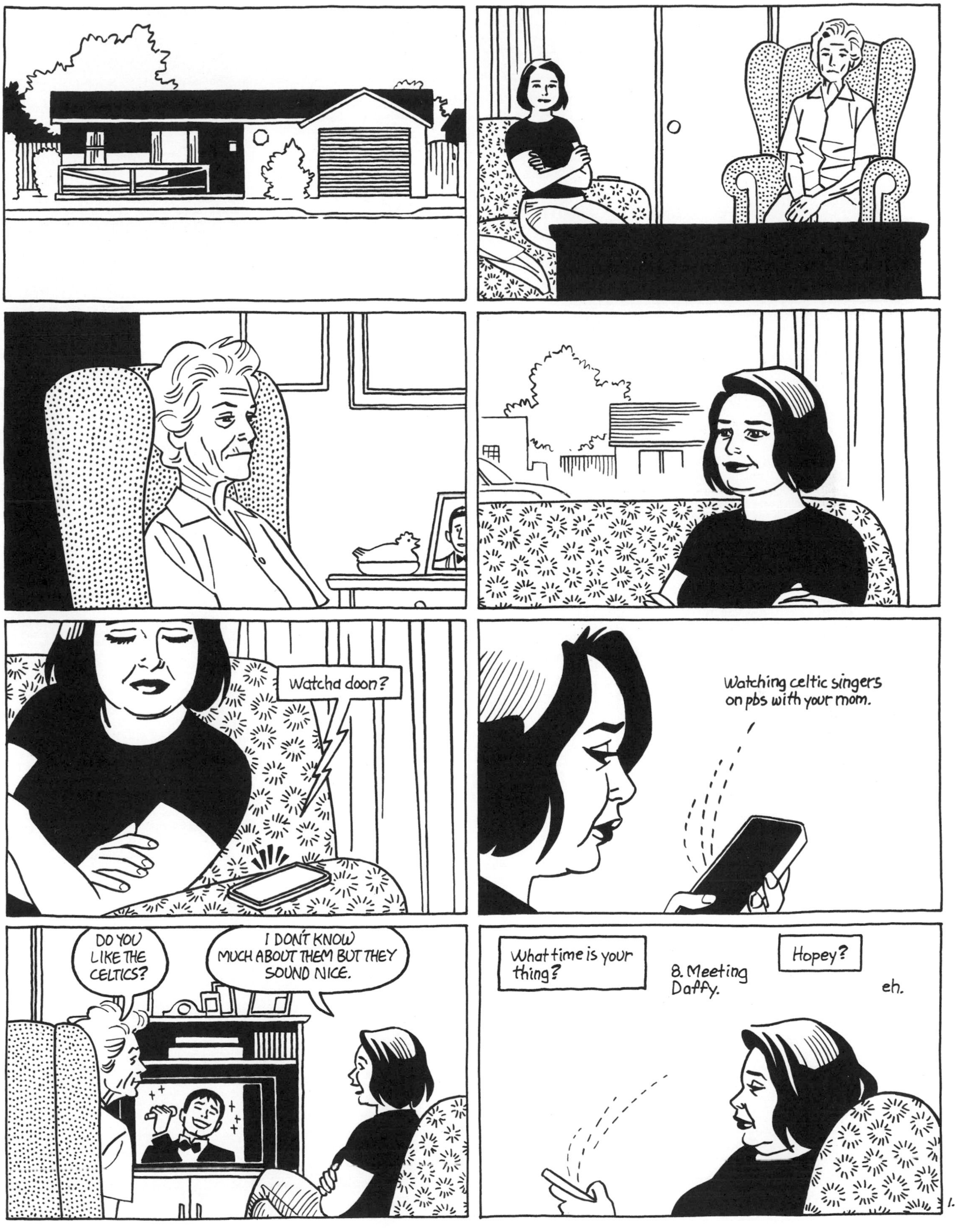
Watcha doon?
Watching celtic singers on pbs with your mom.
DO YOU LIKE THE CELTICS?
I DON'T KNOW MUCH ABOUT THEM BUT THEY SOUND NICE.
What time is your thing?
8. Meeting Daffy.
Hopey?
eh.
1.

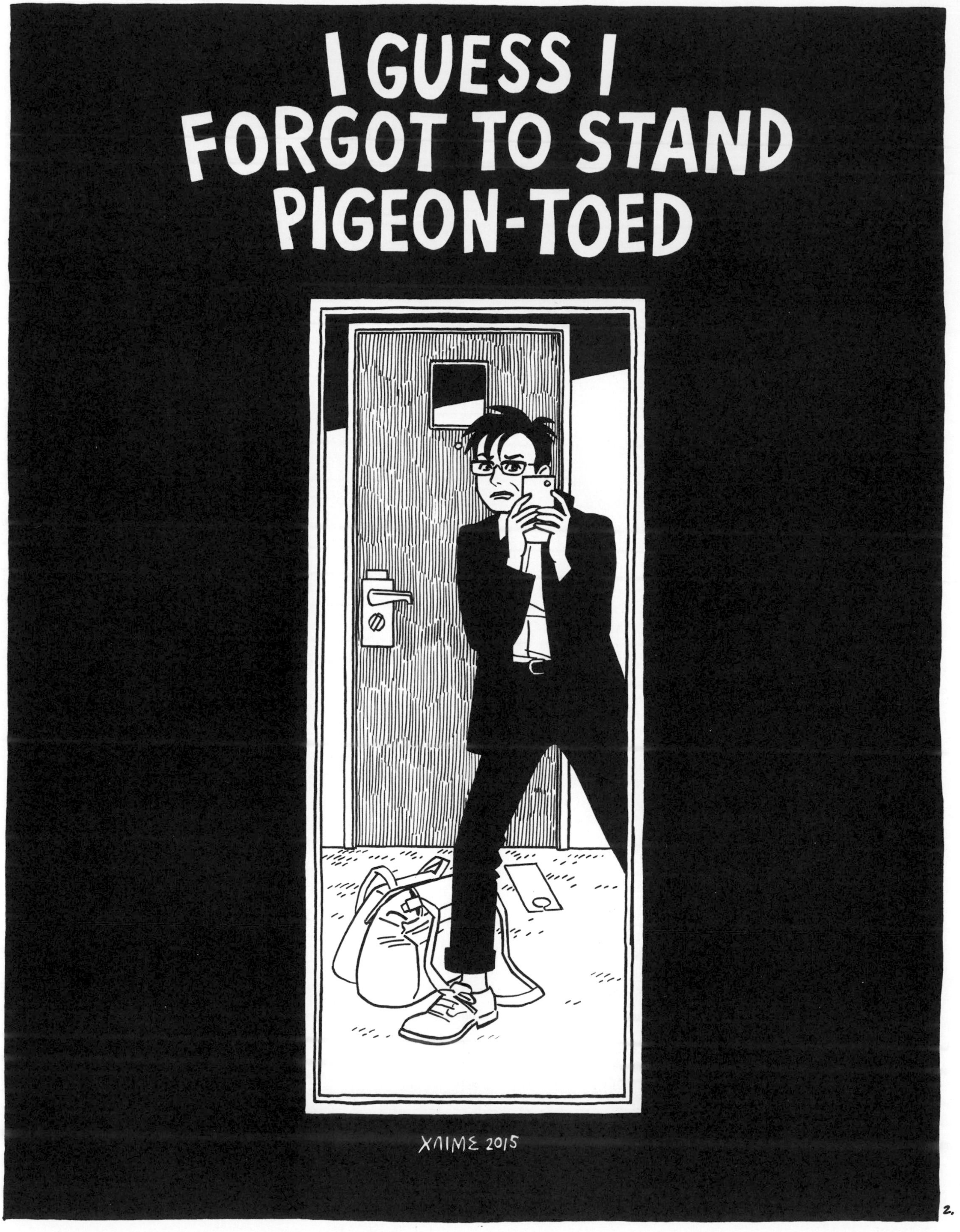
I GUESS I FORGOT TO STAND PIGEON-TOED
XAIME 2015
2.

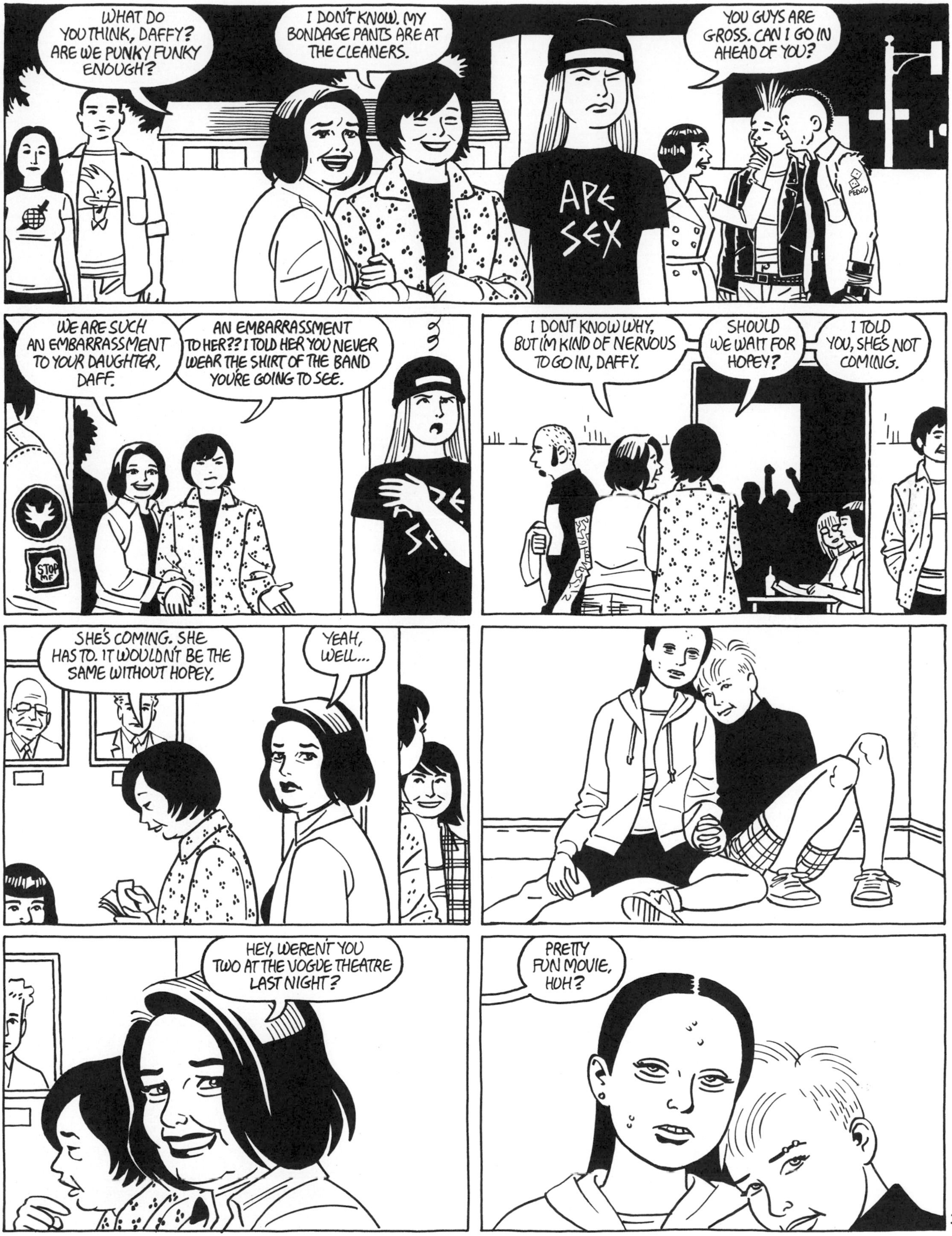
WHAT DO YOU THINK, DAFFY? ARE WE PUNKY FUNKY ENOUGH?
I DON'T KNOW. MY BONDAGE PANTS ARE AT THE CLEANERS.
YOU GUYS ARE GROSS. CAN I GO IN AHEAD OF YOU?
APE SEX
PEDOS
WE ARE SUCH AN EMBARRASSMENT TO YOUR DAUGHTER, DAFF.
AN EMBARRASSMENT TO HER?? I TOLD HER YOU NEVER WEAR THE SHIRT OF THE BAND YOU'RE GOING TO SEE.
STOP ME
I DON'T KNOW WHY, BUT I'M KIND OF NERVOUS TO GO IN, DAFFY.
SHOULD WE WAIT FOR HOPEY?
I TOLD YOU, SHE'S NOT COMING.
SHE'S COMING. SHE HAS TO. IT WOULDN'T BE THE SAME WITHOUT HOPEY.
YEAH, WELL...
HEY, WEREN'T YOU TWO AT THE VOGUE THEATRE LAST NIGHT?
PRETTY FUN MOVIE, HUH?
3.

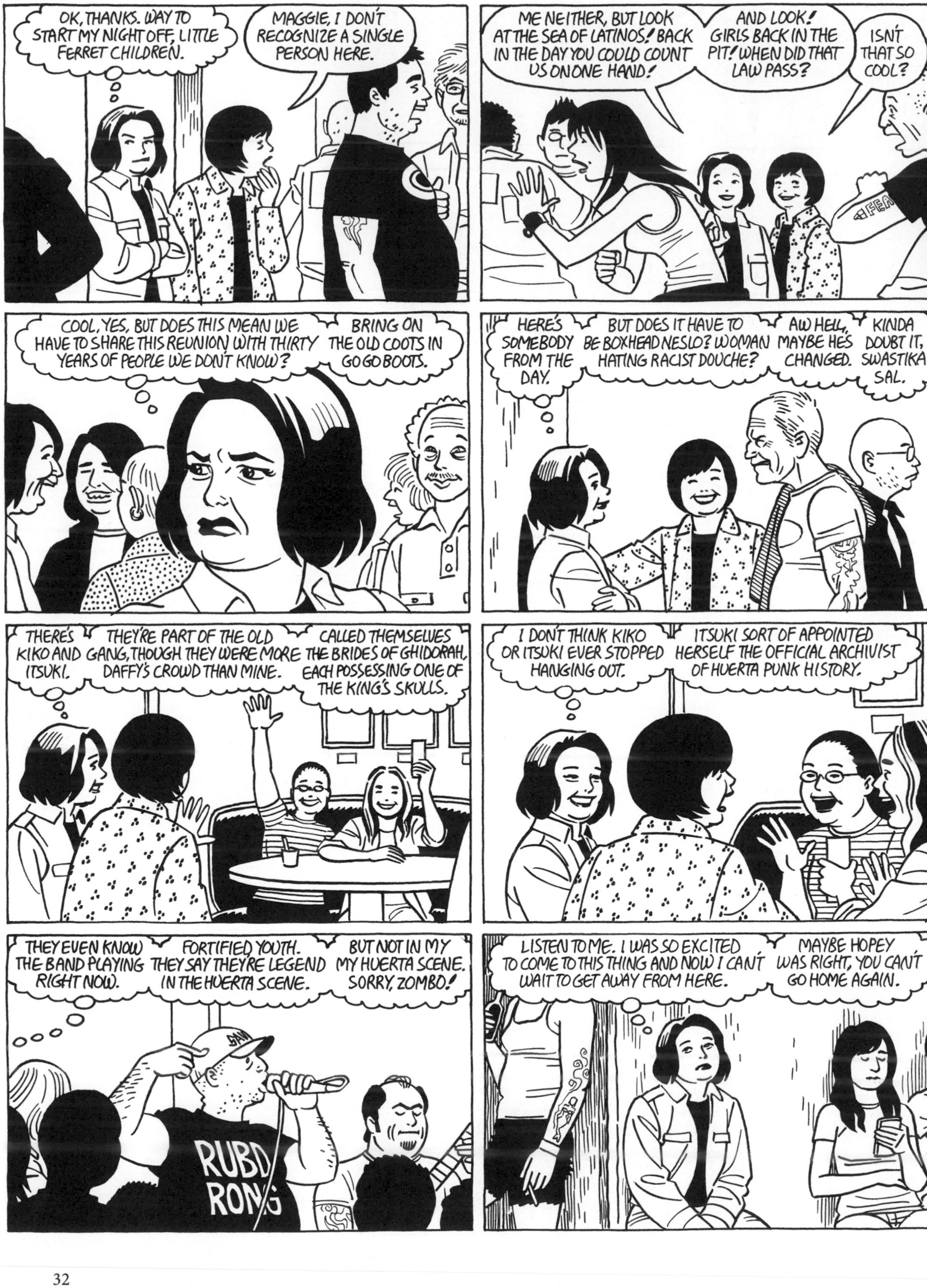
OK, THANKS. WAY TO START MY NIGHT OFF, LITTLE FERRET CHILDREN.
MAGGIE, I DON'T RECOGNIZE A SINGLE PERSON HERE.
ME NEITHER, BUT LOOK AT THE SEA OF LATINOS! BACK IN THE DAY YOU COULD COUNT US ON ONE HAND!
AND LOOK! GIRLS BACK IN THE PIT! WHEN DID THAT LAW PASS?
ISN'T THAT SO COOL?
COOL, YES, BUT DOES THIS MEAN WE HAVE TO SHARE THIS REUNION WITH THIRTY YEARS OF PEOPLE WE DON'T KNOW?
BRING ON THE OLD COOTS IN GO GO BOOTS.
HERE'S SOMEBODY FROM THE DAY.
BUT DOES IT HAVE TO BE BOXHEAD NESLO? WOMAN HATING RACIST DOUCHE?
AW HELL, MAYBE HE'S CHANGED.
KINDA DOUBT IT, SWASTIKA SAL.
THERE'S KIKO AND ITSUKI.
THEY'RE PART OF THE OLD GANG, THOUGH THEY WERE MORE DAFFY'S CROWD THAN MINE.
CALLED THEMSELVES THE BRIDES OF GHIDORAH, EACH POSSESSING ONE OF THE KING'S SKULLS.
I DON'T THINK KIKO OR ITSUKI EVER STOPPED HANGING OUT.
ITSUKI SORT OF APPOINTED HERSELF THE OFFICIAL ARCHIVIST OF HUERTA PUNK HISTORY.
THEY EVEN KNOW THE BAND PLAYING RIGHT NOW.
FORTIFIED YOUTH. THEY SAY THEY'RE LEGEND IN THE HUERTA SCENE.
BUT NOT IN MY MY HUERTA SCENE. SORRY, ZOMBO!
RUBD RONG
LISTEN TO ME. I WAS SO EXCITED TO COME TO THIS THING AND NOW I CAN'T WAIT TO GET AWAY FROM HERE.
MAYBE HOPEY WAS RIGHT, YOU CAN'T GO HOME AGAIN.
4.

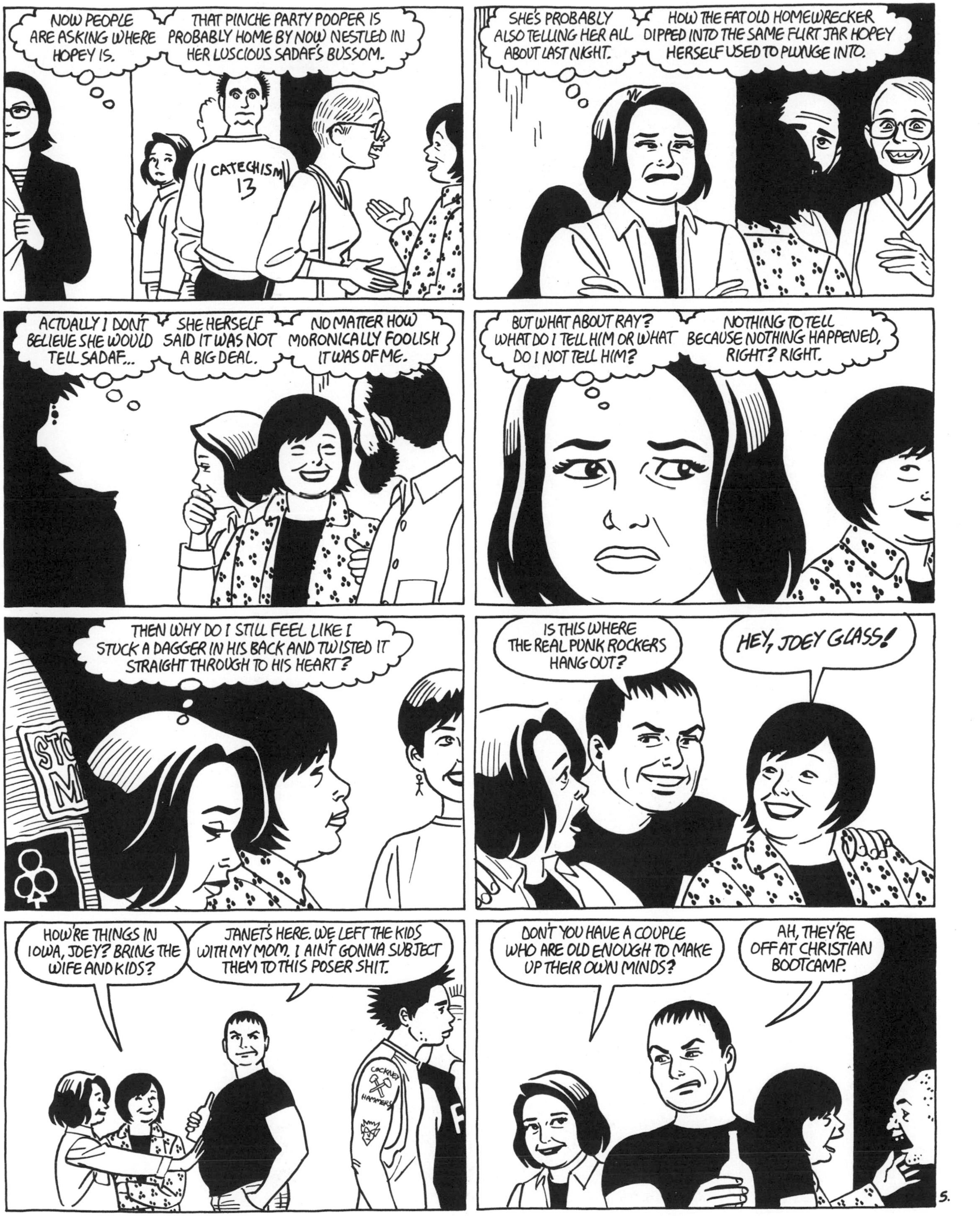
NOW PEOPLE ARE ASKING WHERE HOPEY IS.
THAT PINCHE PARTY POOPER IS PROBABLY HOME BY NOW NESTLED IN HER LUSCIOUS SADAF'S BUSSOM.
CATECHISM 13
SHE'S PROBABLY ALSO TELLING HER ALL ABOUT LAST NIGHT.
HOW THE FAT OLD HOMEWRECKER DIPPED INTO THE SAME FLIRT JAR HOPEY HERSELF USED TO PLUNGE INTO.
ACTUALLY I DON'T BELIEVE SHE WOULD TELL SADAF...
SHE HERSELF SAID IT WAS NOT A BIG DEAL.
NO MATTER HOW MORONICALLY FOOLISH IT WAS OF ME.
BUT WHAT ABOUT RAY? WHAT DO I TELL HIM OR WHAT DO I NOT TELL HIM?
NOTHING TO TELL BECAUSE NOTHING HAPPENED, RIGHT? RIGHT.
THEN WHY DO I STILL FEEL LIKE I STUCK A DAGGER IN HIS BACK AND TWISTED IT STRAIGHT THROUGH TO HIS HEART?
IS THIS WHERE THE REAL PUNK ROCKERS HANG OUT?
HEY, JOEY GLASS!
HOW'RE THINGS IN IOWA, JOEY? BRING THE WIFE AND KIDS?
JANET'S HERE. WE LEFT THE KIDS WITH MY MOM. I AIN'T GONNA SUBJECT THEM TO THIS POSER SHIT.
COCKNEY HAMMERS
DON'T YOU HAVE A COUPLE WHO ARE OLD ENOUGH TO MAKE UP THEIR OWN MINDS?
AH, THEY'RE OFF AT CHRISTIAN BOOTCAMP.
5.

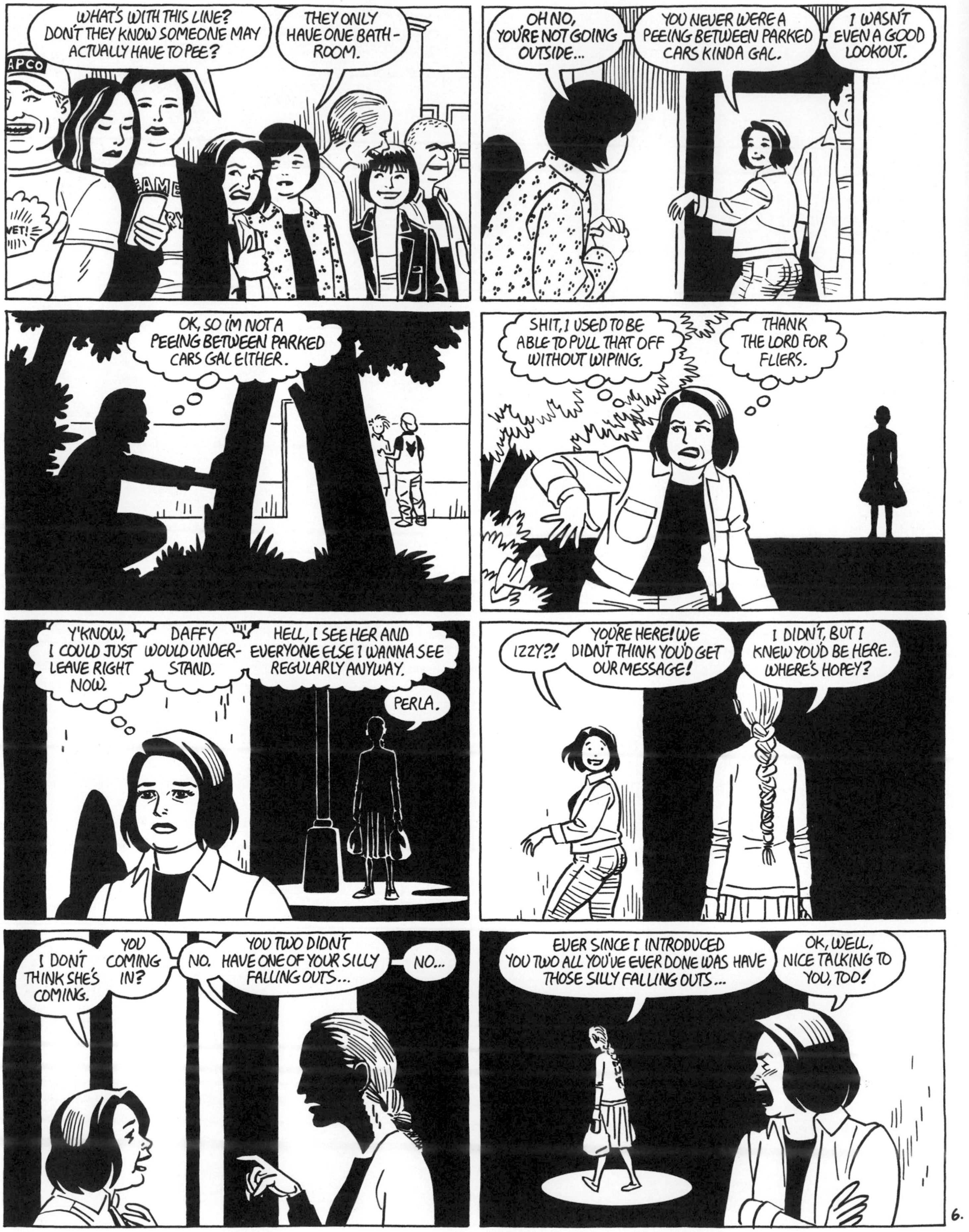
WHAT'S WITH THIS LINE? DON'T THEY KNOW SOMEONE MAY ACTUALLY HAVE TO PEE?
THEY ONLY HAVE ONE BATH-ROOM.
APCO
OH NO, YOU'RE NOT GOING OUTSIDE...
YOU NEVER WERE A PEEING BETWEEN PARKED CARS KINDA GAL.
I WASN'T EVEN A GOOD LOOKOUT.
OK, SO I'M NOT A PEEING BETWEEN PARKED CARS GAL EITHER.
SHIT, I USED TO BE ABLE TO PULL THAT OFF WITHOUT WIPING.
THANK THE LORD FOR FLIERS.
Y'KNOW, I COULD JUST LEAVE RIGHT NOW.
DAFFY WOULD UNDER-STAND.
HELL, I SEE HER AND EVERYONE ELSE I WANNA SEE REGULARLY ANYWAY.
PERLA.
IZZY?!
YOU'RE HERE! WE DIDN'T THINK YOU'D GET OUR MESSAGE!
I DIDN'T, BUT I KNEW YOU'D BE HERE. WHERE'S HOPEY?
I DON'T THINK SHE'S COMING.
YOU COMING IN?
NO.
YOU TWO DIDN'T HAVE ONE OF YOUR SILLY FALLING OUTS...
NO...
EVER SINCE I INTRODUCED YOU TWO ALL YOU'VE EVER DONE WAS HAVE THOSE SILLY FALLING OUTS...
OK, WELL, NICE TALKING TO YOU, TOO!
6.

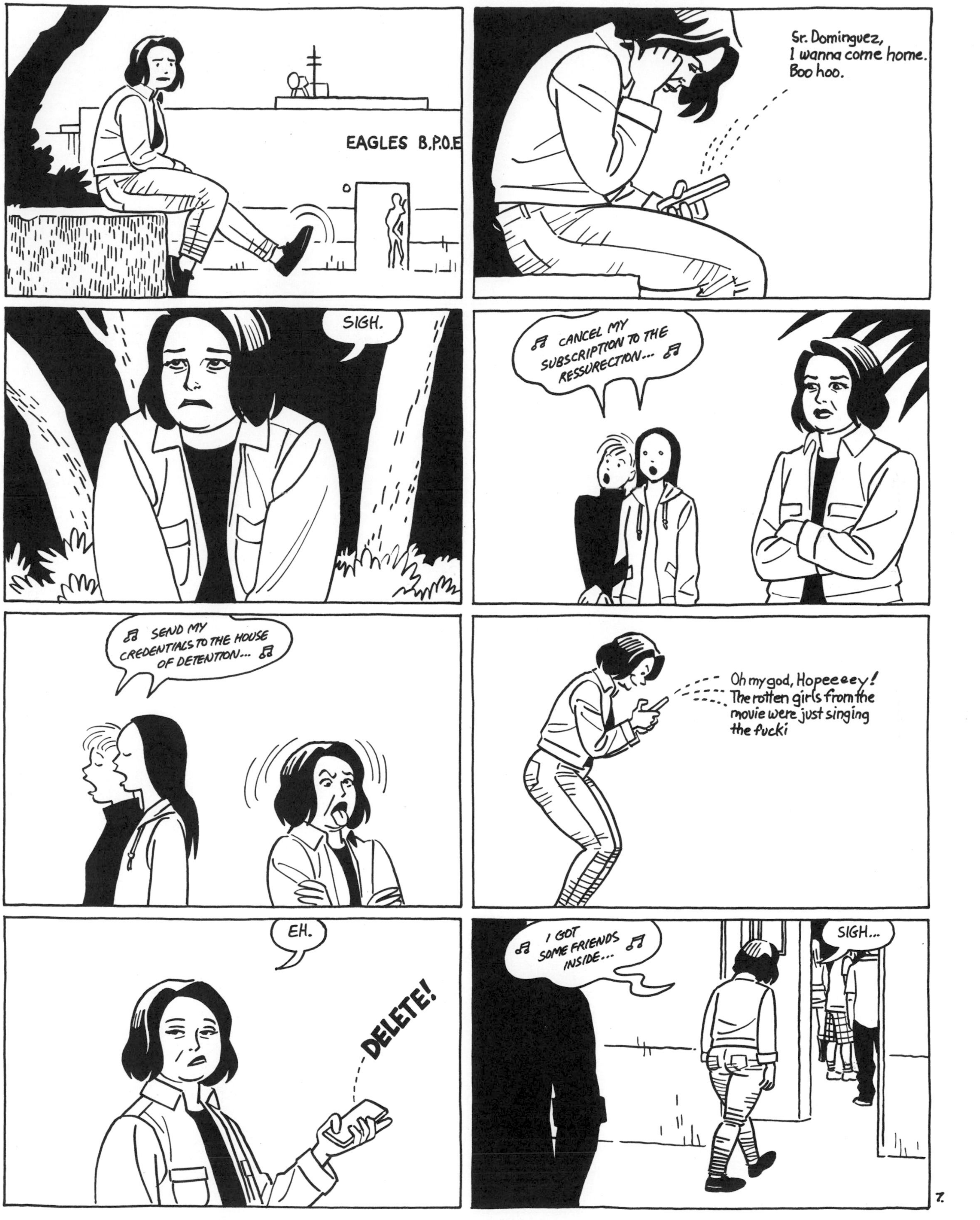
EAGLES B.P.O.E
Sr. Dominguez, I wanna come home. Boo hoo.
SIGH.
♫ CANCEL MY SUBSCRIPTION TO THE RESSURECTION... ♫
♫ SEND MY CREDENTIALS TO THE HOUSE OF DETENTION... ♫
Oh my god, Hopeeeey! The rotten girls from the movie were just singing the fucki
EH.
DELETE!
♫ I GOT SOME FRIENDS INSIDE... ♫
SIGH...
7.

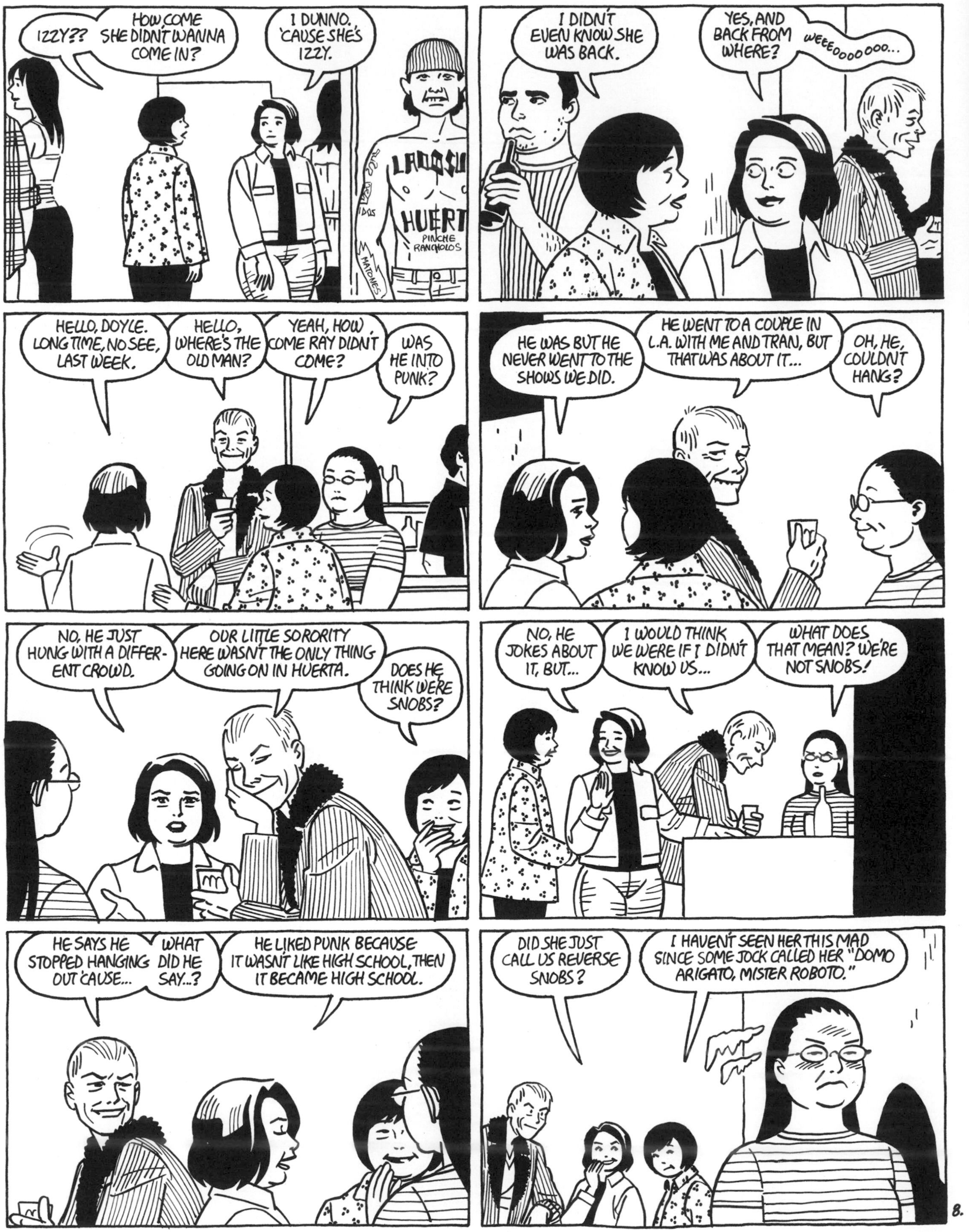
IZZY??
HOW COME SHE DIDN'T WANNA COME IN?
I DUNNO. 'CAUSE SHE'S IZZY.
PINCHE RANCHOLOS
MATONES
I DIDN'T EVEN KNOW SHE WAS BACK.
YES, AND BACK FROM WHERE?
WEEEOOOOOOO...
HELLO, DOYLE. LONG TIME, NO SEE, LAST WEEK.
HELLO, WHERE'S THE OLD MAN?
YEAH, HOW COME RAY DIDN'T COME?
WAS HE INTO PUNK?
HE WAS BUT HE NEVER WENT TO THE SHOWS WE DID.
HE WENT TO A COUPLE IN L.A. WITH ME AND TRAN, BUT THAT WAS ABOUT IT...
OH, HE, COULDN'T HANG?
NO, HE JUST HUNG WITH A DIFFER-ENT CROWD.
OUR LITTLE SORORITY HERE WASN'T THE ONLY THING GOING ON IN HUERTA.
DOES HE THINK WE'RE SNOBS?
NO, HE JOKES ABOUT IT, BUT...
I WOULD THINK WE WERE IF I DIDN'T KNOW US...
WHAT DOES THAT MEAN? WE'RE NOT SNOBS!
HE SAYS HE STOPPED HANGING OUT 'CAUSE...
WHAT DID HE SAY...?
HE LIKED PUNK BECAUSE IT WASN'T LIKE HIGH SCHOOL, THEN IT BECAME HIGH SCHOOL.
DID SHE JUST CALL US REVERSE SNOBS?
I HAVEN'T SEEN HER THIS MAD SINCE SOME JOCK CALLED HER "DOMO ARIGATO, MISTER ROBOTO."
8.

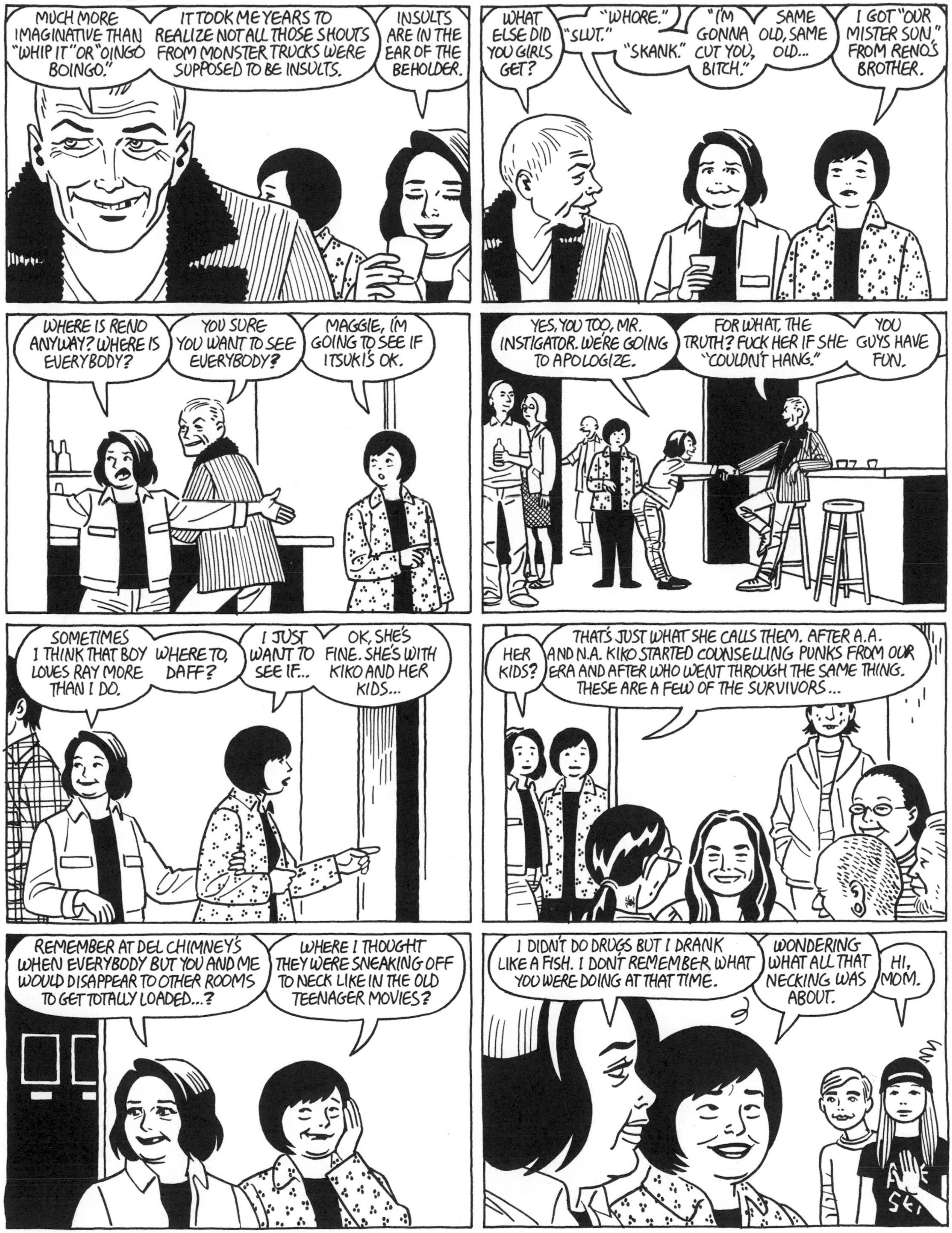
MUCH MORE IMAGINATIVE THAN "WHIP IT" OR "OINGO BOINGO."
IT TOOK ME YEARS TO REALIZE NOT ALL THOSE SHOUTS FROM MONSTER TRUCKS WERE SUPPOSED TO BE INSULTS.
INSULTS ARE IN THE EAR OF THE BEHOLDER.
WHAT ELSE DID YOU GIRLS GET?
"SLUT."
"WHORE."
"SKANK."
"I'M GONNA CUT YOU, BITCH."
SAME OLD, SAME OLD...
I GOT "OUR MISTER SUN," FROM RENO'S BROTHER.
WHERE IS RENO ANYWAY? WHERE IS EVERYBODY?
YOU SURE YOU WANT TO SEE EVERYBODY?
MAGGIE, I'M GOING TO SEE IF ITSUKI'S OK.
YES, YOU TOO, MR. INSTIGATOR. WE'RE GOING TO APOLOGIZE.
FOR WHAT, THE TRUTH? FUCK HER IF SHE "COULDN'T HANG."
YOU GUYS HAVE FUN.
SOMETIMES I THINK THAT BOY LOVES RAY MORE THAN I DO.
WHERE TO, DAFF?
I JUST WANT TO SEE IF...
OK, SHE'S FINE. SHE'S WITH KIKO AND HER KIDS...
HER KIDS?
THAT'S JUST WHAT SHE CALLS THEM. AFTER A.A. AND N.A. KIKO STARTED COUNSELLING PUNKS FROM OUR ERA AND AFTER WHO WENT THROUGH THE SAME THING. THESE ARE A FEW OF THE SURVIVORS...
REMEMBER AT DEL CHIMNEY'S WHEN EVERYBODY BUT YOU AND ME WOULD DISAPPEAR TO OTHER ROOMS TO GET TOTALLY LOADED...?
WHERE I THOUGHT THEY WERE SNEAKING OFF TO NECK LIKE IN THE OLD TEENAGER MOVIES?
I DIDN'T DO DRUGS BUT I DRANK LIKE A FISH. I DON'T REMEMBER WHAT YOU WERE DOING AT THAT TIME.
WONDERING WHAT ALL THAT NECKING WAS ABOUT.
HI, MOM.

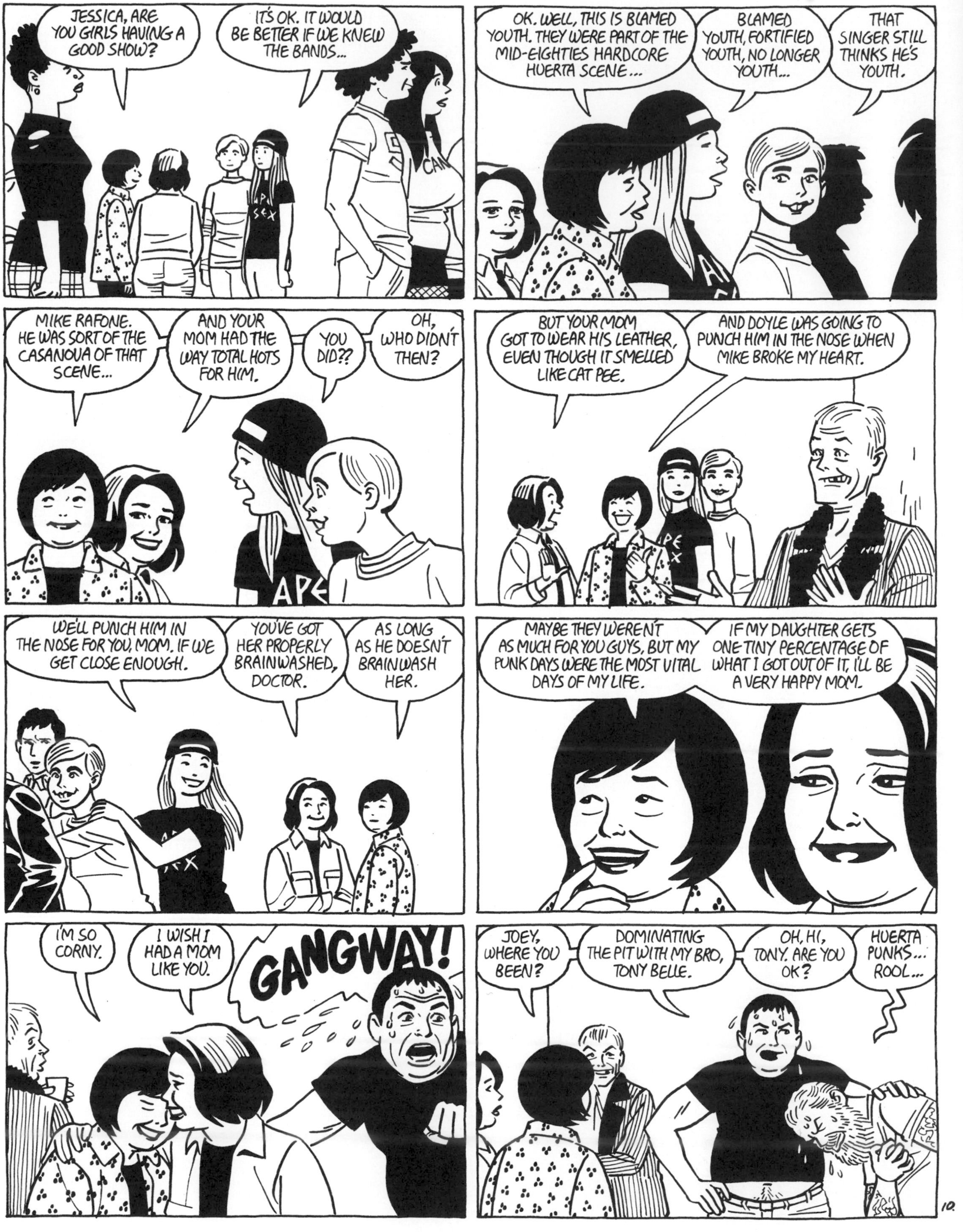
JESSICA, ARE YOU GIRLS HAVING A GOOD SHOW?
IT'S OK. IT WOULD BE BETTER IF WE KNEW THE BANDS...
OK. WELL, THIS IS BLAMED YOUTH. THEY WERE PART OF THE MID-EIGHTIES HARDCORE HUERTA SCENE...
BLAMED YOUTH, FORTIFIED YOUTH, NO LONGER YOUTH...
THAT SINGER STILL THINKS HE'S YOUTH.
MIKE RAFONE. HE WAS SORT OF THE CASANOVA OF THAT SCENE...
AND YOUR MOM HAD THE WAY TOTAL HOTS FOR HIM.
YOU DID??
OH, WHO DIDN'T THEN?
BUT YOUR MOM GOT TO WEAR HIS LEATHER, EVEN THOUGH IT SMELLED LIKE CAT PEE.
AND DOYLE WAS GOING TO PUNCH HIM IN THE NOSE WHEN MIKE BROKE MY HEART.
WE'LL PUNCH HIM IN THE NOSE FOR YOU, MOM. IF WE GET CLOSE ENOUGH.
YOU'VE GOT HER PROPERLY BRAINWASHED, DOCTOR.
AS LONG AS HE DOESN'T BRAINWASH HER.
MAYBE THEY WEREN'T AS MUCH FOR YOU GUYS, BUT MY PUNK DAYS WERE THE MOST VITAL DAYS OF MY LIFE.
IF MY DAUGHTER GETS ONE TINY PERCENTAGE OF WHAT I GOT OUT OF IT, I'LL BE A VERY HAPPY MOM.
I'M SO CORNY.
I WISH I HAD A MOM LIKE YOU.
GANGWAY!
JOEY, WHERE YOU BEEN?
DOMINATING THE PIT WITH MY BRO, TONY BELLE.
OH, HI, TONY. ARE YOU OK?
HUERTA PUNKS... ROOL...
10.

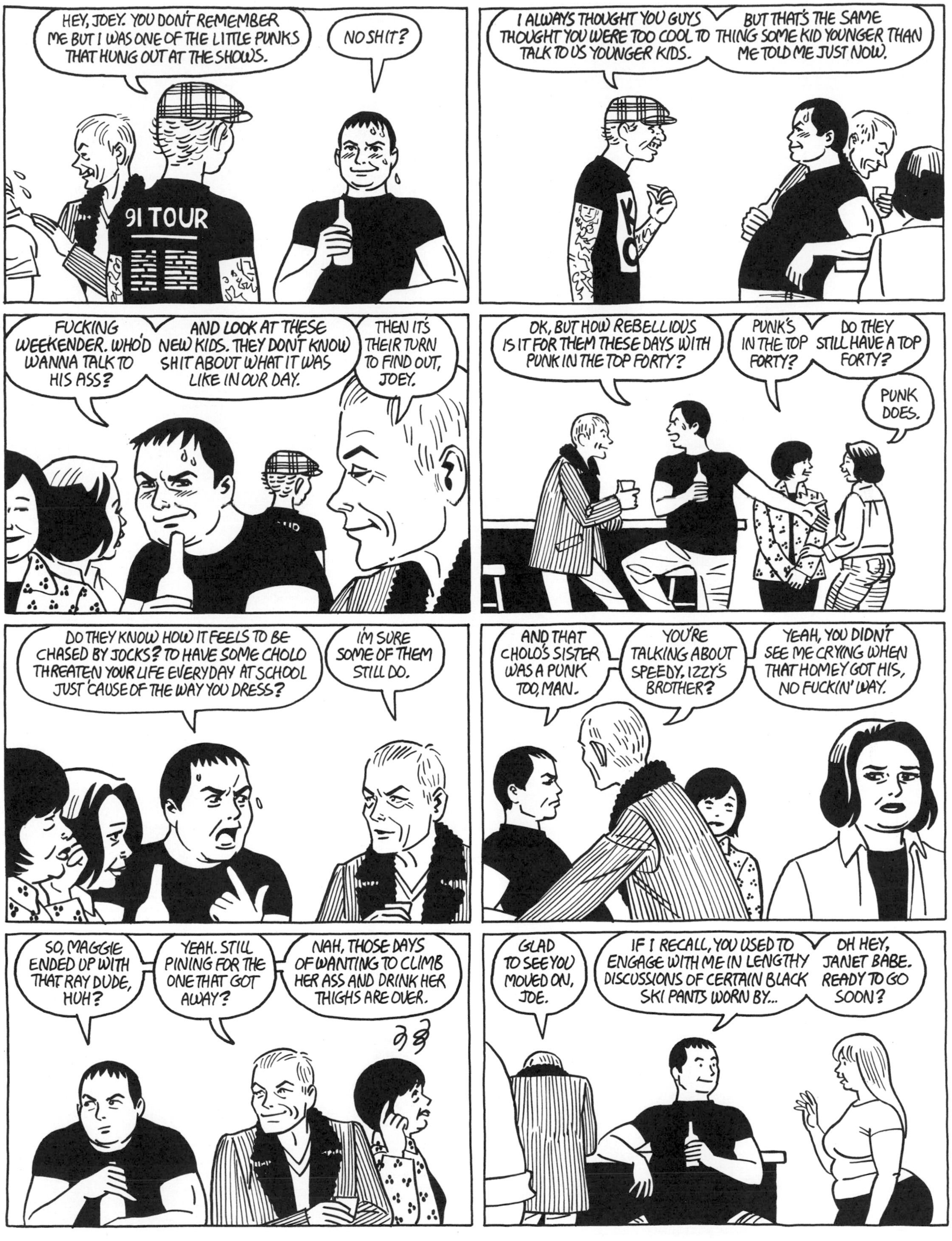
HEY, JOEY. YOU DON'T REMEMBER ME BUT I WAS ONE OF THE LITTLE PUNKS THAT HUNG OUT AT THE SHOWS.
NO SHIT?
91 TOUR
I ALWAYS THOUGHT YOU GUYS THOUGHT YOU WERE TOO COOL TO TALK TO US YOUNGER KIDS.
BUT THAT'S THE SAME THING SOME KID YOUNGER THAN ME TOLD ME JUST NOW.
FUCKING WEEKENDER. WHO'D WANNA TALK TO HIS ASS?
AND LOOK AT THESE NEW KIDS. THEY DON'T KNOW SHIT ABOUT WHAT IT WAS LIKE IN OUR DAY.
THEN IT'S THEIR TURN TO FIND OUT, JOEY.
OK, BUT HOW REBELLIOUS IS IT FOR THEM THESE DAYS WITH PUNK IN THE TOP FORTY?
PUNK'S IN THE TOP FORTY?
DO THEY STILL HAVE A TOP FORTY?
PUNK DOES.
DO THEY KNOW HOW IT FEELS TO BE CHASED BY JOCKS? TO HAVE SOME CHOLO THREATEN YOUR LIFE EVERYDAY AT SCHOOL JUST 'CAUSE OF THE WAY YOU DRESS?
I'M SURE SOME OF THEM STILL DO.
AND THAT CHOLO'S SISTER WAS A PUNK TOO, MAN.
YOU'RE TALKING ABOUT SPEEDY, IZZY'S BROTHER?
YEAH, YOU DIDN'T SEE ME CRYING WHEN THAT HOMEY GOT HIS, NO FUCKIN' WAY.
SO, MAGGIE ENDED UP WITH THAT RAY DUDE, HUH?
YEAH. STILL PINING FOR THE ONE THAT GOT AWAY?
NAH, THOSE DAYS OF WANTING TO CLIMB HER ASS AND DRINK HER THIGHS ARE OVER.
GLAD TO SEE YOU MOVED ON, JOE.
IF I RECALL, YOU USED TO ENGAGE WITH ME IN LENGTHY DISCUSSIONS OF CERTAIN BLACK SKI PANTS WORN BY...
OH HEY, JANET BABE. READY TO GO SOON?
11.

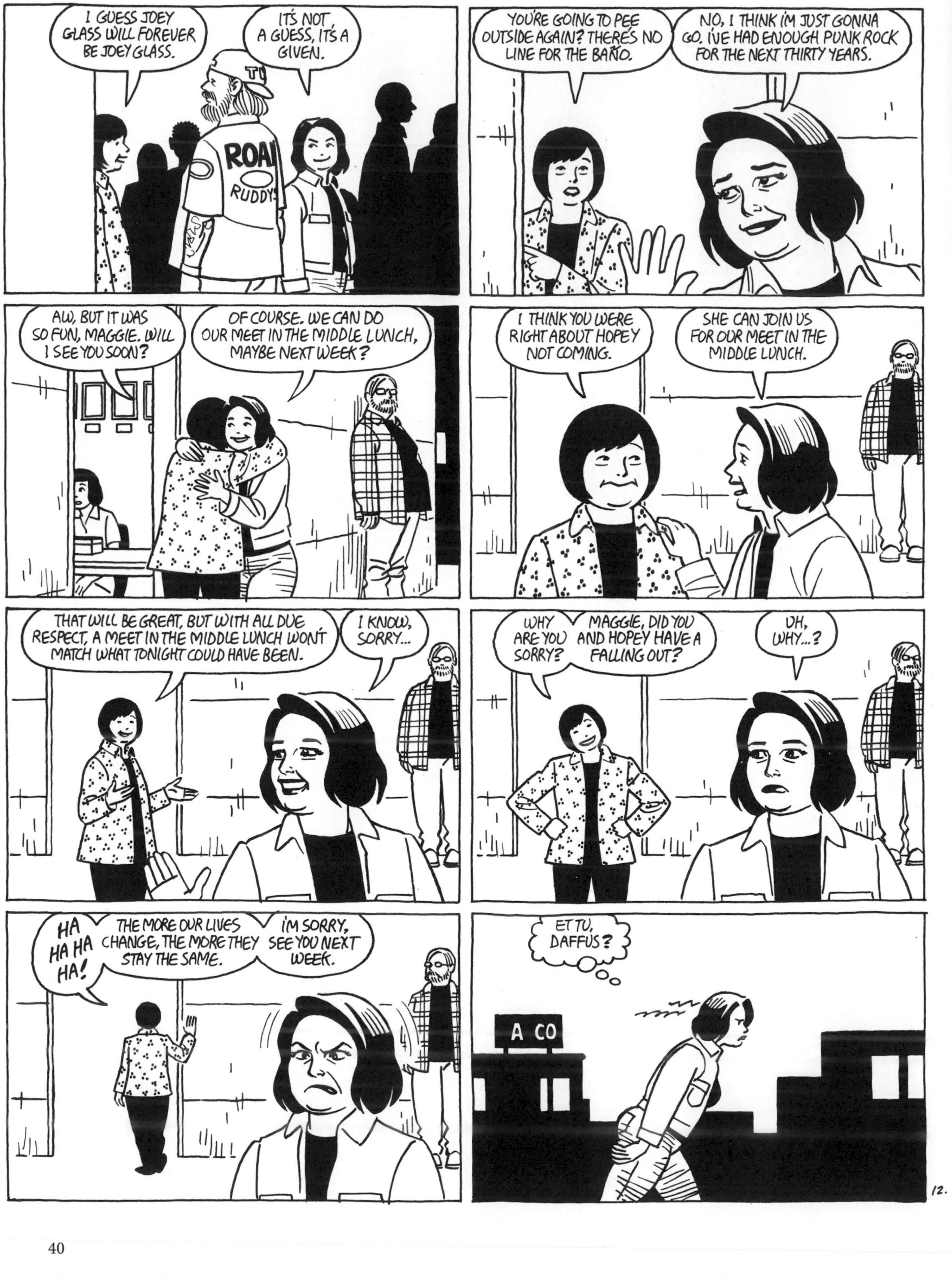

I GUESS JOEY GLASS WILL FOREVER BE JOEY GLASS.
IT'S NOT A GUESS, IT'S A GIVEN.
ROA
RUDDY
YOU'RE GOING TO PEE OUTSIDE AGAIN? THERE'S NO LINE FOR THE BAÑO.
NO, I THINK I'M JUST GONNA GO. I'VE HAD ENOUGH PUNK ROCK FOR THE NEXT THIRTY YEARS.
AW, BUT IT WAS SO FUN, MAGGIE. WILL I SEE YOU SOON?
OF COURSE. WE CAN DO OUR MEET IN THE MIDDLE LUNCH, MAYBE NEXT WEEK?
I THINK YOU WERE RIGHT ABOUT HOPEY NOT COMING.
SHE CAN JOIN US FOR OUR MEET IN THE MIDDLE LUNCH.
THAT WILL BE GREAT, BUT WITH ALL DUE RESPECT, A MEET IN THE MIDDLE LUNCH WON'T MATCH WHAT TONIGHT COULD HAVE BEEN.
I KNOW, SORRY...
WHY ARE YOU SORRY?
MAGGIE, DID YOU AND HOPEY HAVE A FALLING OUT?
UH, WHY...?
HA HA HA HA!
THE MORE OUR LIVES CHANGE, THE MORE THEY STAY THE SAME.
I'M SORRY, SEE YOU NEXT WEEK.
ET TU, DAFFUS?
A CO
12.

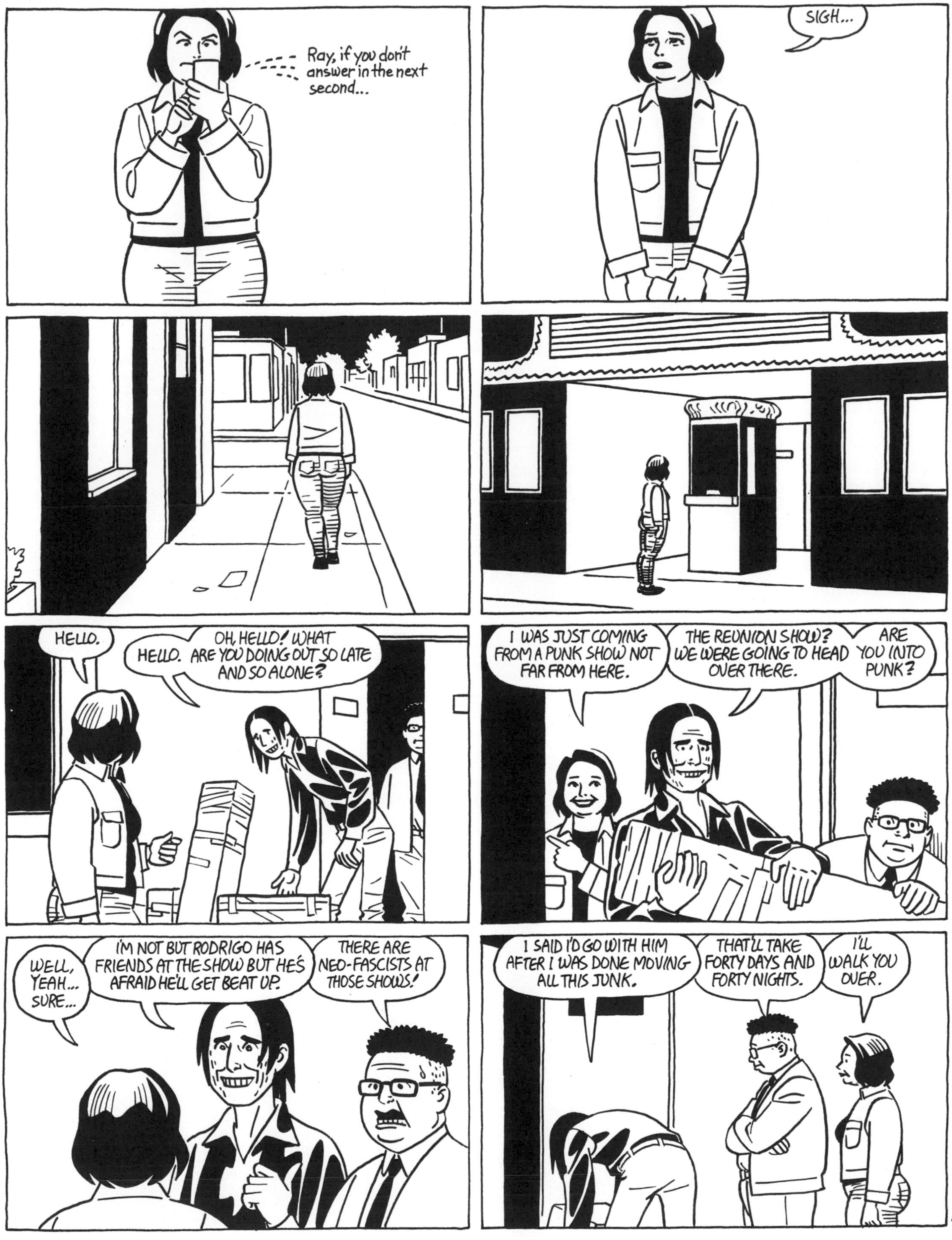

Ray, if you don't answer in the next second...
SIGH...
HELLO.
HELLO.
OH, HELLO! WHAT ARE YOU DOING OUT SO LATE AND SO ALONE?
I WAS JUST COMING FROM A PUNK SHOW NOT FAR FROM HERE.
THE REUNION SHOW? WE WERE GOING TO HEAD OVER THERE.
ARE YOU INTO PUNK?
WELL, YEAH... SURE...
I'M NOT BUT RODRIGO HAS FRIENDS AT THE SHOW BUT HE'S AFRAID HE'LL GET BEAT UP.
THERE ARE NEO-FASCISTS AT THOSE SHOWS!
I SAID I'D GO WITH HIM AFTER I WAS DONE MOVING ALL THIS JUNK.
THAT'LL TAKE FORTY DAYS AND FORTY NIGHTS.
I'LL WALK YOU OVER.
13.

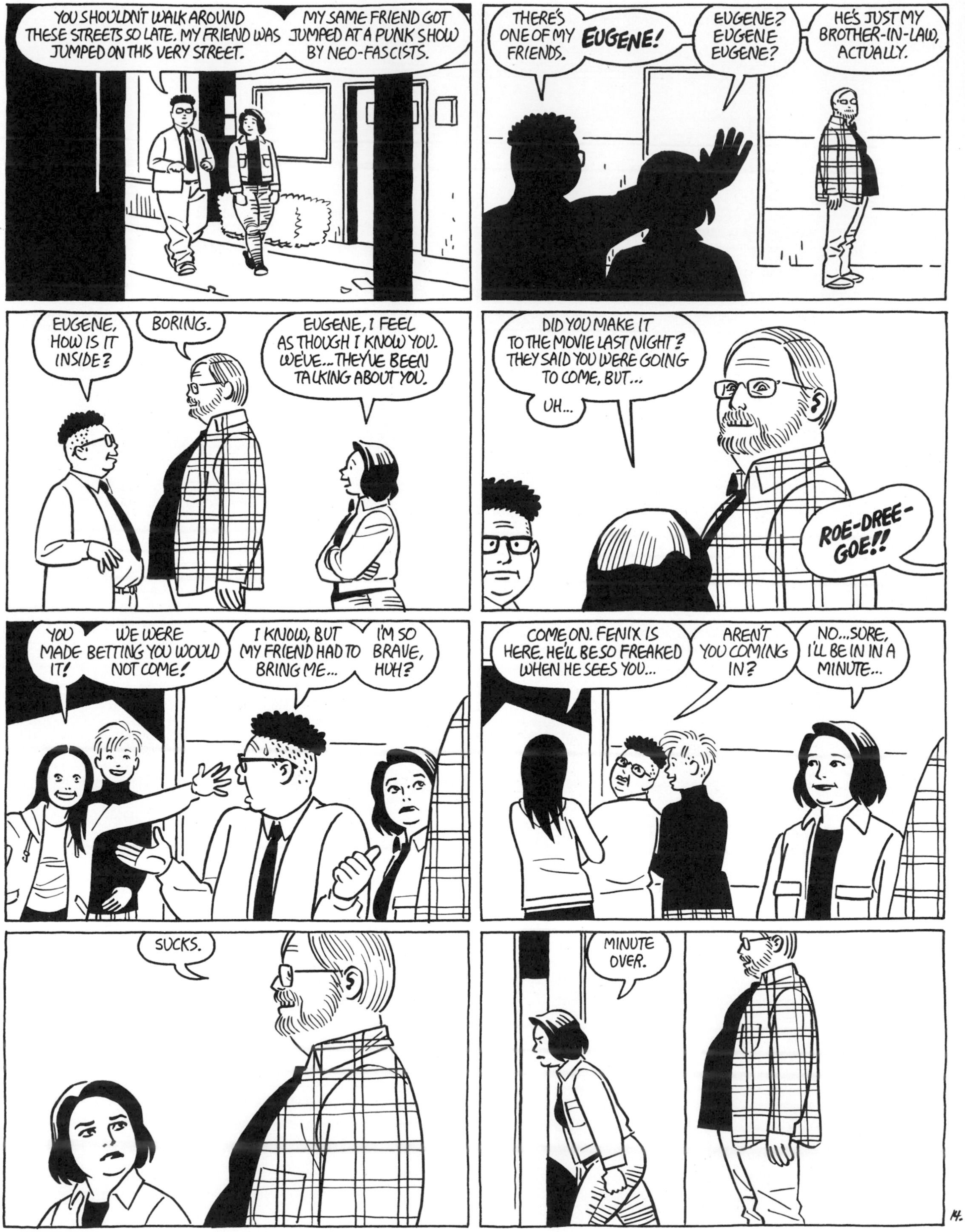
YOU SHOULDN'T WALK AROUND THESE STREETS SO LATE. MY FRIEND WAS JUMPED ON THIS VERY STREET.
MY SAME FRIEND GOT JUMPED AT A PUNK SHOW BY NEO-FASCISTS.
THERE'S ONE OF MY FRIENDS.
EUGENE!
EUGENE? EUGENE EUGENE?
HE'S JUST MY BROTHER-IN-LAW, ACTUALLY.
EUGENE, HOW IS IT INSIDE?
BORING.
EUGENE, I FEEL AS THOUGH I KNOW YOU. WE'VE... THEY'VE BEEN TALKING ABOUT YOU.
DID YOU MAKE IT TO THE MOVIE LAST NIGHT? THEY SAID YOU WERE GOING TO COME, BUT...
UH...
ROE-DREE-GOE!!
YOU MADE IT!
WE WERE BETTING YOU WOULD NOT COME!
I KNOW, BUT MY FRIEND HAD TO BRING ME...
I'M SO BRAVE, HUH?
COME ON. FENIX IS HERE. HE'LL BE SO FREAKED WHEN HE SEES YOU...
AREN'T YOU COMING IN?
NO...SURE, I'LL BE IN IN A MINUTE...
SUCKS.
MINUTE OVER.
14.

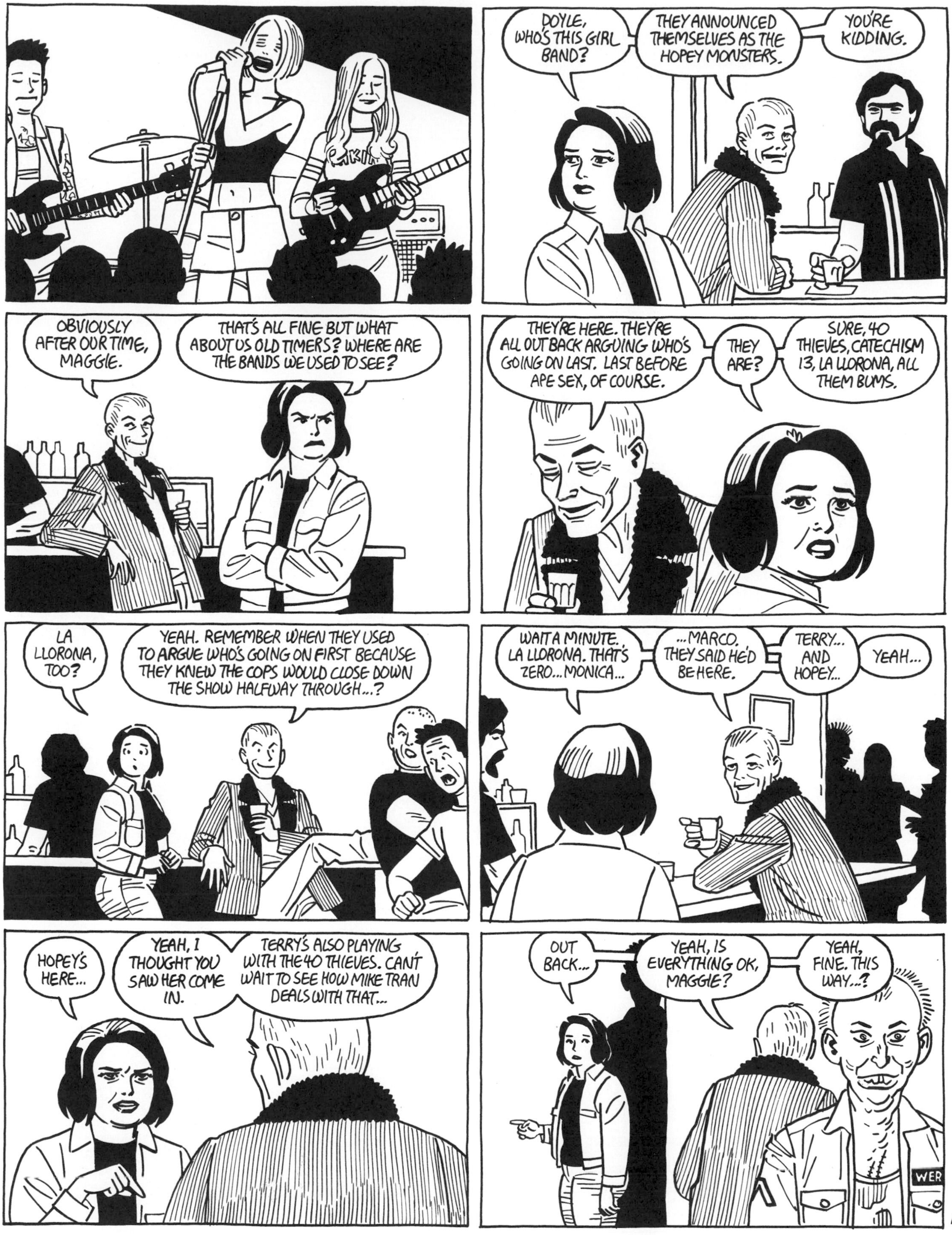
DOYLE, WHO'S THIS GIRL BAND?
THEY ANNOUNCED THEMSELVES AS THE HOPEY MONSTERS.
YOU'RE KIDDING.
OBVIOUSLY AFTER OUR TIME, MAGGIE.
THAT'S ALL FINE BUT WHAT ABOUT US OLD TIMERS? WHERE ARE THE BANDS WE USED TO SEE?
THEY'RE HERE. THEY'RE ALL OUT BACK ARGUING WHO'S GOING ON LAST. LAST BEFORE APE SEX, OF COURSE.
THEY ARE?
SURE, 40 THIEVES, CATECHISM 13, LA LLORONA, ALL THEM BUMS.
LA LLORONA, TOO?
YEAH. REMEMBER WHEN THEY USED TO ARGUE WHO'S GOING ON FIRST BECAUSE THEY KNEW THE COPS WOULD CLOSE DOWN THE SHOW HALFWAY THROUGH...?
WAIT A MINUTE. LA LLORONA. THAT'S ZERO...MONICA...
...MARCO. THEY SAID HE'D BE HERE.
TERRY... AND HOPEY...
YEAH...
HOPEY'S HERE...
YEAH, I THOUGHT YOU SAW HER COME IN.
TERRY'S ALSO PLAYING WITH THE 40 THIEVES. CAN'T WAIT TO SEE HOW MIKE TRAN DEALS WITH THAT...
OUT BACK...
YEAH, IS EVERYTHING OK, MAGGIE?
YEAH, FINE. THIS WAY...?
WER

15.

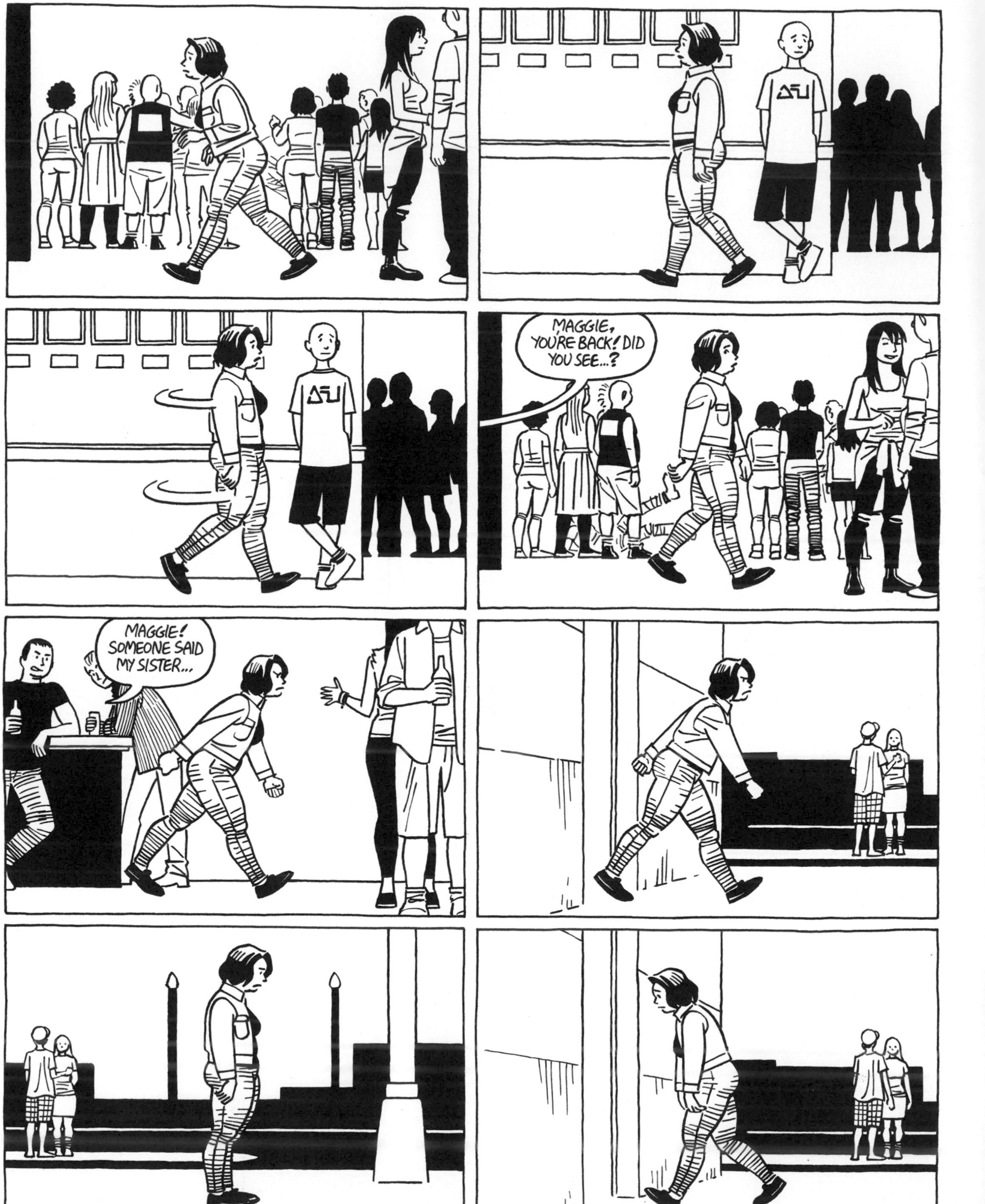
MAGGIE, YOU'RE BACK! DID YOU SEE...?
MAGGIE! SOMEONE SAID MY SISTER...
16.

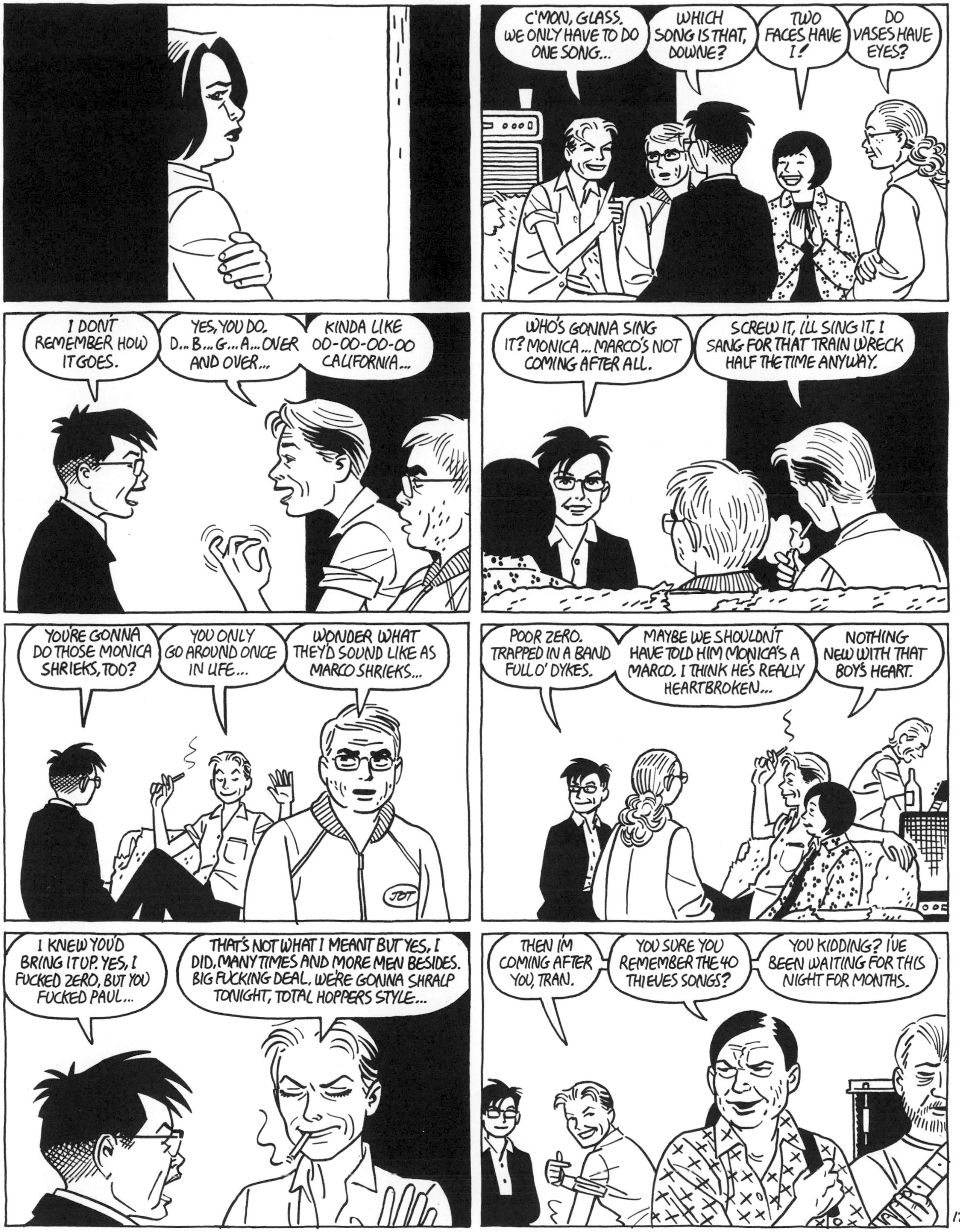
C'MON, GLASS. WE ONLY HAVE TO DO ONE SONG...
WHICH SONG IS THAT, DOWNE?
TWO FACES HAVE I!
DO VASES HAVE EYES?
I DON'T REMEMBER HOW IT GOES.
YES, YOU DO. D...B...G...A...OVER AND OVER...
KINDA LIKE OO-OO-OO-OO CALIFORNIA...
WHO'S GONNA SING IT? MONICA... MARCO'S NOT COMING AFTER ALL.
SCREW IT, I'LL SING IT. I SANG FOR THAT TRAIN WRECK HALF THE TIME ANYWAY.
YOU'RE GONNA DO THOSE MONICA SHRIEKS, TOO?
YOU ONLY GO AROUND ONCE IN LIFE...
WONDER WHAT THEY'D SOUND LIKE AS MARCO SHRIEKS...
JOT
POOR ZERO. TRAPPED IN A BAND FULL O' DYKES.
MAYBE WE SHOULDN'T HAVE TOLD HIM MONICA'S A MARCO. I THINK HE'S REALLY HEARTBROKEN...
NOTHING NEW WITH THAT BOY'S HEART.
I KNEW YOU'D BRING IT UP. YES, I FUCKED ZERO, BUT YOU FUCKED PAUL...
THAT'S NOT WHAT I MEANT BUT YES, I DID, MANY TIMES AND MORE MEN BESIDES. BIG FUCKING DEAL, WE'RE GONNA SHRALP TONIGHT, TOTAL HOPPERS STYLE...
THEN I'M COMING AFTER YOU, TRAN.
YOU SURE YOU REMEMBER THE 40 THIEVES SONGS?
YOU KIDDING? I'VE BEEN WAITING FOR THIS NIGHT FOR MONTHS.
17.

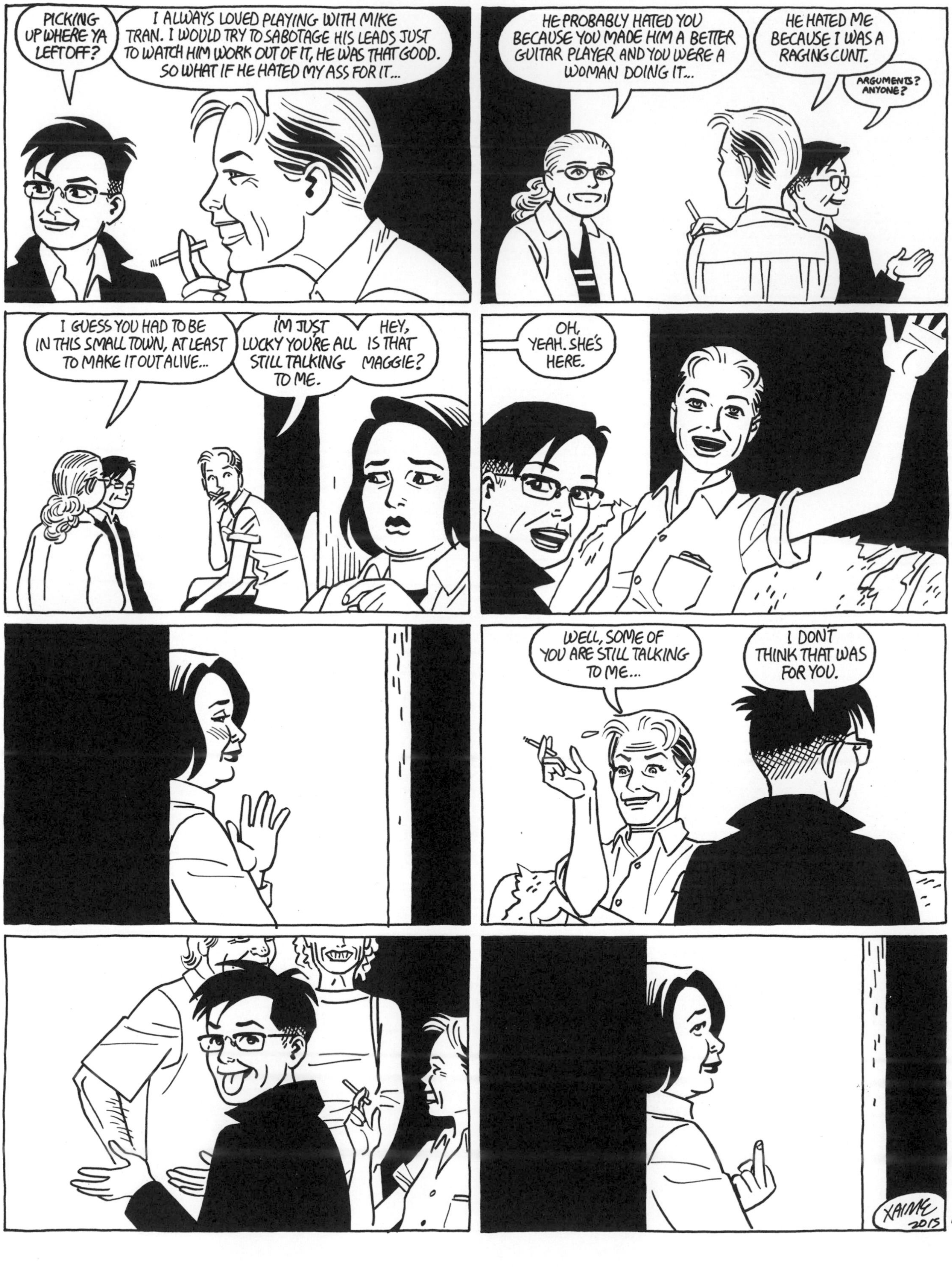
PICKING UP WHERE YA LEFT OFF?
I ALWAYS LOVED PLAYING WITH MIKE TRAN. I WOULD TRY TO SABOTAGE HIS LEADS JUST TO WATCH HIM WORK OUT OF IT, HE WAS THAT GOOD. SO WHAT IF HE HATED MY ASS FOR IT...
HE PROBABLY HATED YOU BECAUSE YOU MADE HIM A BETTER GUITAR PLAYER AND YOU WERE A WOMAN DOING IT...
HE HATED ME BECAUSE I WAS A RAGING CUNT.
ARGUMENTS? ANYONE?
I GUESS YOU HAD TO BE IN THIS SMALL TOWN, AT LEAST TO MAKE IT OUT ALIVE...
I'M JUST LUCKY YOU'RE ALL STILL TALKING TO ME.
HEY, IS THAT MAGGIE?
OH, YEAH. SHE'S HERE.
WELL, SOME OF YOU ARE STILL TALKING TO ME...
I DONT THINK THAT WAS FOR YOU.
XAIME 2015
18.

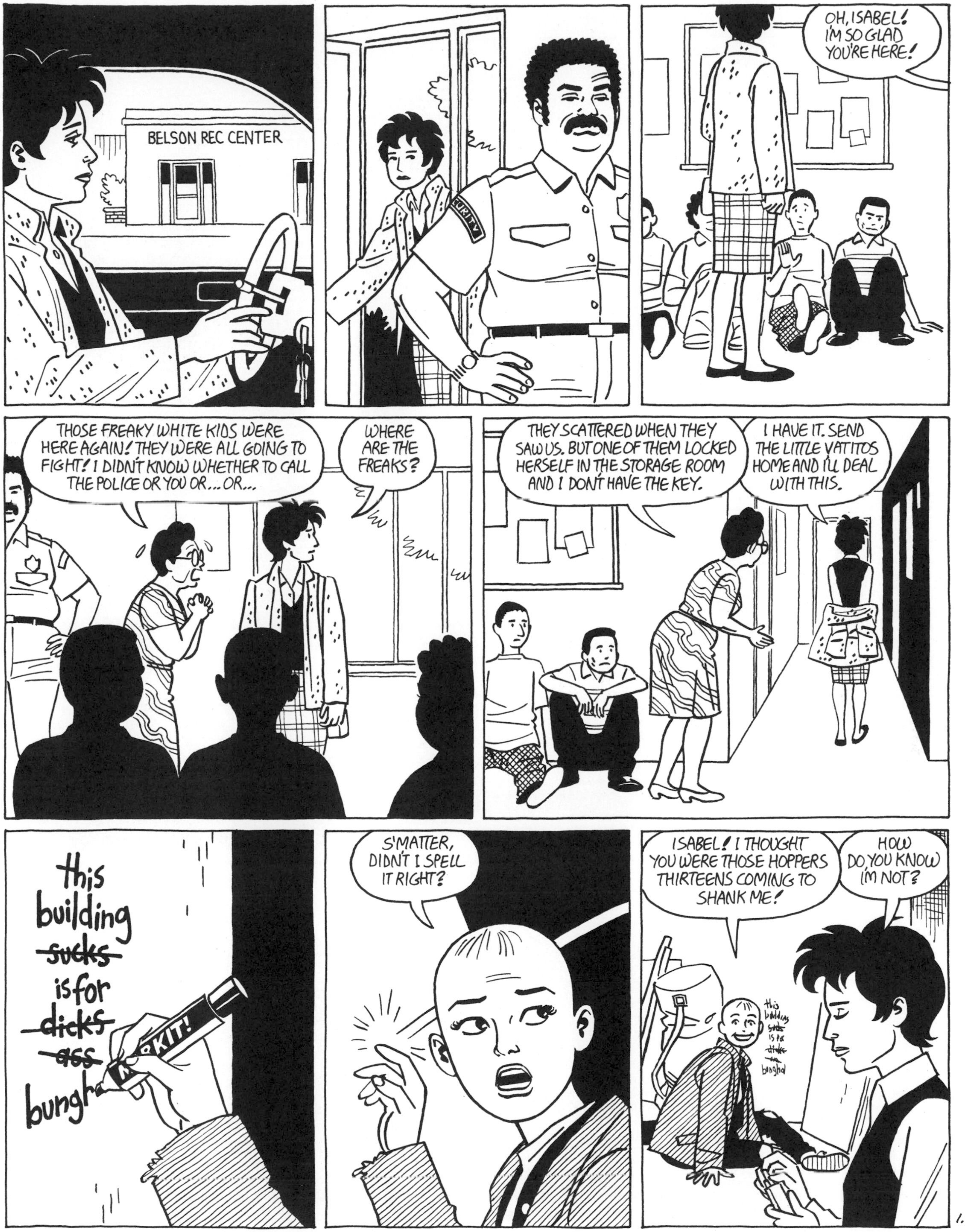
BELSON REC CENTER
OH, ISABEL! I'M SO GLAD YOU'RE HERE!
THOSE FREAKY WHITE KIDS WERE HERE AGAIN! THEY WERE ALL GOING TO FIGHT! I DIDN'T KNOW WHETHER TO CALL THE POLICE OR YOU OR... OR...
WHERE ARE THE FREAKS?
THEY SCATTERED WHEN THEY SAW US. BUT ONE OF THEM LOCKED HERSELF IN THE STORAGE ROOM AND I DON'T HAVE THE KEY.
I HAVE IT. SEND THE LITTLE VATITOS HOME AND I'LL DEAL WITH THIS.
this building ~~sucks~~ is for ~~dicks~~ ~~ass~~ bungh
S'MATTER, DIDN'T I SPELL IT RIGHT?
ISABEL! I THOUGHT YOU WERE THOSE HOPPERS THIRTEENS COMING TO SHANK ME!
HOW DO, YOU KNOW I'M NOT?
1.

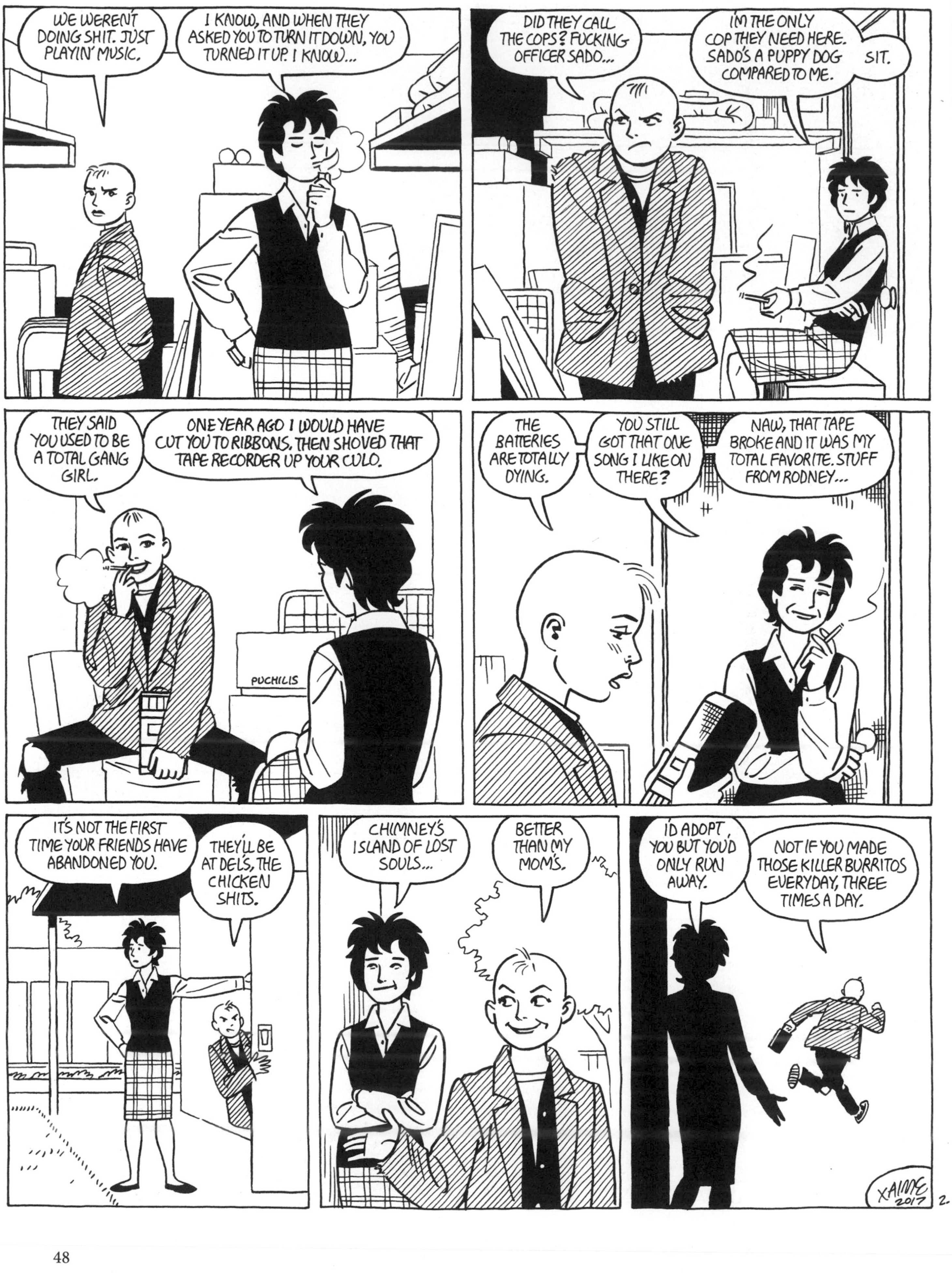
WE WEREN'T DOING SHIT. JUST PLAYIN' MUSIC.
I KNOW, AND WHEN THEY ASKED YOU TO TURN IT DOWN, YOU TURNED IT UP. I KNOW...
DID THEY CALL THE COPS? FUCKING OFFICER SADO...
I'M THE ONLY COP THEY NEED HERE. SADO'S A PUPPY DOG COMPARED TO ME.
SIT.
THEY SAID YOU USED TO BE A TOTAL GANG GIRL.
ONE YEAR AGO I WOULD HAVE CUT YOU TO RIBBONS, THEN SHOVED THAT TAPE RECORDER UP YOUR CULO.
PUCHILIS
THE BATTERIES ARE TOTALLY DYING.
YOU STILL GOT THAT ONE SONG I LIKE ON THERE?
NAW, THAT TAPE BROKE AND IT WAS MY TOTAL FAVORITE. STUFF FROM RODNEY...
IT'S NOT THE FIRST TIME YOUR FRIENDS HAVE ABANDONED YOU.
THEY'LL BE AT DEL'S, THE CHICKEN SHITS.
CHIMNEY'S ISLAND OF LOST SOULS...
BETTER THAN MY MOM'S.
I'D ADOPT YOU BUT YOU'D ONLY RUN AWAY.
NOT IF YOU MADE THOSE KILLER BURRITOS EVERYDAY, THREE TIMES A DAY.
XAIME 2017
2.

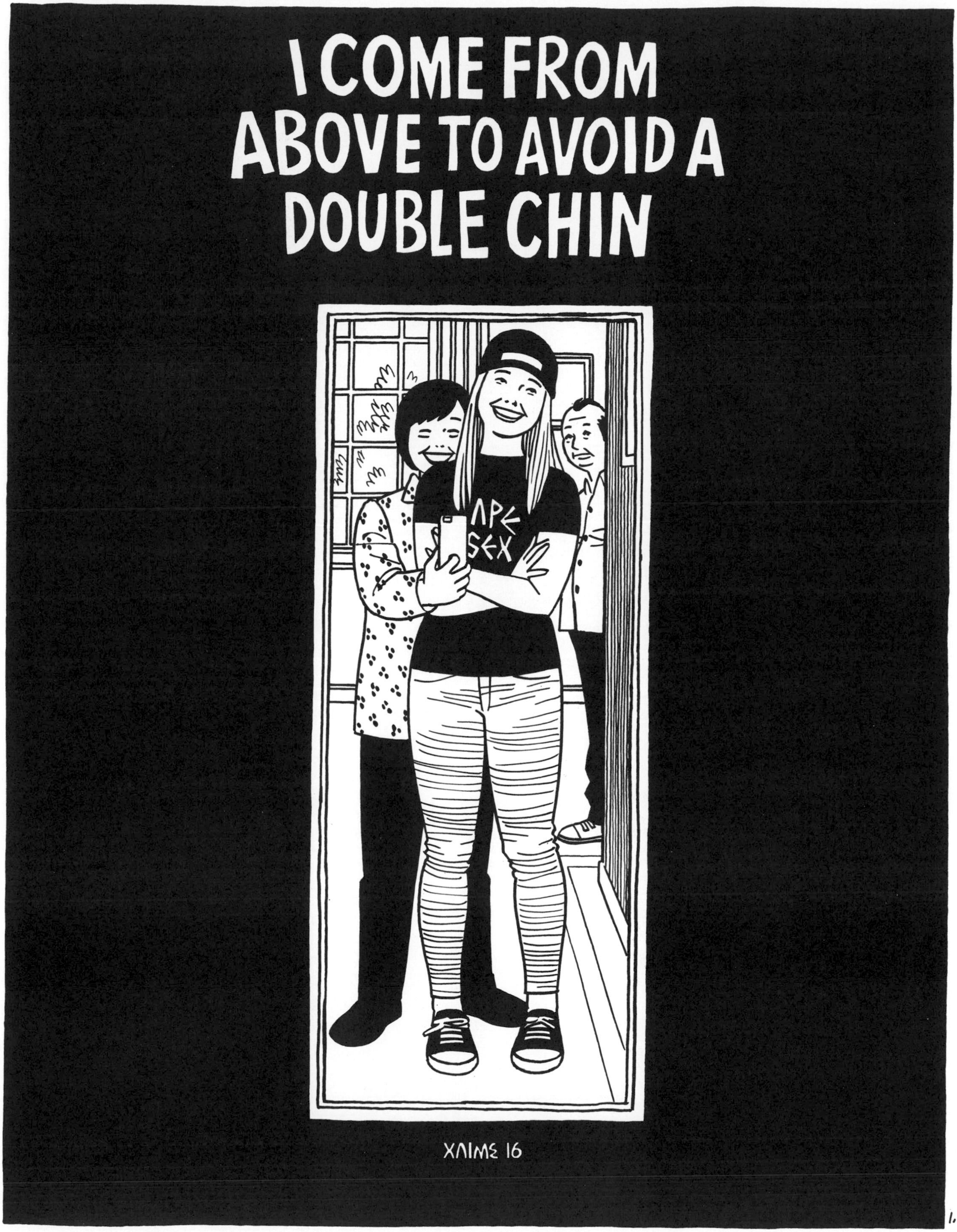
I COME FROM
ABOVE TO AVOID A
DOUBLE CHIN
APE
SEX
XAIME 16

1.

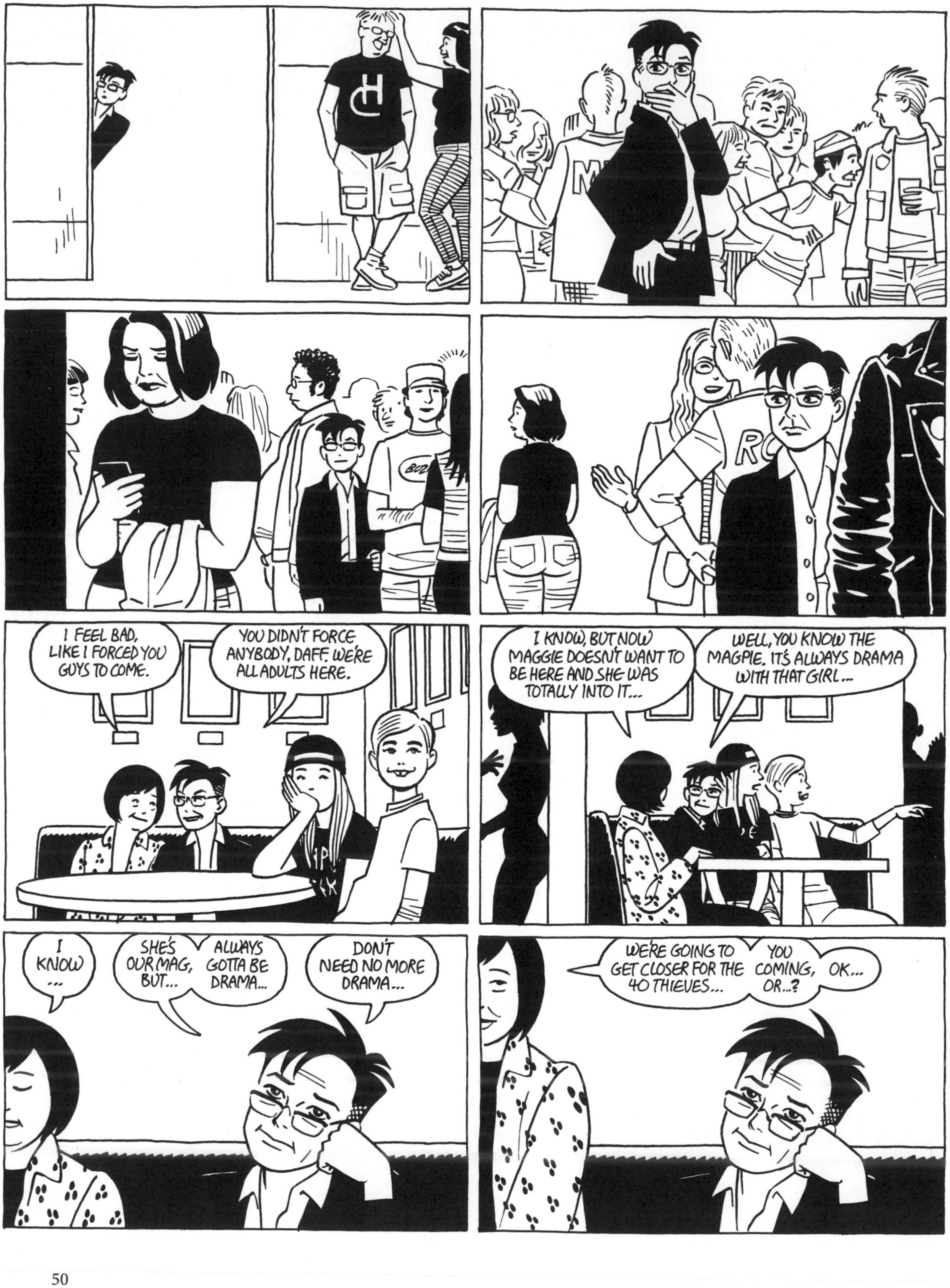

I FEEL BAD, LIKE I FORCED YOU GUYS TO COME.
YOU DIDN'T FORCE ANYBODY, DAFF. WE'RE ALL ADULTS HERE.
I KNOW, BUT NOW MAGGIE DOESN'T WANT TO BE HERE AND SHE WAS TOTALLY INTO IT...
WELL, YOU KNOW THE MAGPIE. IT'S ALWAYS DRAMA WITH THAT GIRL...
I KNOW ...
SHE'S OUR MAG, BUT...
ALWAYS GOTTA BE DRAMA...
DON'T NEED NO MORE DRAMA...
WE'RE GOING TO GET CLOSER FOR THE 40 THIEVES...
YOU COMING, OR...?
OK...
2.

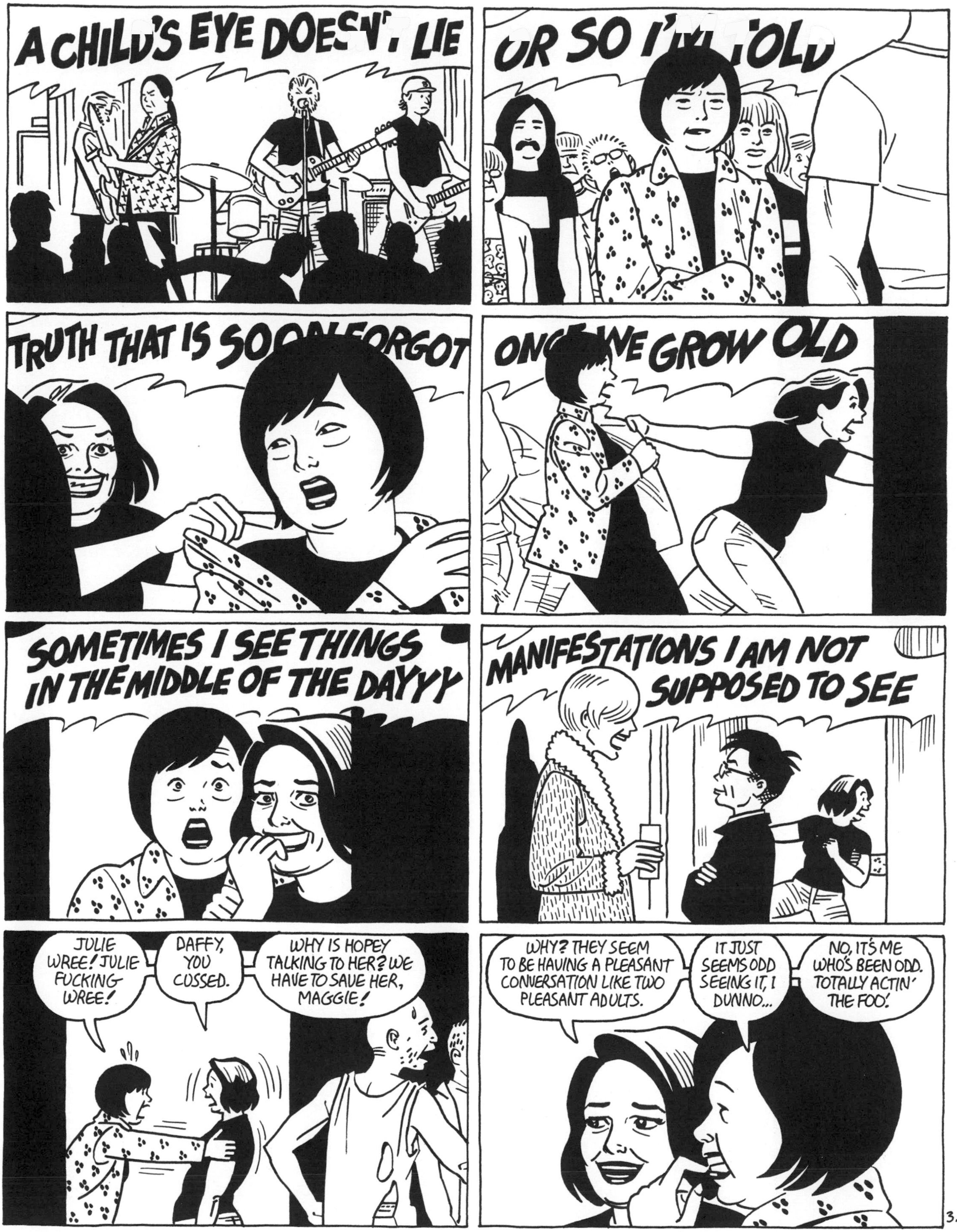
A CHILD'S EYE DOESN'T LIE
OR SO I'M TOLD
TRUTH THAT IS SOON FORGOT
ONCE WE GROW OLD
SOMETIMES I SEE THINGS IN THE MIDDLE OF THE DAYYY
MANIFESTATIONS I AM NOT SUPPOSED TO SEE
JULIE WREE! JULIE FUCKING WREE!
DAFFY, YOU CUSSED.
WHY IS HOPEY TALKING TO HER? WE HAVE TO SAVE HER, MAGGIE!
WHY? THEY SEEM TO BE HAVING A PLEASANT CONVERSATION LIKE TWO PLEASANT ADULTS.
IT JUST SEEMS ODD SEEING IT, I DUNNO...
NO, IT'S ME WHO'S BEEN ODD. TOTALLY ACTIN' THE FOO'.
3.

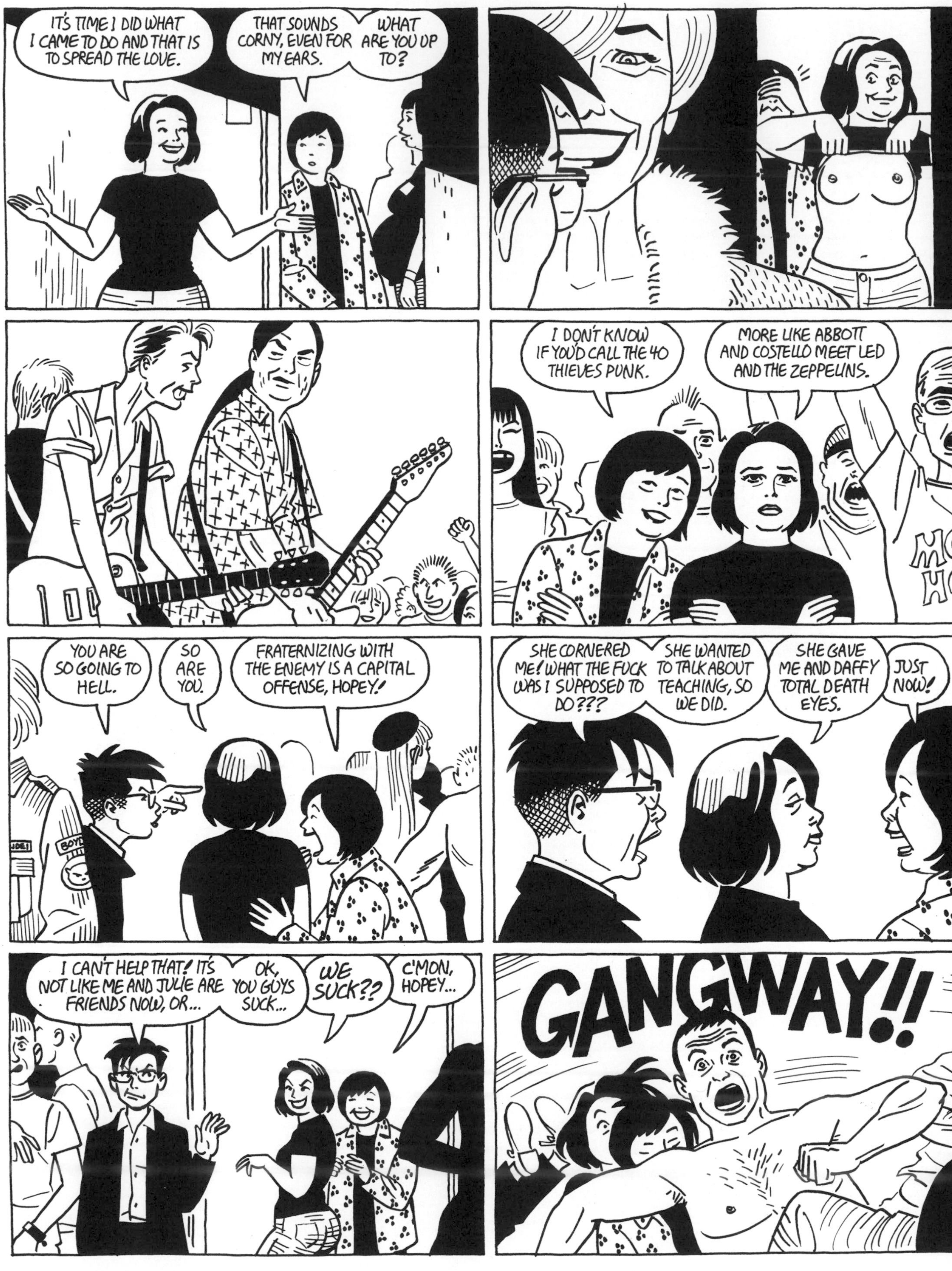
IT'S TIME I DID WHAT I CAME TO DO AND THAT IS TO SPREAD THE LOVE.
THAT SOUNDS CORNY, EVEN FOR MY EARS.
WHAT ARE YOU UP TO?
I DON'T KNOW IF YOU'D CALL THE 40 THIEVES PUNK.
MORE LIKE ABBOTT AND COSTELLO MEET LED AND THE ZEPPELINS.
YOU ARE SO GOING TO HELL.
SO ARE YOU.
FRATERNIZING WITH THE ENEMY IS A CAPITAL OFFENSE, HOPEY!
SHE CORNERED ME! WHAT THE FUCK WAS I SUPPOSED TO DO???
SHE WANTED TO TALK ABOUT TEACHING, SO WE DID.
SHE GAVE ME AND DAFFY TOTAL DEATH EYES.
JUST NOW!
I CAN'T HELP THAT! IT'S NOT LIKE ME AND JULIE ARE FRIENDS NOW, OR...
OK, YOU GUYS SUCK...
WE SUCK??
C'MON, HOPEY...
GANGWAY!!
4.

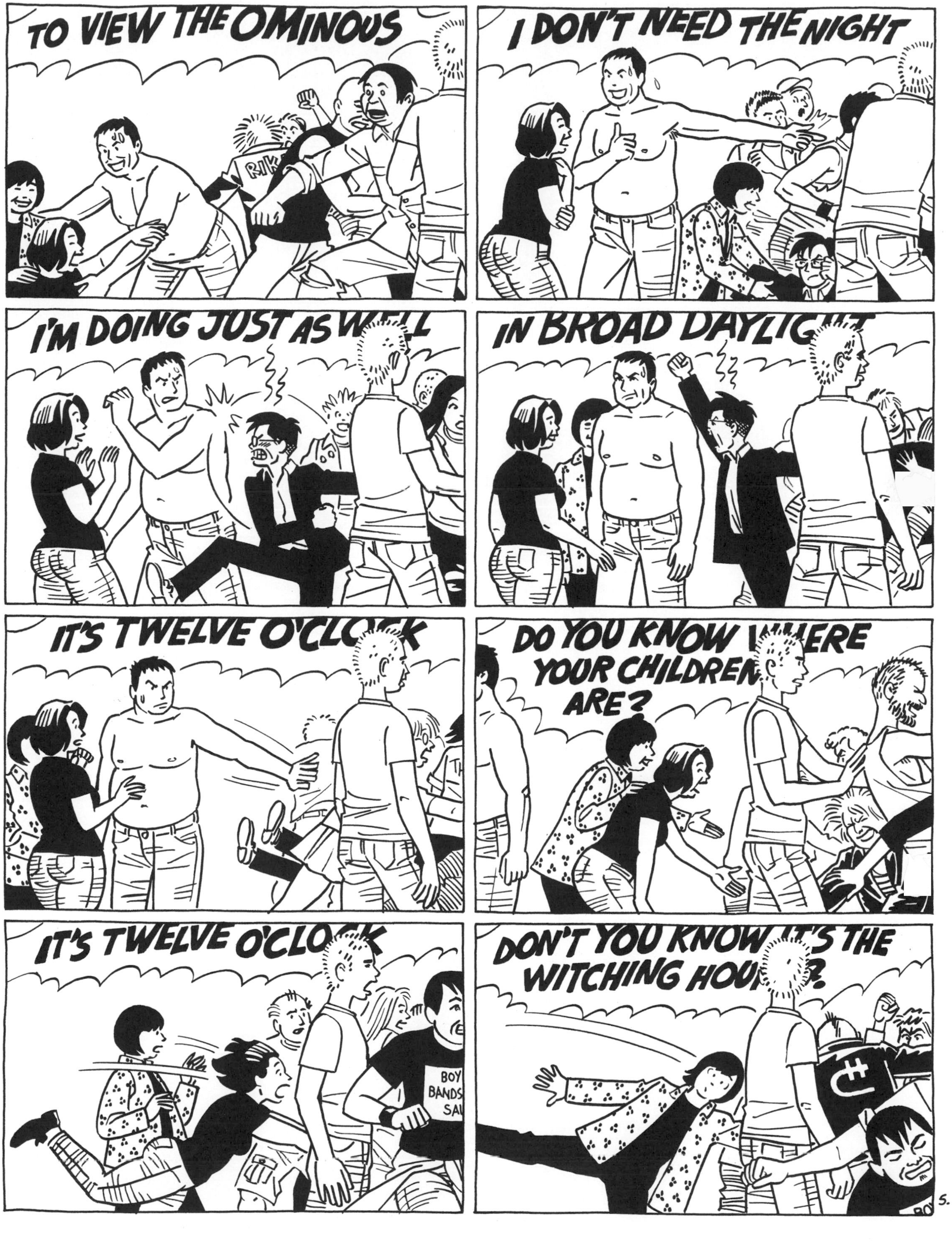
TO VIEW THE OMINOUS
I DON'T NEED THE NIGHT
I'M DOING JUST AS WELL
IN BROAD DAYLIGHT
IT'S TWELVE O'CLOCK
DO YOU KNOW WHERE YOUR CHILDREN ARE?
IT'S TWELVE O'CLOCK
BOY BANDS SA
DON'T YOU KNOW IT'S THE WITCHING HOUR?
S.

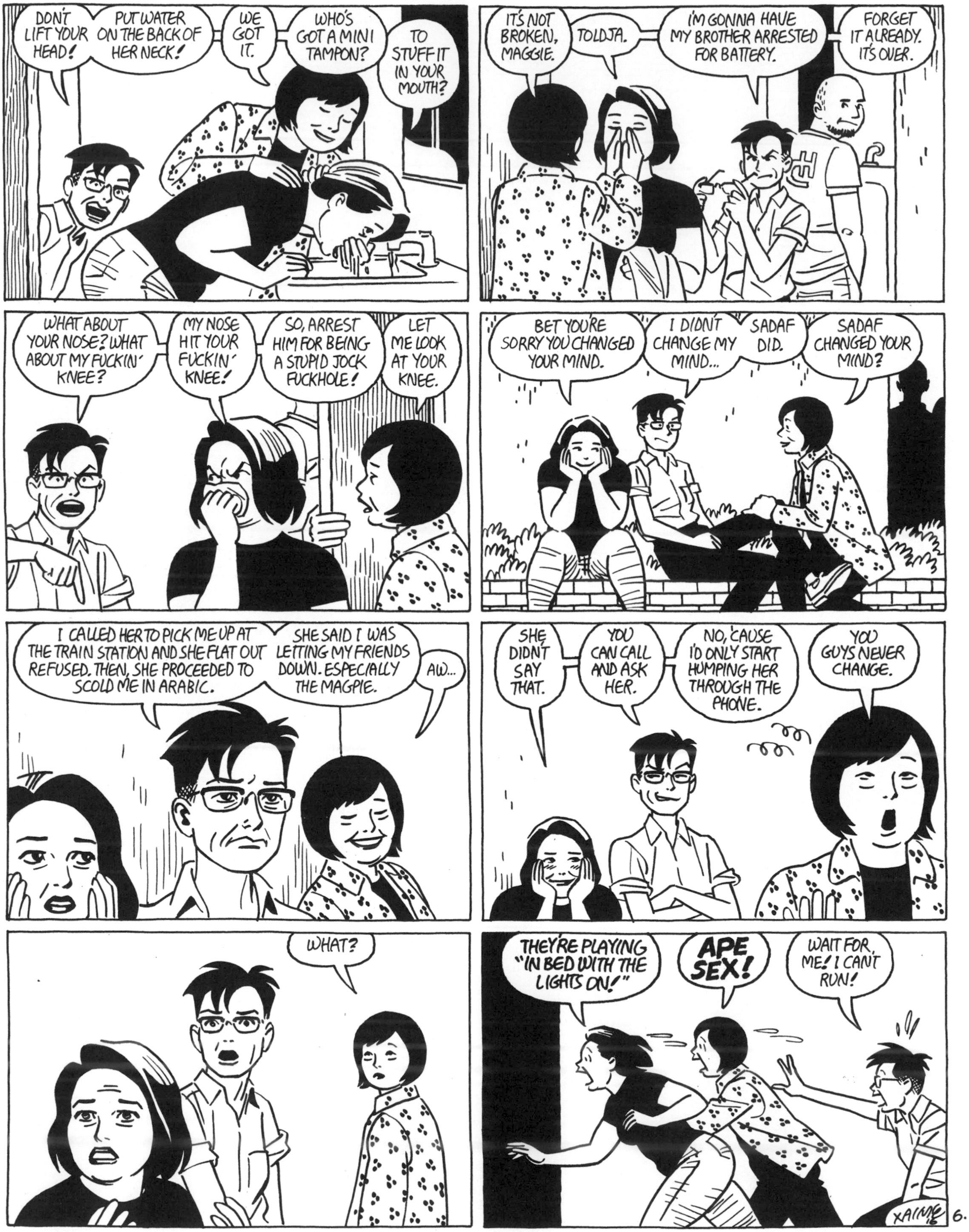
DON'T LIFT YOUR HEAD!
PUT WATER ON THE BACK OF HER NECK!
WE GOT IT.
WHO'S GOT A MINI TAMPON?
TO STUFF IT IN YOUR MOUTH?
IT'S NOT BROKEN, MAGGIE.
TOLDJA.
I'M GONNA HAVE MY BROTHER ARRESTED FOR BATTERY.
FORGET IT ALREADY. IT'S OVER.
WHAT ABOUT YOUR NOSE? WHAT ABOUT MY FUCKIN' KNEE?
MY NOSE HIT YOUR FUCKIN' KNEE!
SO, ARREST HIM FOR BEING A STUPID JOCK FUCKHOLE!
LET ME LOOK AT YOUR KNEE.
BET YOU'RE SORRY YOU CHANGED YOUR MIND.
I DIDN'T CHANGE MY MIND...
SADAF DID.
SADAF CHANGED YOUR MIND?
I CALLED HER TO PICK ME UP AT THE TRAIN STATION AND SHE FLAT OUT REFUSED. THEN, SHE PROCEEDED TO SCOLD ME IN ARABIC.
SHE SAID I WAS LETTING MY FRIENDS DOWN. ESPECIALLY THE MAGPIE.
AW...
SHE DIDN'T SAY THAT.
YOU CAN CALL AND ASK HER.
NO, 'CAUSE I'D ONLY START HUMPING HER THROUGH THE PHONE.
YOU GUYS NEVER CHANGE.
WHAT?
THEY'RE PLAYING "IN BED WITH THE LIGHTS ON!"
APE SEX!
WAIT FOR ME! I CAN'T RUN!
XAIME
6.

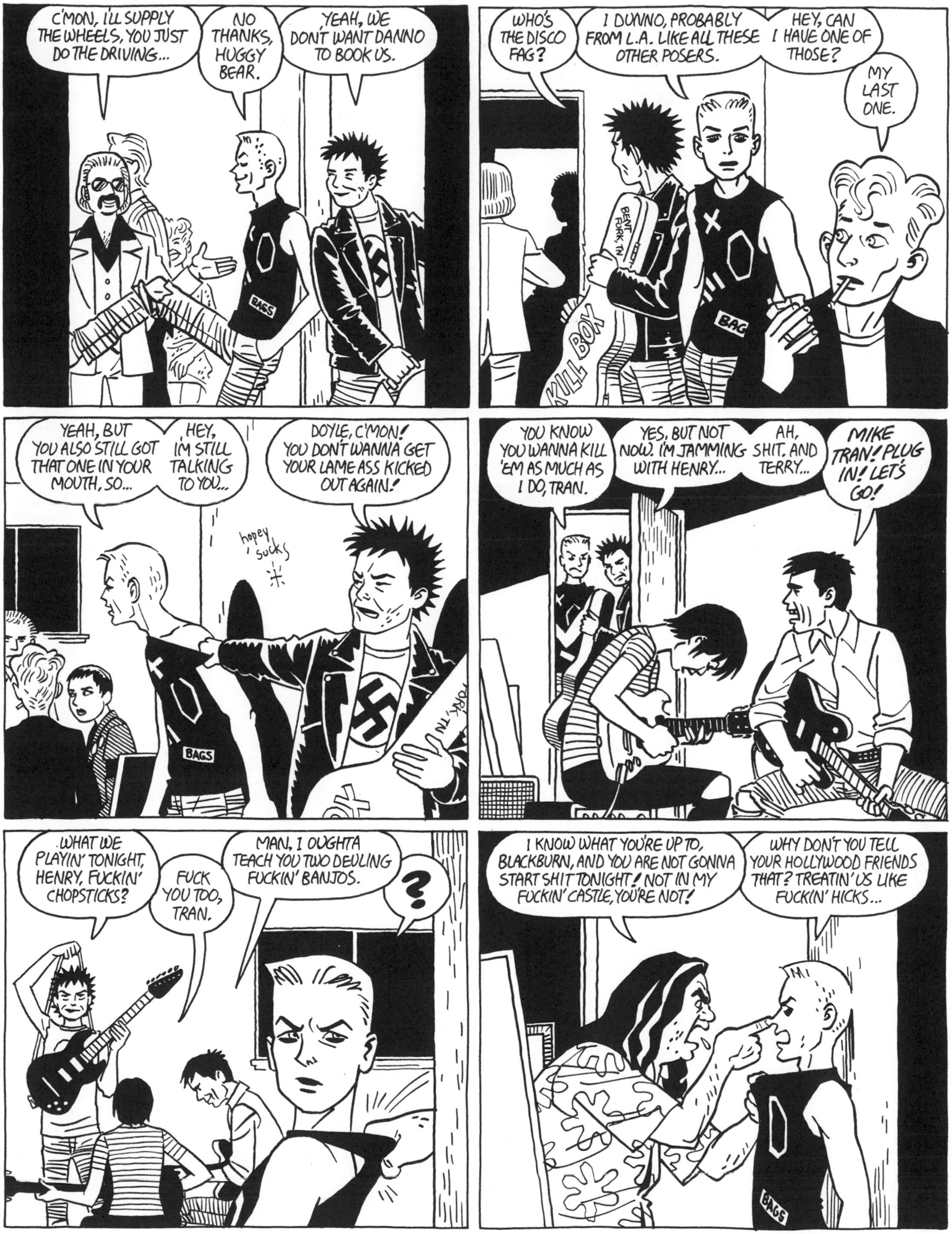
C'MON, I'LL SUPPLY THE WHEELS, YOU JUST DO THE DRIVING...
NO THANKS, HUGGY BEAR.
YEAH, WE DON'T WANT DANNO TO BOOK US.
BAGS
WHO'S THE DISCO FAG?
I DUNNO, PROBABLY FROM L.A. LIKE ALL THESE OTHER POSERS.
HEY, CAN I HAVE ONE OF THOSE?
MY LAST ONE.
BENT FORK, TN
KILL BOX
BAG
YEAH, BUT YOU ALSO STILL GOT THAT ONE IN YOUR MOUTH, SO...
HEY, I'M STILL TALKING TO YOU...
DOYLE, C'MON! YOU DON'T WANNA GET YOUR LAME ASS KICKED OUT AGAIN!
hopey sucks
BAGS
YOU KNOW YOU WANNA KILL 'EM AS MUCH AS I DO, TRAN.
YES, BUT NOT NOW. I'M JAMMING WITH HENRY...
AH, SHIT. AND TERRY...
MIKE TRAN! PLUG IN! LET'S GO!
WHAT WE PLAYIN' TONIGHT, HENRY, FUCKIN' CHOPSTICKS?
FUCK YOU TOO, TRAN.
MAN, I OUGHTA TEACH YOU TWO DEVLING FUCKIN' BANJOS.
?
I KNOW WHAT YOU'RE UP TO, BLACKBURN, AND YOU ARE NOT GONNA START SHIT TONIGHT! NOT IN MY FUCKIN' CASTLE, YOU'RE NOT!
WHY DON'T YOU TELL YOUR HOLLYWOOD FRIENDS THAT? TREATIN' US LIKE FUCKIN' HICKS...
BAGS
1.

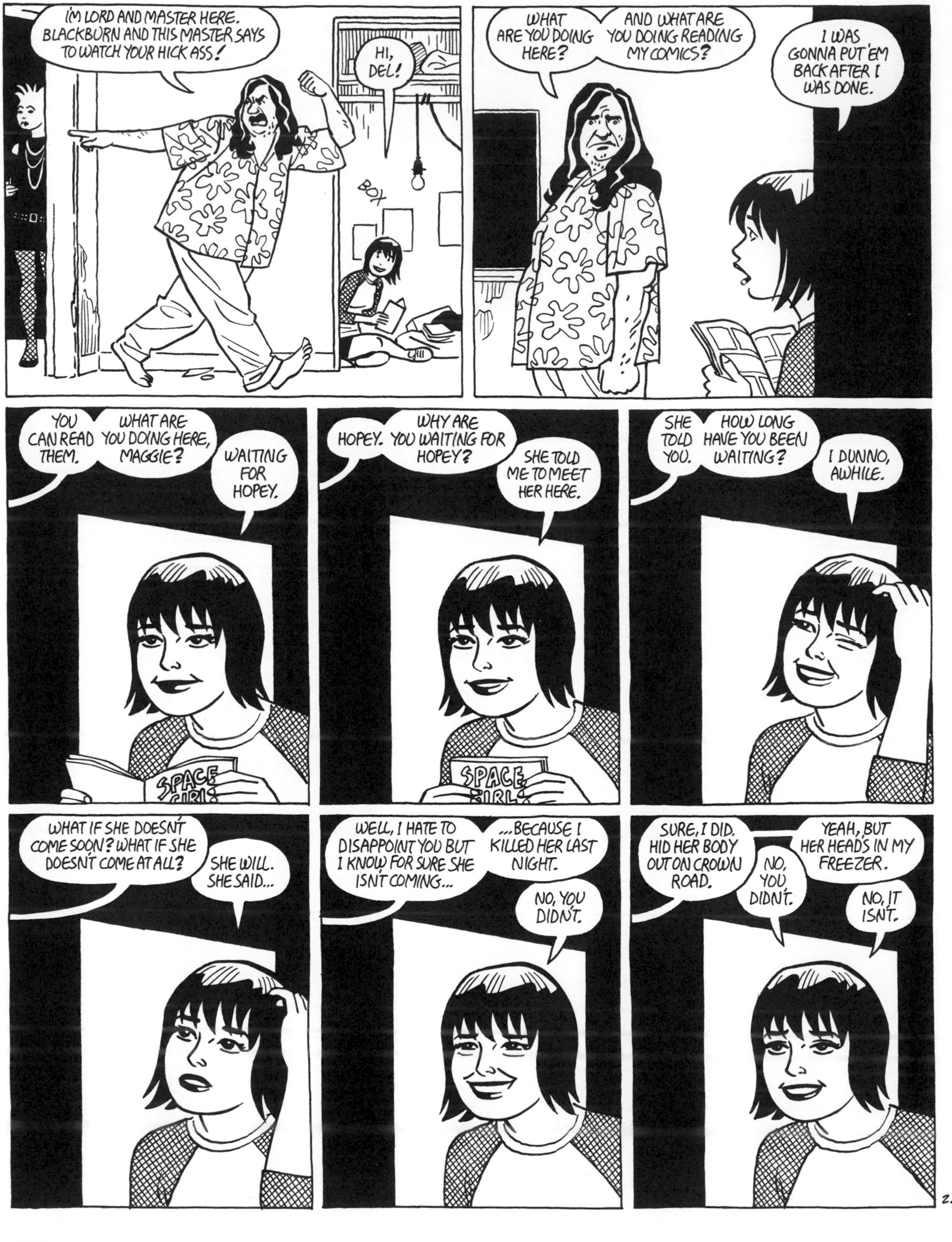
I'M LORD AND MASTER HERE. BLACKBURN AND THIS MASTER SAYS TO WATCH YOUR HICK ASS!
HI, DEL!
BOX
WHAT ARE YOU DOING HERE?
AND WHAT ARE YOU DOING READING MY COMICS?
I WAS GONNA PUT 'EM BACK AFTER I WAS DONE.
YOU CAN READ THEM.
WHAT ARE YOU DOING HERE, MAGGIE?
WAITING FOR HOPEY.
HOPEY.
YOU WAITING FOR HOPEY?
SHE TOLD ME TO MEET HER HERE.
SPACE GIRLS
SHE TOLD YOU.
HOW LONG HAVE YOU BEEN WAITING?
I DUNNO, AWHILE.
WHAT IF SHE DOESN'T COME SOON? WHAT IF SHE DOESN'T COME AT ALL?
SHE WILL. SHE SAID...
WELL, I HATE TO DISAPPOINT YOU BUT I KNOW FOR SURE SHE ISN'T COMING...
...BECAUSE I KILLED HER LAST NIGHT.
NO, YOU DIDN'T.
SURE, I DID. HID HER BODY OUT ON CROWN ROAD.
NO, YOU DIDN'T.
YEAH, BUT HER HEAD'S IN MY FREEZER.
NO, IT ISN'T.
2.

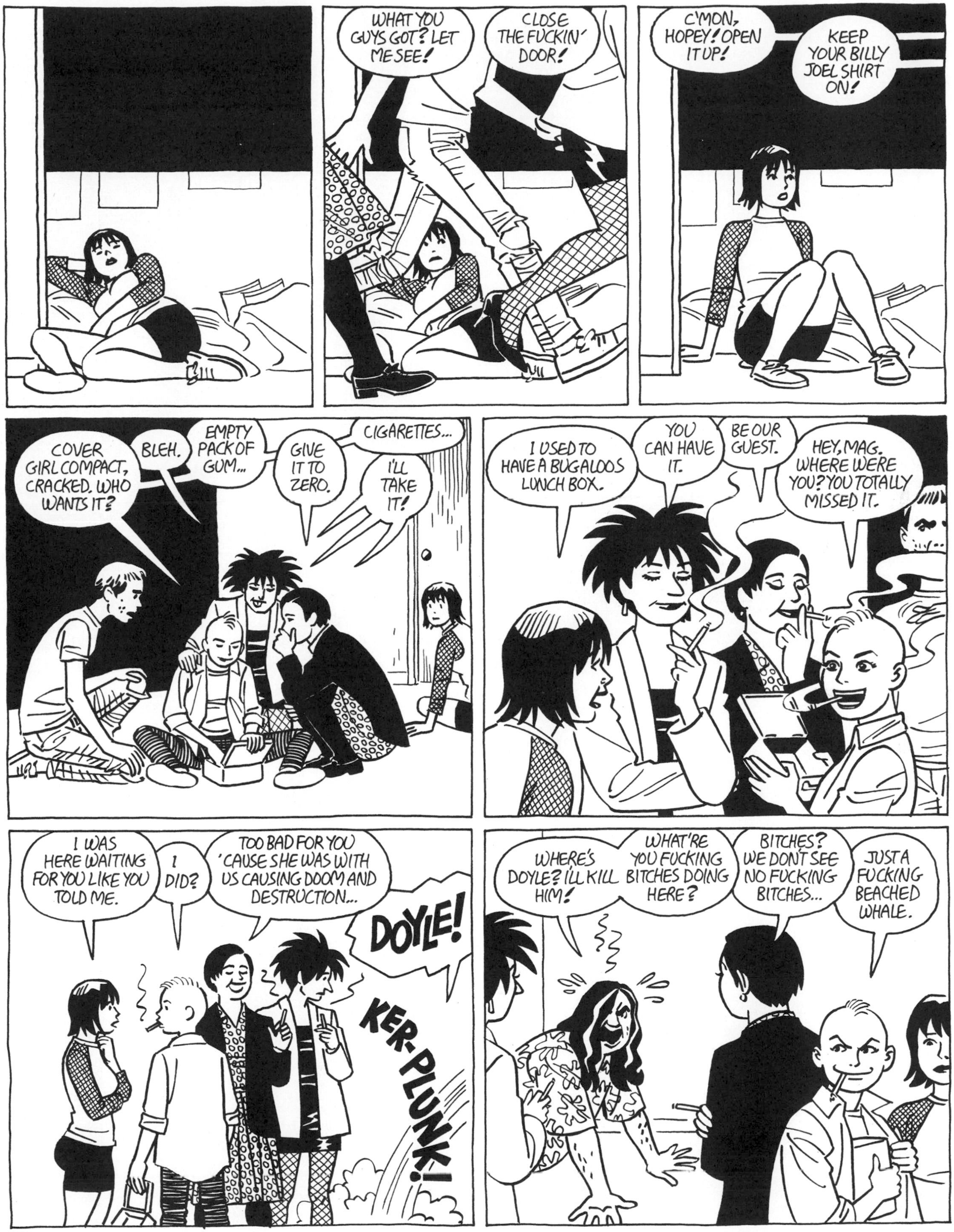
WHAT YOU GUYS GOT? LET ME SEE!
CLOSE THE FUCKIN' DOOR!
C'MON, HOPEY! OPEN IT UP!
KEEP YOUR BILLY JOEL SHIRT ON!
COVER GIRL COMPACT, CRACKED. WHO WANTS IT?
BLEH.
EMPTY PACK OF GUM...
GIVE IT TO ZERO.
CIGARETTES...
I'LL TAKE IT!
I USED TO HAVE A BUGALOOS LUNCH BOX.
YOU CAN HAVE IT.
BE OUR GUEST.
HEY, MAG. WHERE WERE YOU? YOU TOTALLY MISSED IT.
I WAS HERE WAITING FOR YOU LIKE YOU TOLD ME.
I DID?
TOO BAD FOR YOU 'CAUSE SHE WAS WITH US CAUSING DOOM AND DESTRUCTION...
DOYLE!
KER-PLUNK!!
WHERE'S DOYLE? I'LL KILL HIM!
WHAT'RE YOU FUCKING BITCHES DOING HERE?
BITCHES? WE DON'T SEE NO FUCKING BITCHES...
JUST A FUCKING BEACHED WHALE.
3.

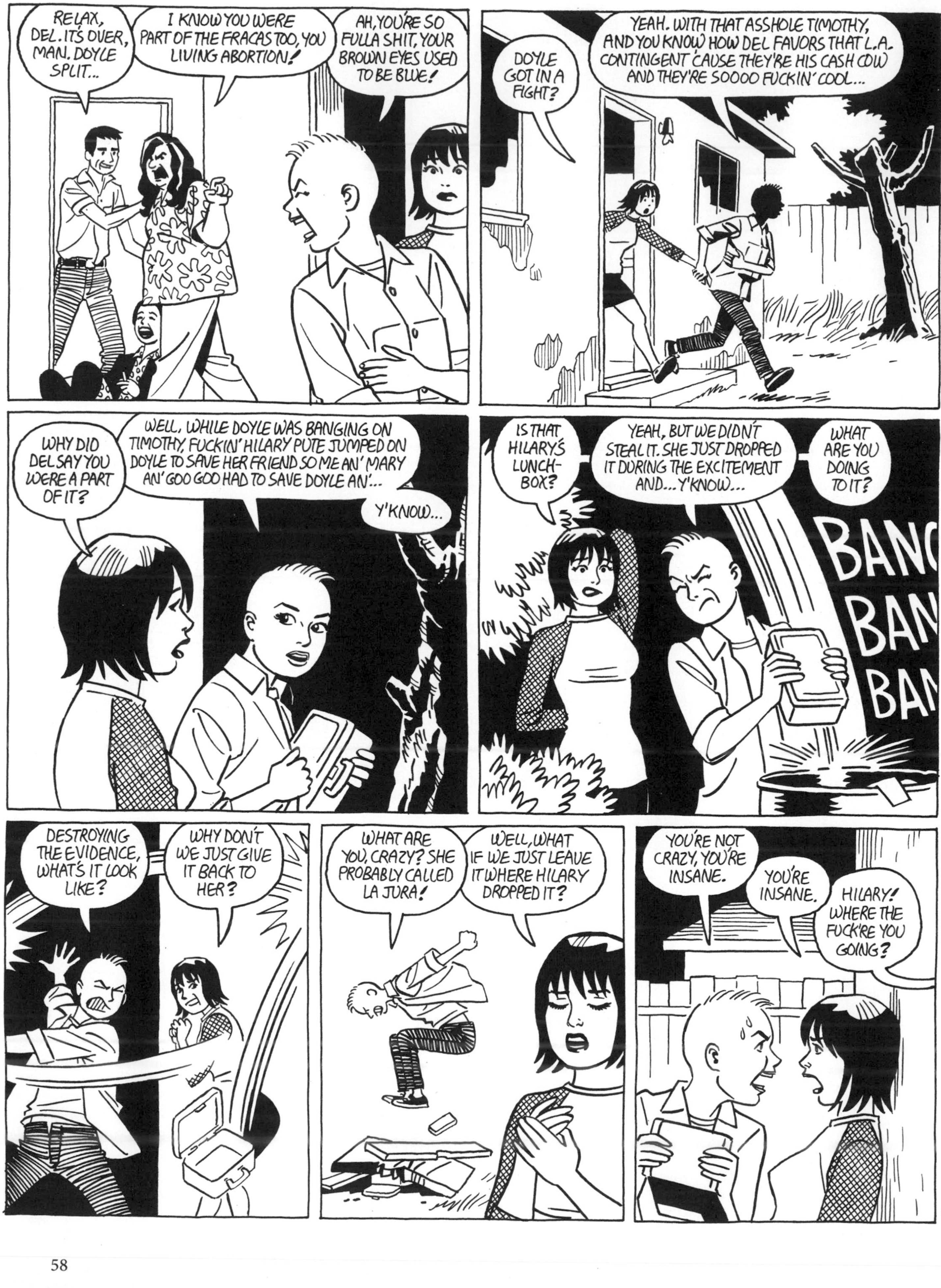

RELAX, DEL. IT'S OVER, MAN. DOYLE SPLIT...
I KNOW YOU WERE PART OF THE FRACAS TOO, YOU LIVING ABORTION!
AH, YOU'RE SO FULLA SHIT, YOUR BROWN EYES USED TO BE BLUE!
DOYLE GOT IN A FIGHT?
YEAH. WITH THAT ASSHOLE TIMOTHY, AND YOU KNOW HOW DEL FAVORS THAT L.A. CONTINGENT 'CAUSE THEY'RE HIS CASH COW AND THEY'RE SOOOO FUCKIN' COOL...
WHY DID DEL SAY YOU WERE A PART OF IT?
WELL, WHILE DOYLE WAS BANGING ON TIMOTHY, FUCKIN' HILARY PUTE JUMPED ON DOYLE TO SAVE HER FRIEND SO ME AN' MARY AN' GOO GOO HAD TO SAVE DOYLE AN'...
Y'KNOW...
IS THAT HILARY'S LUNCH-BOX?
YEAH, BUT WE DIDN'T STEAL IT. SHE JUST DROPPED IT DURING THE EXCITEMENT AND... Y'KNOW...
WHAT ARE YOU DOING TO IT?
BANG
BAN
BAN
DESTROYING THE EVIDENCE, WHAT'S IT LOOK LIKE?
WHY DON'T WE JUST GIVE IT BACK TO HER?
WHAT ARE YOU, CRAZY? SHE PROBABLY CALLED LA JURA!
WELL, WHAT IF WE JUST LEAVE IT WHERE HILARY DROPPED IT?
YOU'RE NOT CRAZY, YOU'RE INSANE.
YOU'RE INSANE.
HILARY! WHERE THE FUCK'RE YOU GOING?
4.

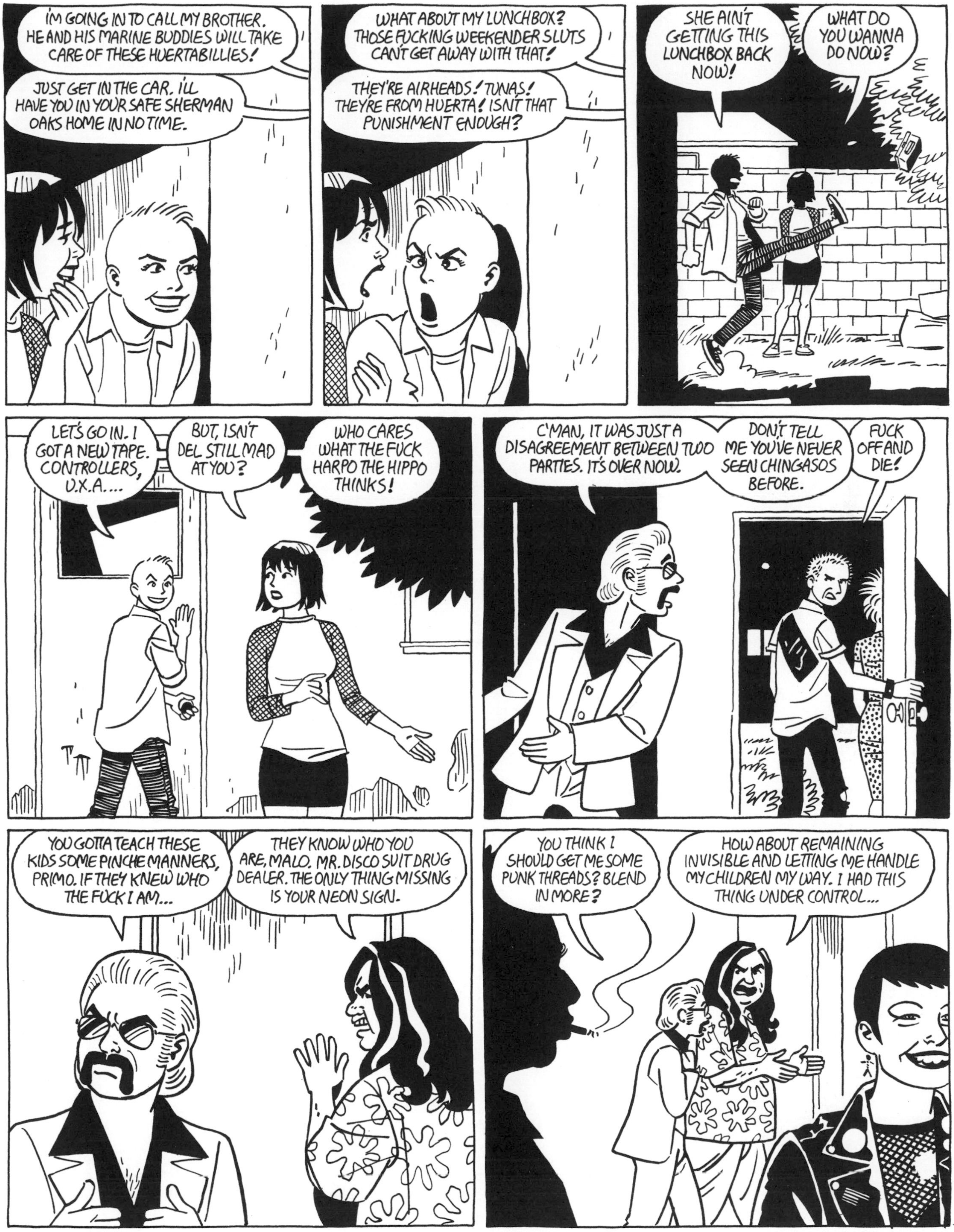
I'M GOING IN TO CALL MY BROTHER. HE AND HIS MARINE BUDDIES WILL TAKE CARE OF THESE HUERTABILLIES!
JUST GET IN THE CAR. I'LL HAVE YOU IN YOUR SAFE SHERMAN OAKS HOME IN NO TIME.
WHAT ABOUT MY LUNCHBOX? THOSE FUCKING WEEKENDER SLUTS CAN'T GET AWAY WITH THAT!
THEY'RE AIRHEADS! TUNAS! THEY'RE FROM HUERTA! ISN'T THAT PUNISHMENT ENOUGH?
SHE AIN'T GETTING THIS LUNCHBOX BACK NOW!
WHAT DO YOU WANNA DO NOW?
LET'S GO IN. I GOT A NEW TAPE. CONTROLLERS, U.X.A....
BUT, ISN'T DEL STILL MAD AT YOU?
WHO CARES WHAT THE FUCK HARPO THE HIPPO THINKS!
C'MAN, IT WAS JUST A DISAGREEMENT BETWEEN TWO PARTIES. IT'S OVER NOW.
DON'T TELL ME YOU'VE NEVER SEEN CHINGASOS BEFORE.
FUCK OFF AND DIE!
YOU GOTTA TEACH THESE KIDS SOME PINCHE MANNERS, PRIMO. IF THEY KNEW WHO THE FUCK I AM...
THEY KNOW WHO YOU ARE, MALO. MR. DISCO SUIT DRUG DEALER. THE ONLY THING MISSING IS YOUR NEON SIGN.
YOU THINK I SHOULD GET ME SOME PUNK THREADS? BLEND IN MORE?
HOW ABOUT REMAINING INVISIBLE AND LETTING ME HANDLE MY CHILDREN MY WAY. I HAD THIS THING UNDER CONTROL...
5.

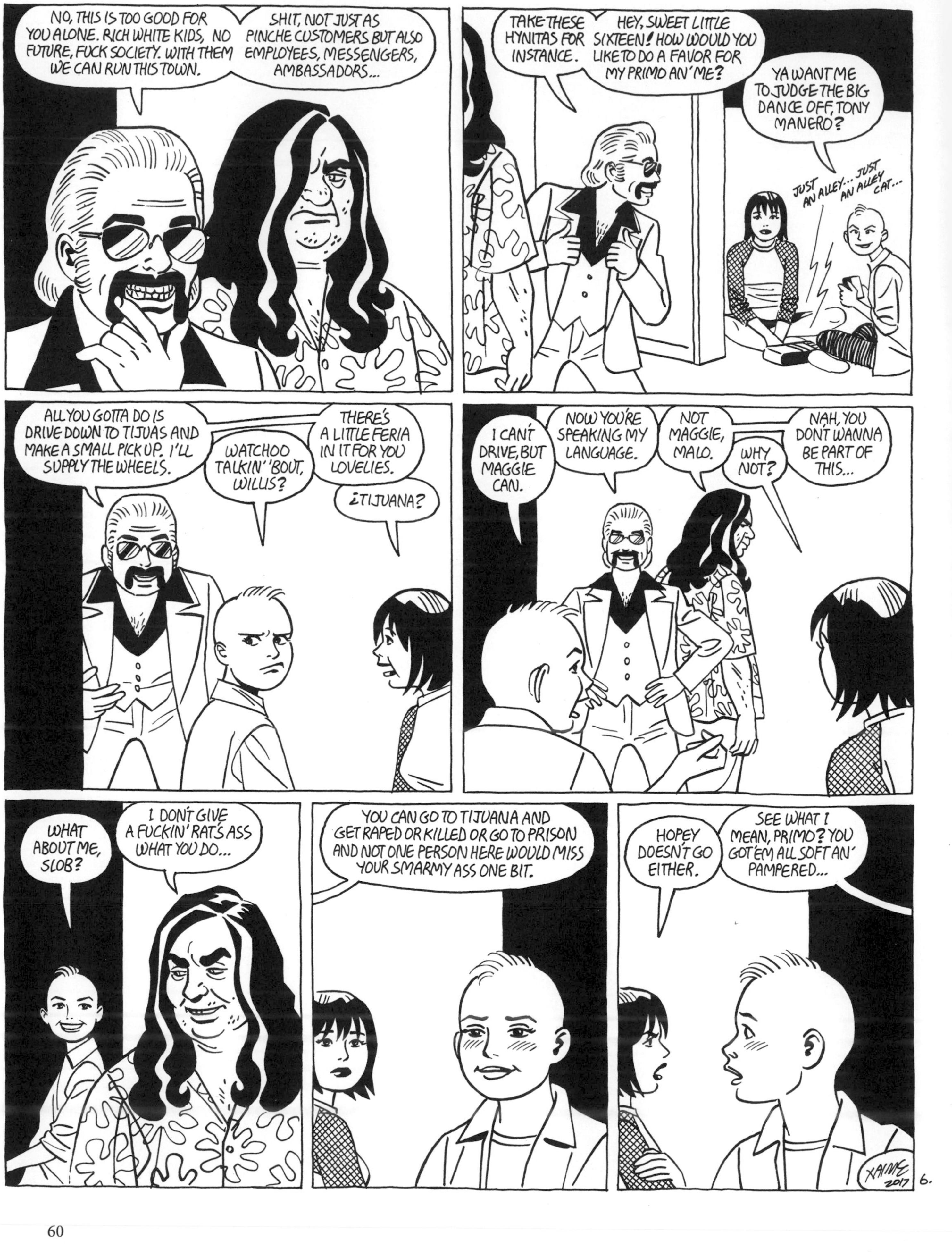
NO, THIS IS TOO GOOD FOR YOU ALONE. RICH WHITE KIDS, NO FUTURE, FUCK SOCIETY. WITH THEM WE CAN RUN THIS TOWN.
SHIT, NOT JUST AS PINCHE CUSTOMERS BUT ALSO EMPLOYEES, MESSENGERS, AMBASSADORS...
TAKE THESE HYNITAS FOR INSTANCE.
HEY, SWEET LITTLE SIXTEEN! HOW WOULD YOU LIKE TO DO A FAVOR FOR MY PRIMO AN' ME?
YA WANT ME TO JUDGE THE BIG DANCE OFF, TONY MANERO?
JUST AN ALLEY... JUST AN ALLEY CAT...
ALL YOU GOTTA DO IS DRIVE DOWN TO TIJUAS AND MAKE A SMALL PICK UP. I'LL SUPPLY THE WHEELS.
THERE'S A LITTLE FERIA IN IT FOR YOU LOVELIES.
WATCHOO TALKIN' 'BOUT, WILLIS?
¿TIJUANA?
I CAN'T DRIVE, BUT MAGGIE CAN.
NOW YOU'RE SPEAKING MY LANGUAGE.
NOT MAGGIE, MALO.
WHY NOT?
NAH, YOU DON'T WANNA BE PART OF THIS...
WHAT ABOUT ME, SLOB?
I DON'T GIVE A FUCKIN' RAT'S ASS WHAT YOU DO...
YOU CAN GO TO TIJUANA AND GET RAPED OR KILLED OR GO TO PRISON AND NOT ONE PERSON HERE WOULD MISS YOUR SMARMY ASS ONE BIT.
HOPEY DOESN'T GO EITHER.
SEE WHAT I MEAN, PRIMO? YOU GOT'EM ALL SOFT AN' PAMPERED...
XAIME 2017
6.

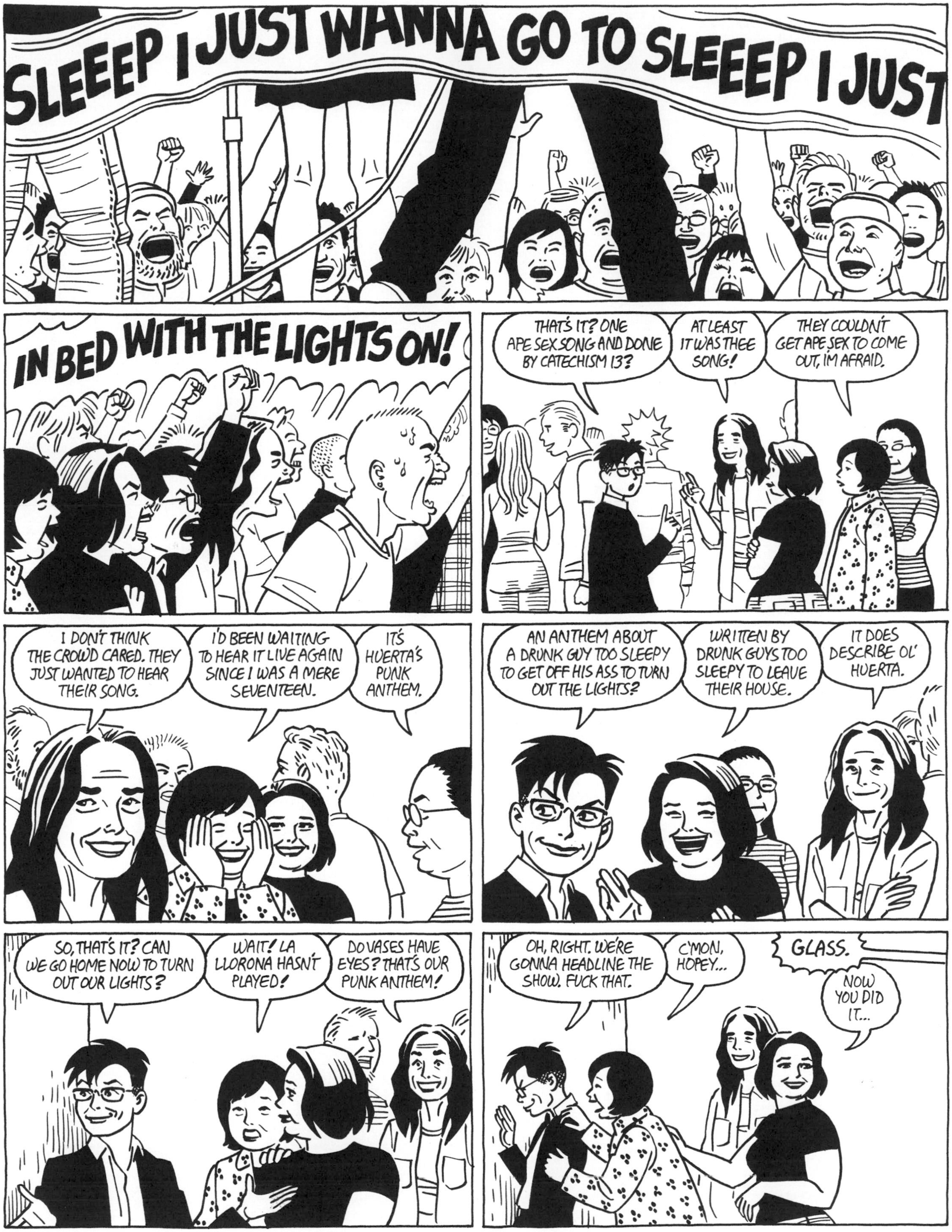
SLEEEP I JUST WANNA GO TO SLEEEP I JUST
IN BED WITH THE LIGHTS ON!
THAT'S IT? ONE APE SEX SONG AND DONE BY CATECHISM 13?
AT LEAST IT WAS THEE SONG!
THEY COULDN'T GET APE SEX TO COME OUT, I'M AFRAID.
I DON'T THINK THE CROWD CARED. THEY JUST WANTED TO HEAR THEIR SONG.
I'D BEEN WAITING TO HEAR IT LIVE AGAIN SINCE I WAS A MERE SEVENTEEN.
IT'S HUERTA'S PUNK ANTHEM.
AN ANTHEM ABOUT A DRUNK GUY TOO SLEEPY TO GET OFF HIS ASS TO TURN OUT THE LIGHTS?
WRITTEN BY DRUNK GUYS TOO SLEEPY TO LEAVE THEIR HOUSE.
IT DOES DESCRIBE OL' HUERTA.
SO, THAT'S IT? CAN WE GO HOME NOW TO TURN OUT OUR LIGHTS?
WAIT! LA LLORONA HASN'T PLAYED!
DO VASES HAVE EYES? THAT'S OUR PUNK ANTHEM!
OH, RIGHT. WE'RE GONNA HEADLINE THE SHOW. FUCK THAT.
C'MON, HOPEY...
GLASS.
NOW YOU DID IT...
1.

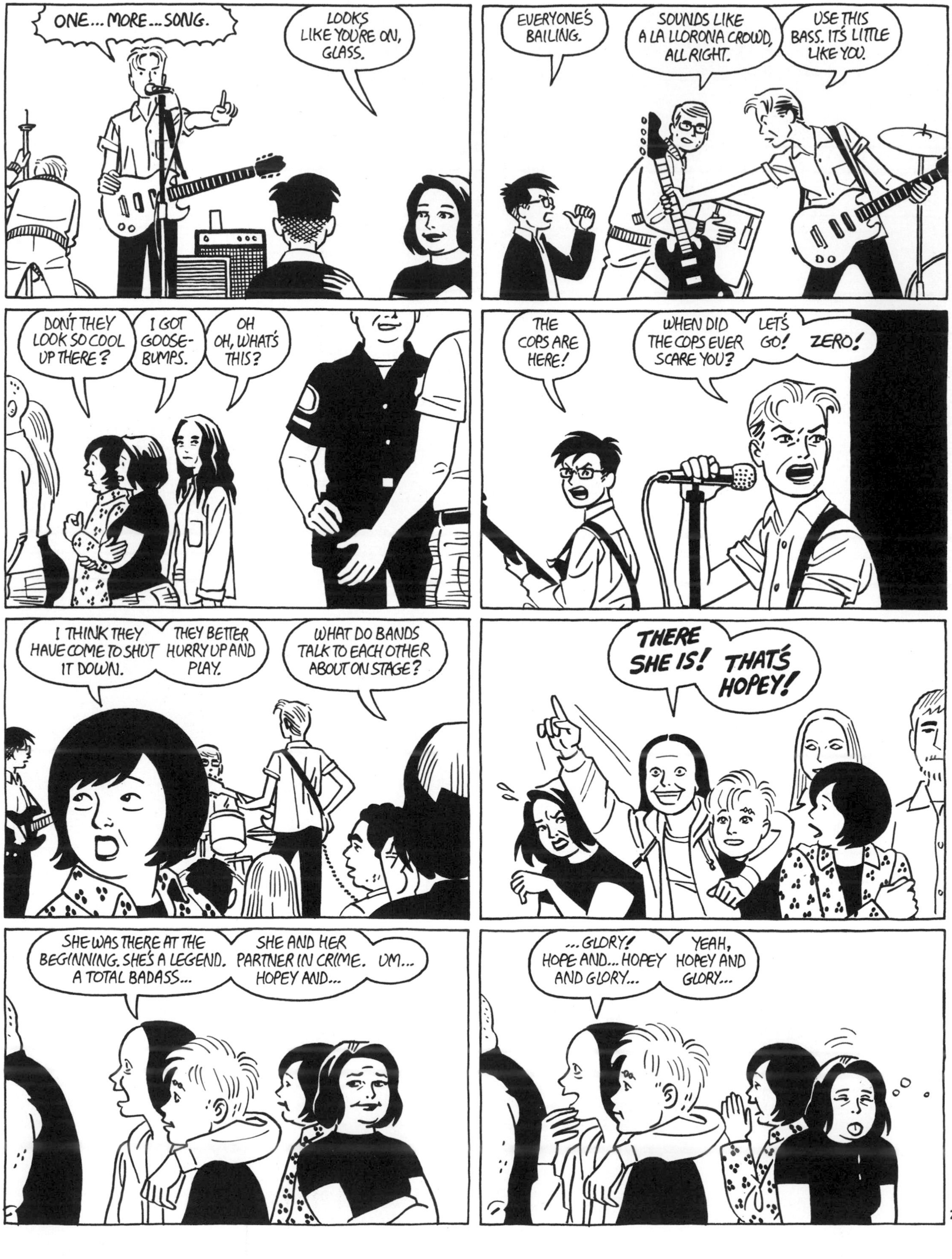
ONE... MORE... SONG.
LOOKS LIKE YOU'RE ON, GLASS.
EVERYONE'S BAILING.
SOUNDS LIKE A LA LLORONA CROWD, ALL RIGHT.
USE THIS BASS. IT'S LITTLE LIKE YOU.
DON'T THEY LOOK SO COOL UP THERE?
I GOT GOOSE-BUMPS.
OH OH, WHAT'S THIS?
THE COPS ARE HERE!
WHEN DID THE COPS EVER SCARE YOU?
LET'S GO!
ZERO!
I THINK THEY HAVE COME TO SHUT IT DOWN.
THEY BETTER HURRY UP AND PLAY.
WHAT DO BANDS TALK TO EACH OTHER ABOUT ON STAGE?
THERE SHE IS!
THAT'S HOPEY!
SHE WAS THERE AT THE BEGINNING. SHE'S A LEGEND. A TOTAL BADASS...
SHE AND HER PARTNER IN CRIME. HOPEY AND...
UM...
...GLORY! HOPE AND... HOPEY AND GLORY...
YEAH, HOPEY AND GLORY...
2.

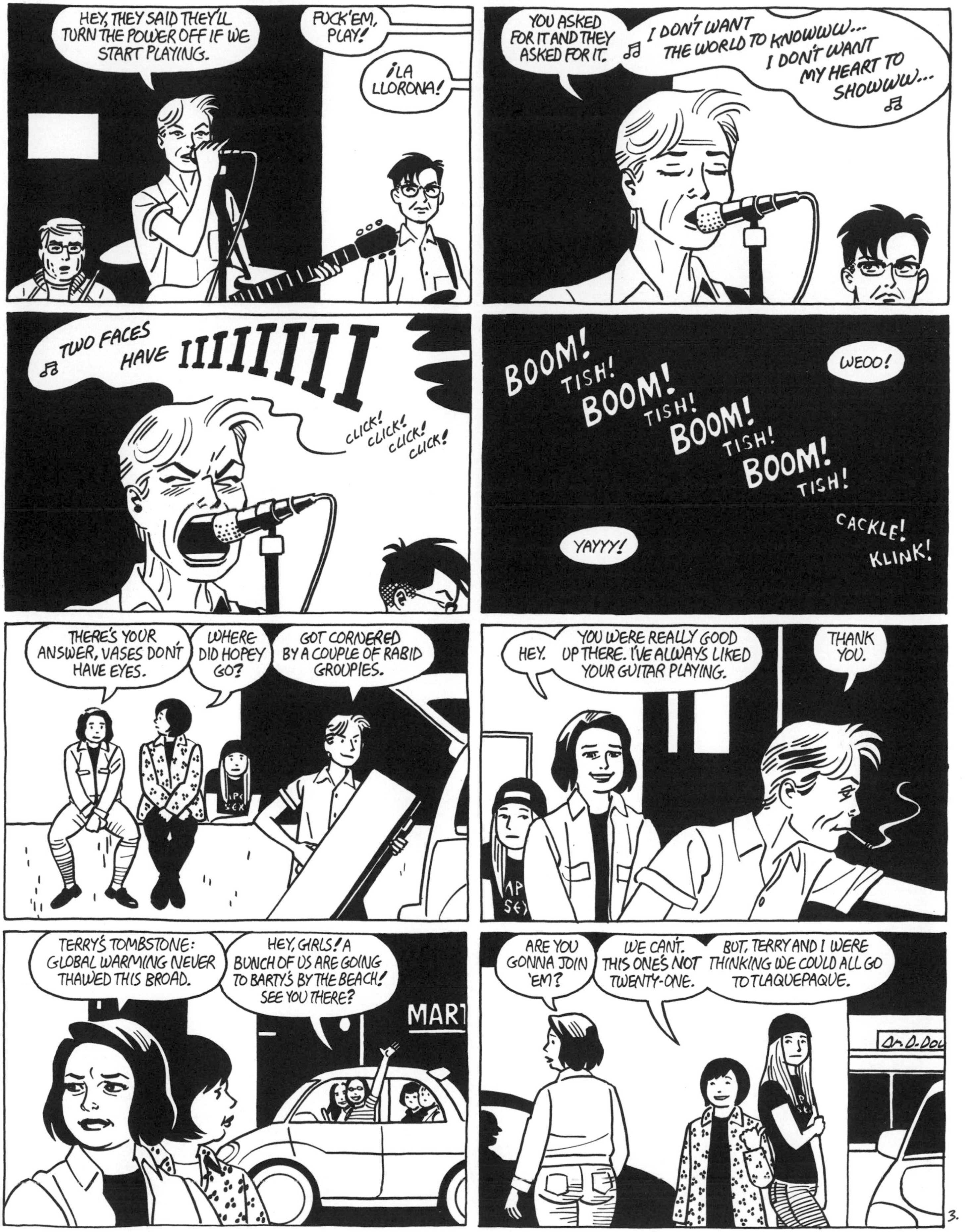

HEY, THEY SAID THEY'LL TURN THE POWER OFF IF WE START PLAYING.
FUCK'EM, PLAY!
¡LA LLORONA!
YOU ASKED FOR IT AND THEY ASKED FOR IT.
I DON'T WANT THE WORLD TO KNOWWW... I DON'T WANT MY HEART TO SHOWWW...
TWO FACES HAVE IIIIIIII
CLICK! CLICK! CLICK! CLICK!
BOOM! TISH! BOOM! TISH! BOOM! TISH! BOOM! TISH!
WEOO!
YAYYY!
CACKLE! KLINK!
THERE'S YOUR ANSWER, VASES DON'T HAVE EYES.
WHERE DID HOPEY GO?
GOT CORNERED BY A COUPLE OF RABID GROUPIES.
HEY.
YOU WERE REALLY GOOD UP THERE. I'VE ALWAYS LIKED YOUR GUITAR PLAYING.
THANK YOU.
TERRY'S TOMBSTONE: GLOBAL WARMING NEVER THAWED THIS BROAD.
HEY, GIRLS! A BUNCH OF US ARE GOING TO BARTY'S BY THE BEACH! SEE YOU THERE?
MART
ARE YOU GONNA JOIN 'EM?
WE CAN'T. THIS ONE'S NOT TWENTY-ONE.
BUT, TERRY AND I WERE THINKING WE COULD ALL GO TO TLAQUEPAQUE.
3.

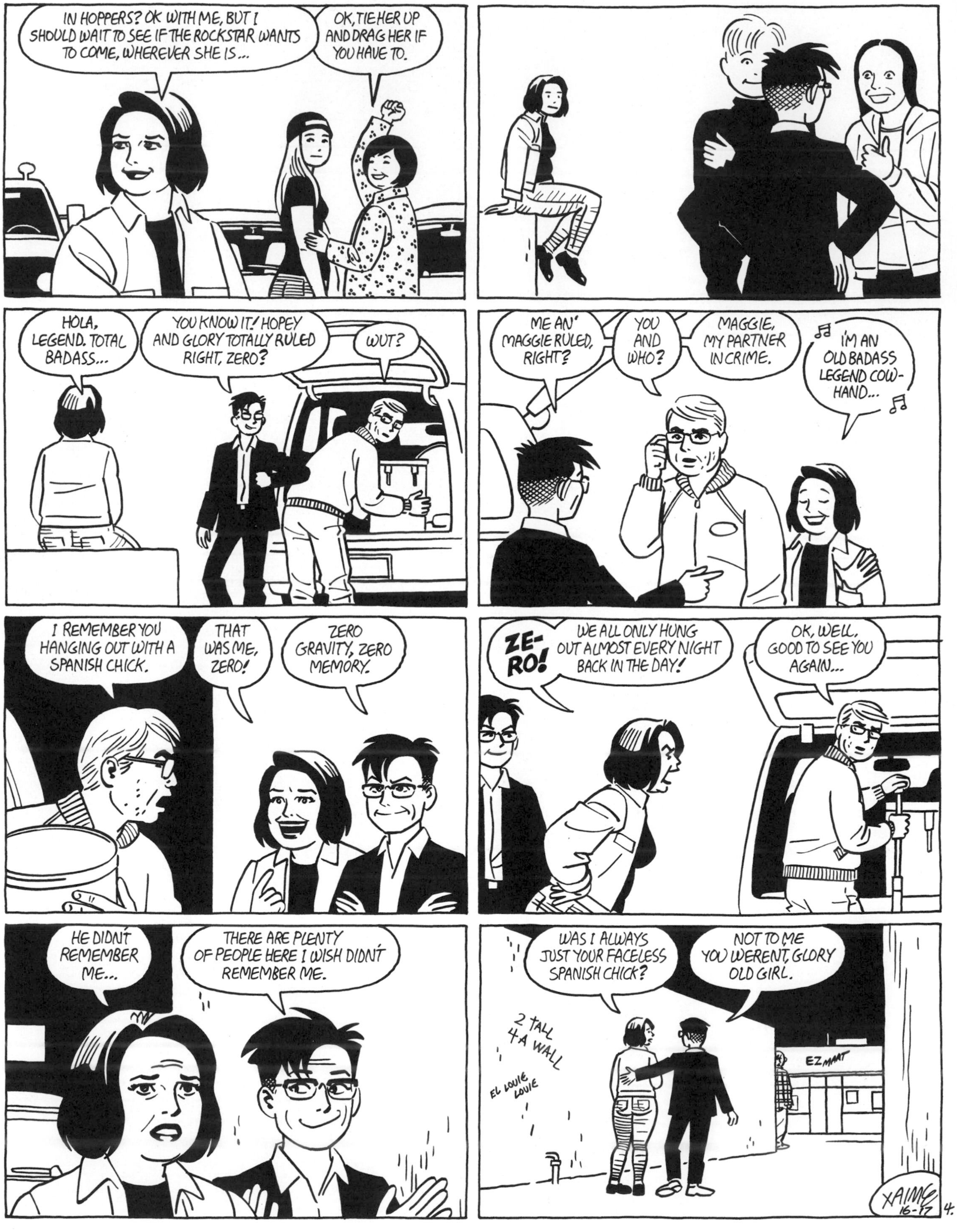
IN HOPPERS? OK WITH ME, BUT I SHOULD WAIT TO SEE IF THE ROCKSTAR WANTS TO COME, WHEREVER SHE IS...
OK, TIE HER UP AND DRAG HER IF YOU HAVE TO.
HOLA, LEGEND. TOTAL BADASS...
YOU KNOW IT! HOPEY AND GLORY TOTALLY RULED RIGHT, ZERO?
WUT?
ME AN' MAGGIE RULED, RIGHT?
YOU AND WHO?
MAGGIE, MY PARTNER IN CRIME.
I'M AN OLD BADASS LEGEND COW-HAND...
I REMEMBER YOU HANGING OUT WITH A SPANISH CHICK.
THAT WAS ME, ZERO!
ZERO GRAVITY, ZERO MEMORY.
ZE-RO!
WE ALL ONLY HUNG OUT ALMOST EVERY NIGHT BACK IN THE DAY!
OK, WELL, GOOD TO SEE YOU AGAIN...
HE DIDN'T REMEMBER ME...
THERE ARE PLENTY OF PEOPLE HERE I WISH DIDN'T REMEMBER ME.
WAS I ALWAYS JUST YOUR FACELESS SPANISH CHICK?
NOT TO ME YOU WEREN'T, GLORY OLD GIRL.
2 TALL 4 A WALL
EL LOUIE LOUIE
EZ MART
XAIME 16-17
4.

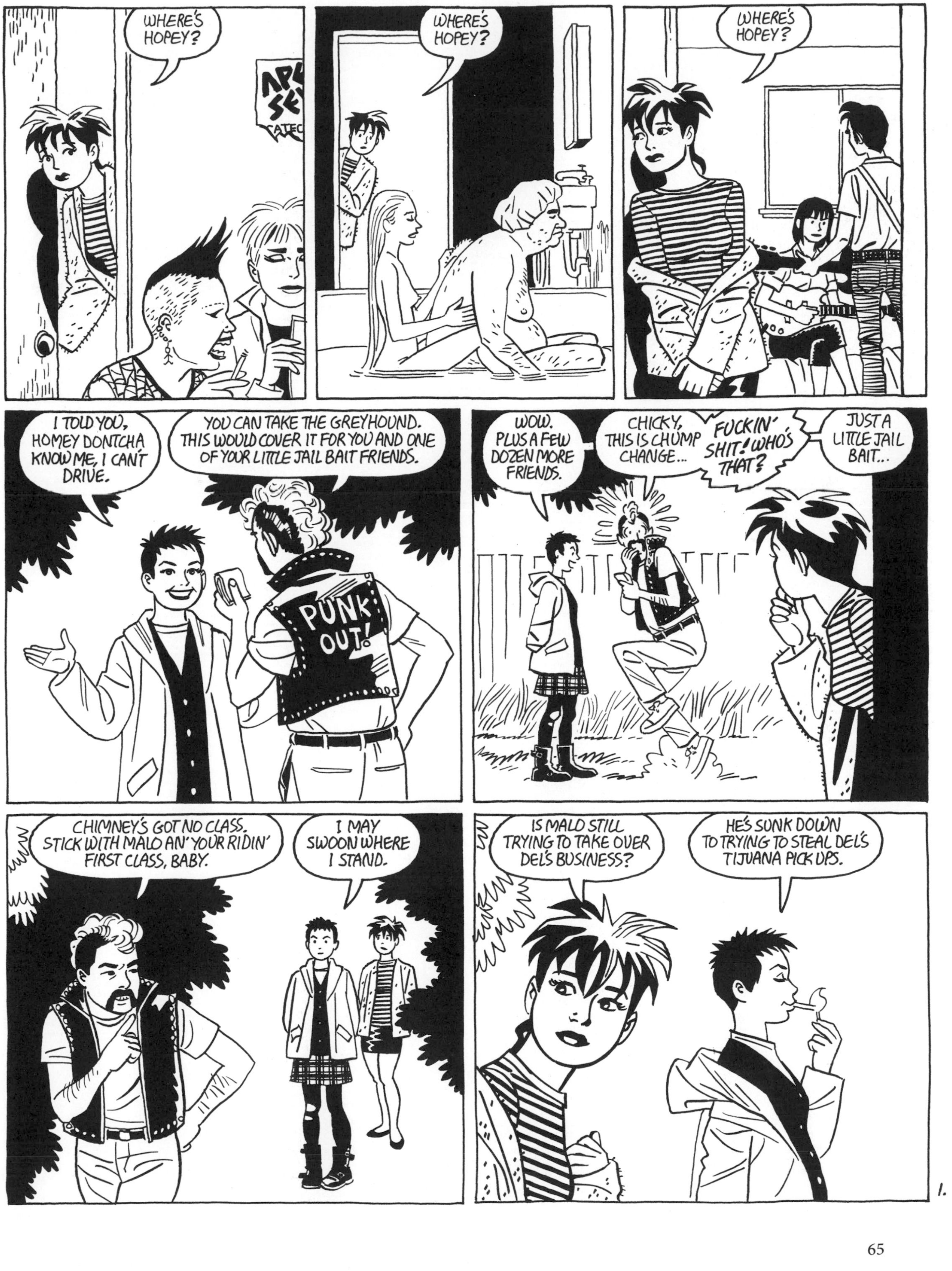
WHERE'S HOPEY?
WHERE'S HOPEY?
WHERE'S HOPEY?
I TOLD YOU, HOMEY DONTCHA KNOW ME, I CAN'T DRIVE.
YOU CAN TAKE THE GREYHOUND. THIS WOULD COVER IT FOR YOU AND ONE OF YOUR LITTLE JAIL BAIT FRIENDS.
PUNK OUT!
WOW. PLUS A FEW DOZEN MORE FRIENDS.
CHICKY, THIS IS CHUMP CHANGE...
FUCKIN' SHIT! WHO'S THAT?
JUST A LITTLE JAIL BAIT...
CHIMNEY'S GOT NO CLASS. STICK WITH MALO AN' YOUR RIDIN' FIRST CLASS, BABY.
I MAY SWOON WHERE I STAND.
IS MALO STILL TRYING TO TAKE OVER DEL'S BUSINESS?
HE'S SUNK DOWN TO TRYING TO STEAL DEL'S TIJUANA PICK UPS.
1.

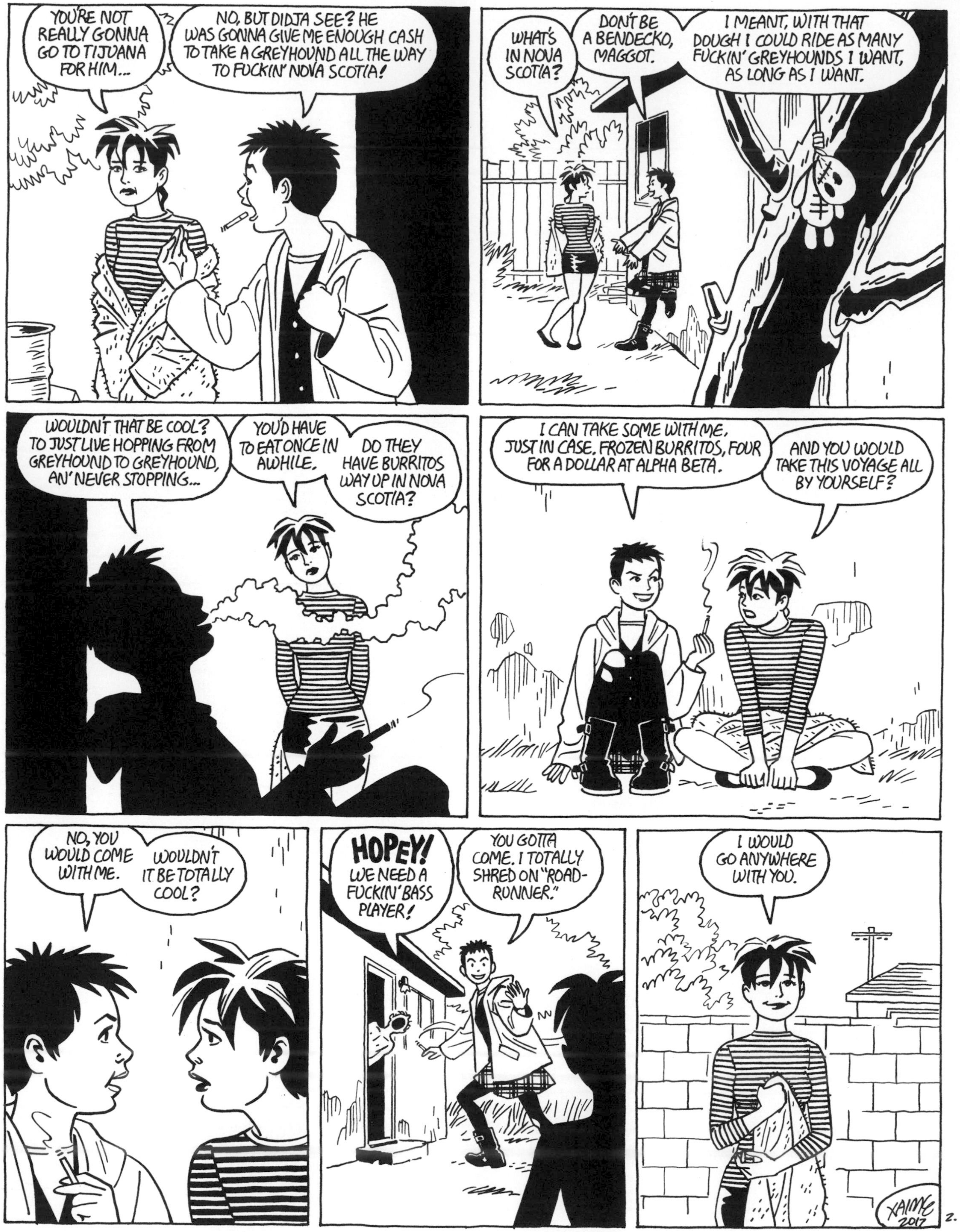
YOU'RE NOT REALLY GONNA GO TO TIJUANA FOR HIM...
NO, BUT DIDJA SEE? HE WAS GONNA GIVE ME ENOUGH CASH TO TAKE A GREYHOUND ALL THE WAY TO FUCKIN' NOVA SCOTIA!
WHAT'S IN NOVA SCOTIA?
DON'T BE A BENDECKO, MAGGOT.
I MEANT, WITH THAT DOUGH I COULD RIDE AS MANY FUCKIN' GREYHOUNDS I WANT, AS LONG AS I WANT.
WOULDN'T THAT BE COOL? TO JUST LIVE HOPPING FROM GREYHOUND TO GREYHOUND, AN' NEVER STOPPING...
YOU'D HAVE TO EAT ONCE IN AWHILE.
DO THEY HAVE BURRITOS WAY UP IN NOVA SCOTIA?
I CAN TAKE SOME WITH ME, JUST IN CASE. FROZEN BURRITOS, FOUR FOR A DOLLAR AT ALPHA BETA.
AND YOU WOULD TAKE THIS VOYAGE ALL BY YOURSELF?
NO, YOU WOULD COME WITH ME.
WOULDN'T IT BE TOTALLY COOL?
HOPEY! WE NEED A FUCKIN' BASS PLAYER!
YOU GOTTA COME. I TOTALLY SHRED ON "ROAD-RUNNER."
I WOULD GO ANYWHERE WITH YOU.
XAIME 2017
2.

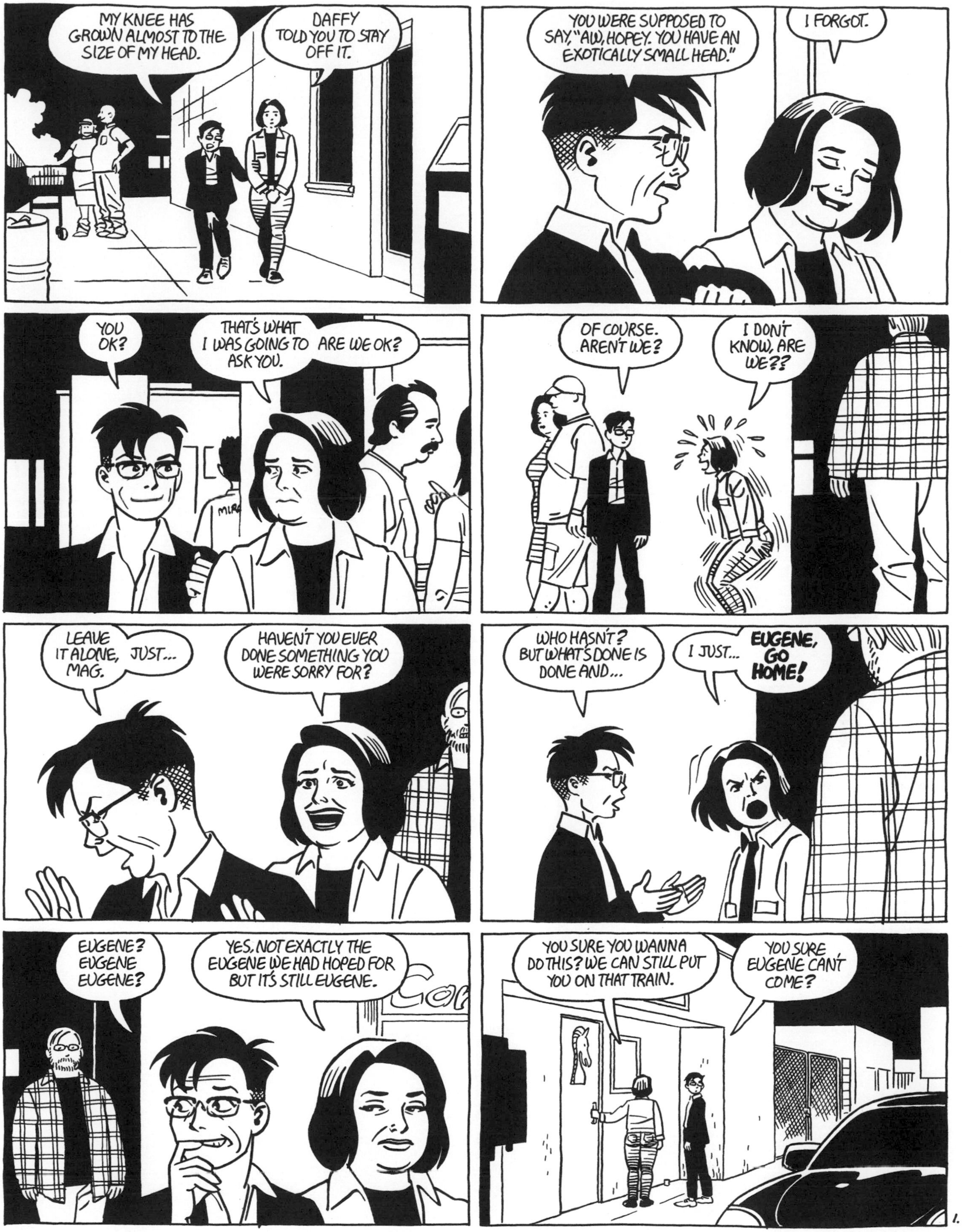
MY KNEE HAS GROWN ALMOST TO THE SIZE OF MY HEAD.
DAFFY TOLD YOU TO STAY OFF IT.
YOU WERE SUPPOSED TO SAY, "AW, HOPEY. YOU HAVE AN EXOTICALLY SMALL HEAD."
I FORGOT.
YOU OK?
THAT'S WHAT I WAS GOING TO ASK YOU.
ARE WE OK?
OF COURSE. AREN'T WE?
I DON'T KNOW, ARE WE??
LEAVE IT ALONE, MAG.
JUST...
HAVEN'T YOU EVER DONE SOMETHING YOU WERE SORRY FOR?
WHO HASN'T? BUT WHAT'S DONE IS DONE AND...
I JUST...
EUGENE, GO HOME!
EUGENE? EUGENE EUGENE?
YES, NOT EXACTLY THE EUGENE WE HAD HOPED FOR BUT IT'S STILL EUGENE.
YOU SURE YOU WANNA DO THIS? WE CAN STILL PUT YOU ON THAT TRAIN.
YOU SURE EUGENE CAN'T COME?
1.

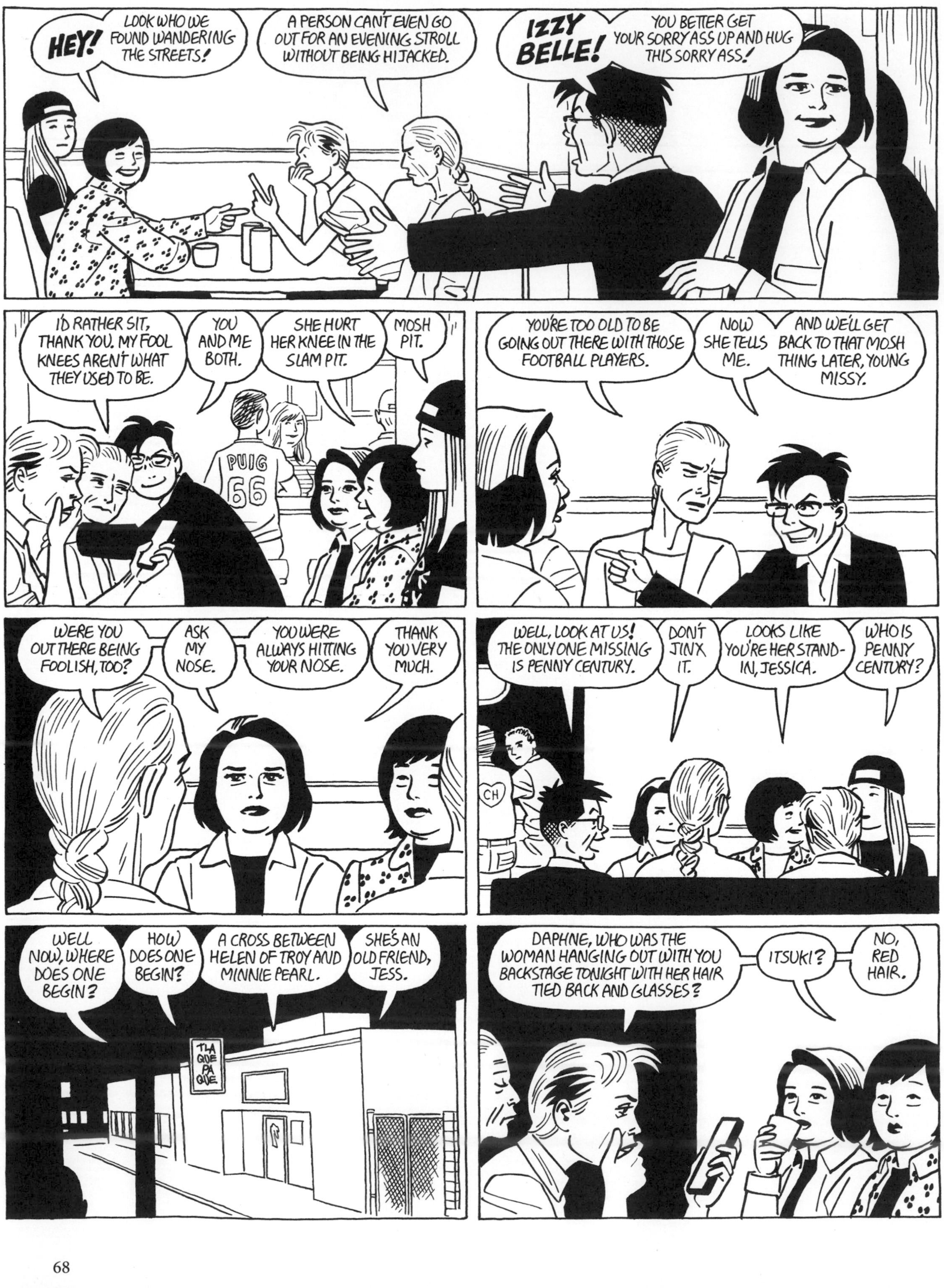
HEY!
LOOK WHO WE FOUND WANDERING THE STREETS!
A PERSON CAN'T EVEN GO OUT FOR AN EVENING STROLL WITHOUT BEING HIJACKED.
IZZY BELLE!
YOU BETTER GET YOUR SORRY ASS UP AND HUG THIS SORRY ASS!
I'D RATHER SIT, THANK YOU. MY FOOL KNEES AREN'T WHAT THEY USED TO BE.
YOU AND ME BOTH.
SHE HURT HER KNEE IN THE SLAM PIT.
MOSH PIT.
PUIG 66
YOU'RE TOO OLD TO BE GOING OUT THERE WITH THOSE FOOTBALL PLAYERS.
NOW SHE TELLS ME.
AND WE'LL GET BACK TO THAT MOSH THING LATER, YOUNG MISSY.
WERE YOU OUT THERE BEING FOOLISH, TOO?
ASK MY NOSE.
YOU WERE ALWAYS HITTING YOUR NOSE.
THANK YOU VERY MUCH.
WELL, LOOK AT US! THE ONLY ONE MISSING IS PENNY CENTURY.
DON'T JINX IT.
LOOKS LIKE YOU'RE HER STAND-IN, JESSICA.
WHO IS PENNY CENTURY?
CH
WELL NOW, WHERE DOES ONE BEGIN?
HOW DOES ONE BEGIN?
A CROSS BETWEEN HELEN OF TROY AND MINNIE PEARL.
SHE'S AN OLD FRIEND, JESS.
TLA QUE PA QUE
DAPHNE, WHO WAS THE WOMAN HANGING OUT WITH YOU BACKSTAGE TONIGHT WITH HER HAIR TIED BACK AND GLASSES?
ITSUKI?
NO, RED HAIR.
2.

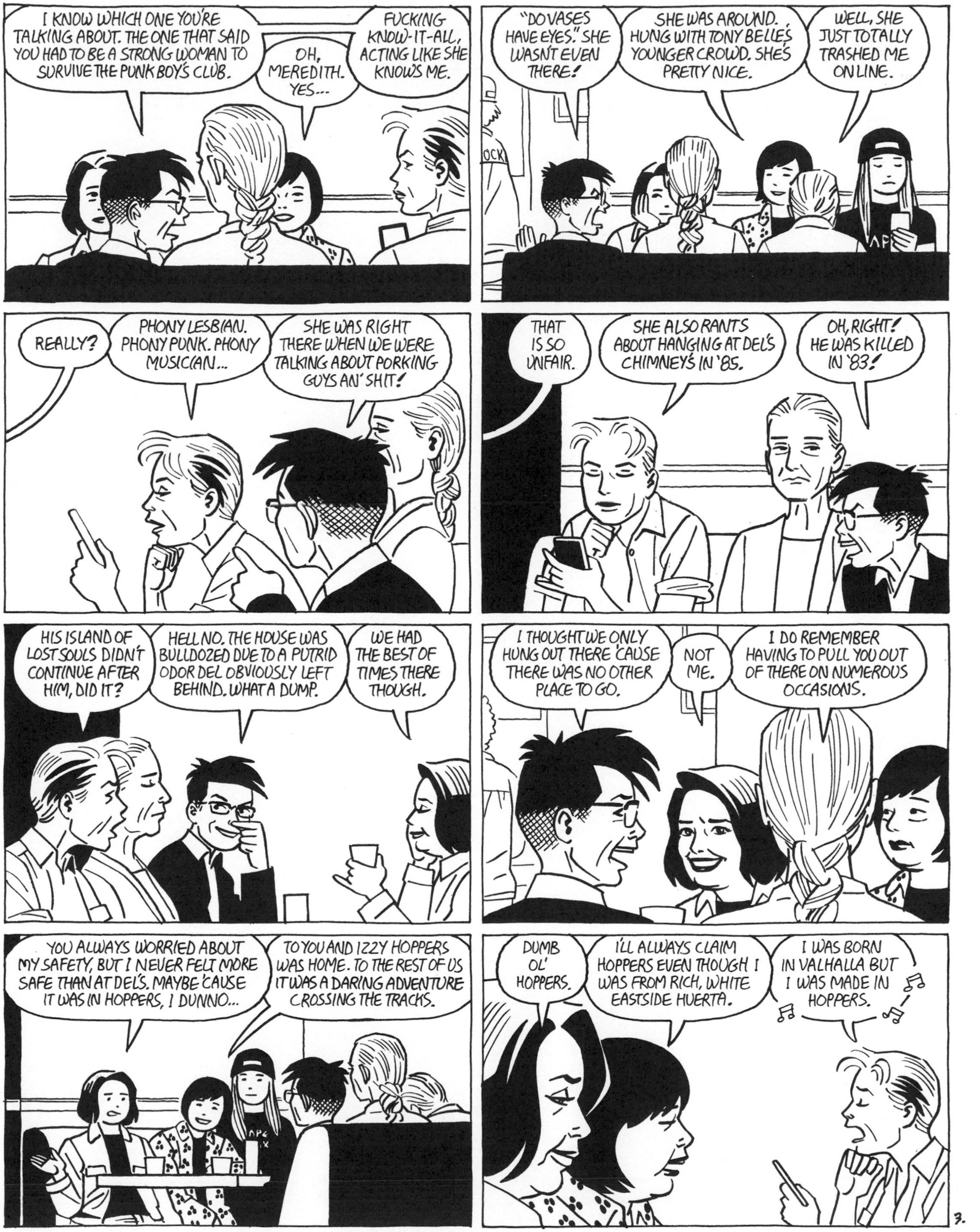
I KNOW WHICH ONE YOU'RE TALKING ABOUT. THE ONE THAT SAID YOU HAD TO BE A STRONG WOMAN TO SURVIVE THE PUNK BOY'S CLUB.
OH, MEREDITH. YES...
FUCKING KNOW-IT-ALL, ACTING LIKE SHE KNOWS ME.
"DO VASES HAVE EYES." SHE WASN'T EVEN THERE!
SHE WAS AROUND. HUNG WITH TONY BELLE'S YOUNGER CROWD. SHE'S PRETTY NICE.
WELL, SHE JUST TOTALLY TRASHED ME ONLINE.
REALLY?
PHONY LESBIAN. PHONY PUNK. PHONY MUSICIAN...
SHE WAS RIGHT THERE WHEN WE WERE TALKING ABOUT PORKING GUYS AN' SHIT!
THAT IS SO UNFAIR.
SHE ALSO RANTS ABOUT HANGING AT DEL'S CHIMNEY'S IN '85.
OH, RIGHT! HE WAS KILLED IN '83!
HIS ISLAND OF LOST SOULS DIDN'T CONTINUE AFTER HIM, DID IT?
HELL NO. THE HOUSE WAS BULLDOZED DUE TO A PUTRID ODOR DEL OBVIOUSLY LEFT BEHIND. WHAT A DUMP.
WE HAD THE BEST OF TIMES THERE THOUGH.
I THOUGHT WE ONLY HUNG OUT THERE 'CAUSE THERE WAS NO OTHER PLACE TO GO.
NOT ME.
I DO REMEMBER HAVING TO PULL YOU OUT OF THERE ON NUMEROUS OCCASIONS.
YOU ALWAYS WORRIED ABOUT MY SAFETY, BUT I NEVER FELT MORE SAFE THAN AT DEL'S. MAYBE 'CAUSE IT WAS IN HOPPERS, I DUNNO...
TO YOU AND IZZY HOPPERS WAS HOME. TO THE REST OF US IT WAS A DARING ADVENTURE CROSSING THE TRACKS.
DUMB OL' HOPPERS.
I'LL ALWAYS CLAIM HOPPERS EVEN THOUGH I WAS FROM RICH, WHITE EASTSIDE HUERTA.
I WAS BORN IN VALHALLA BUT I WAS MADE IN HOPPERS.
3.

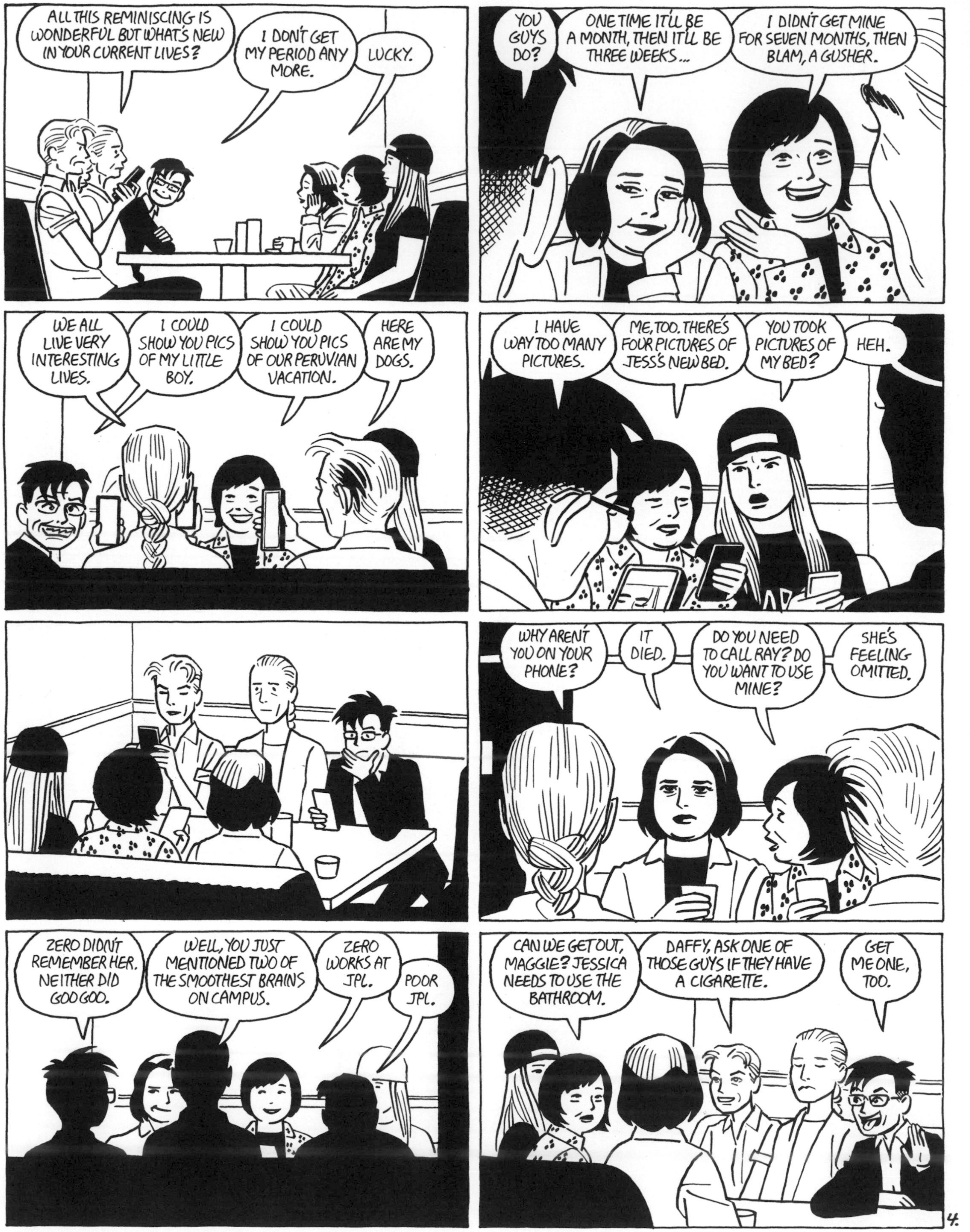
ALL THIS REMINISCING IS WONDERFUL BUT WHAT'S NEW IN YOUR CURRENT LIVES?
I DON'T GET MY PERIOD ANY MORE.
LUCKY.
YOU GUYS DO?
ONE TIME IT'LL BE A MONTH, THEN IT'LL BE THREE WEEKS...
I DIDN'T GET MINE FOR SEVEN MONTHS, THEN BLAM, A GUSHER.
WE ALL LIVE VERY INTERESTING LIVES.
I COULD SHOW YOU PICS OF MY LITTLE BOY.
I COULD SHOW YOU PICS OF OUR PERUVIAN VACATION.
HERE ARE MY DOGS.
I HAVE WAY TOO MANY PICTURES.
ME, TOO. THERE'S FOUR PICTURES OF JESS'S NEW BED.
YOU TOOK PICTURES OF MY BED?
HEH.
WHY AREN'T YOU ON YOUR PHONE?
IT DIED.
DO YOU NEED TO CALL RAY? DO YOU WANT TO USE MINE?
SHE'S FEELING OMITTED.
ZERO DIDN'T REMEMBER HER. NEITHER DID GOOGOO.
WELL, YOU JUST MENTIONED TWO OF THE SMOOTHEST BRAINS ON CAMPUS.
ZERO WORKS AT JPL.
POOR JPL.
CAN WE GET OUT, MAGGIE? JESSICA NEEDS TO USE THE BATHROOM.
DAFFY, ASK ONE OF THOSE GUYS IF THEY HAVE A CIGARETTE.
GET ME ONE, TOO.
4.

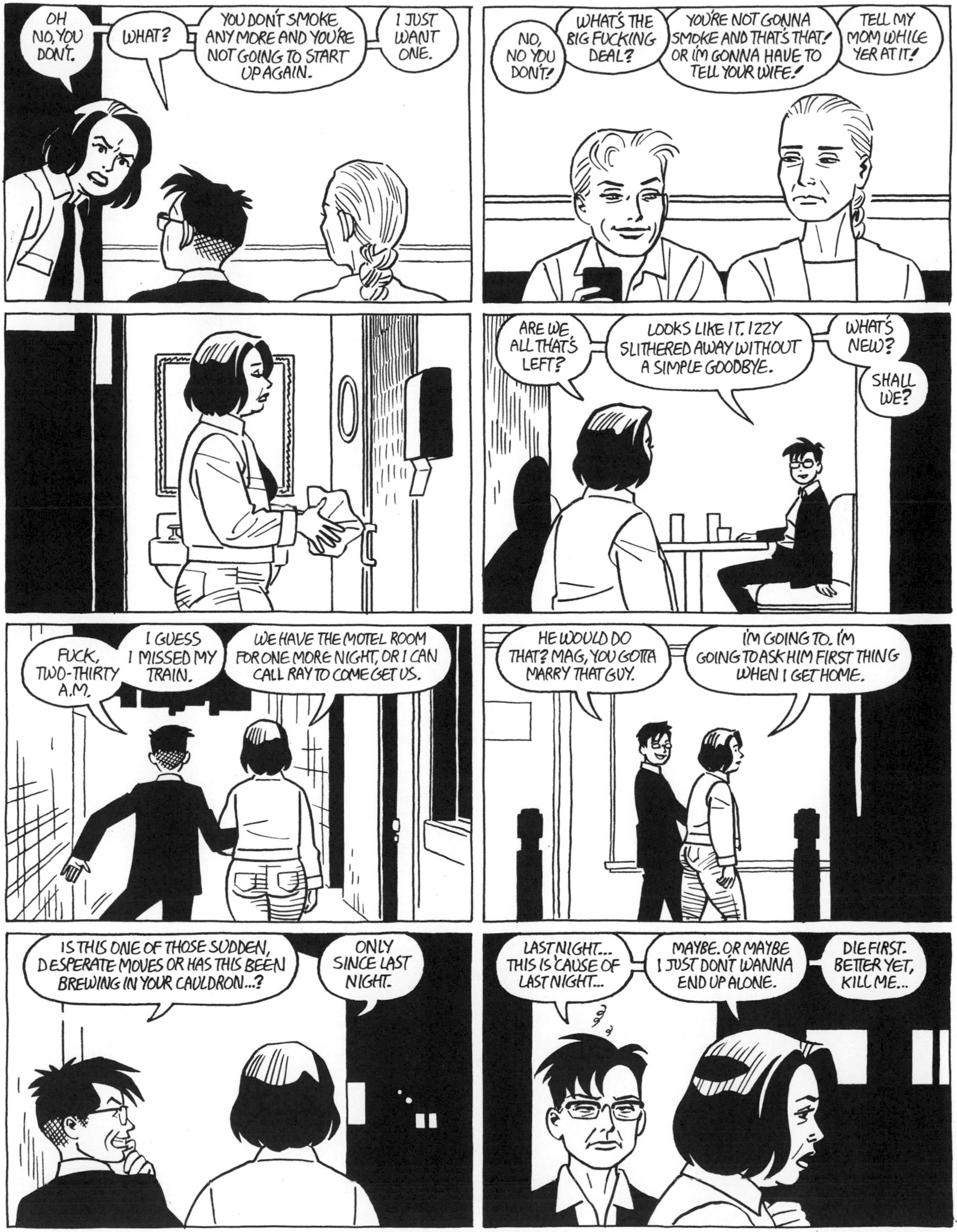
OH NO, YOU DON'T.
WHAT?
YOU DON'T SMOKE ANY MORE AND YOU'RE NOT GOING TO START UP AGAIN.
I JUST WANT ONE.
NO, NO YOU DON'T!
WHAT'S THE BIG FUCKING DEAL?
YOU'RE NOT GONNA SMOKE AND THAT'S THAT! OR I'M GONNA HAVE TO TELL YOUR WIFE!
TELL MY MOM WHILE YER AT IT!
ARE WE ALL THAT'S LEFT?
LOOKS LIKE IT. IZZY SLITHERED AWAY WITHOUT A SIMPLE GOODBYE.
WHAT'S NEW?
SHALL WE?
FUCK, TWO-THIRTY A.M.
I GUESS I MISSED MY TRAIN.
WE HAVE THE MOTEL ROOM FOR ONE MORE NIGHT, OR I CAN CALL RAY TO COME GET US.
HE WOULD DO THAT? MAG, YOU GOTTA MARRY THAT GUY.
I'M GOING TO. I'M GOING TO ASK HIM FIRST THING WHEN I GET HOME.
IS THIS ONE OF THOSE SUDDEN, DESPERATE MOVES OR HAS THIS BEEN BREWING IN YOUR CAULDRON...?
ONLY SINCE LAST NIGHT.
LAST NIGHT... THIS IS 'CAUSE OF LAST NIGHT...
MAYBE. OR MAYBE I JUST DON'T WANNA END UP ALONE.
DIE FIRST. BETTER YET, KILL ME...

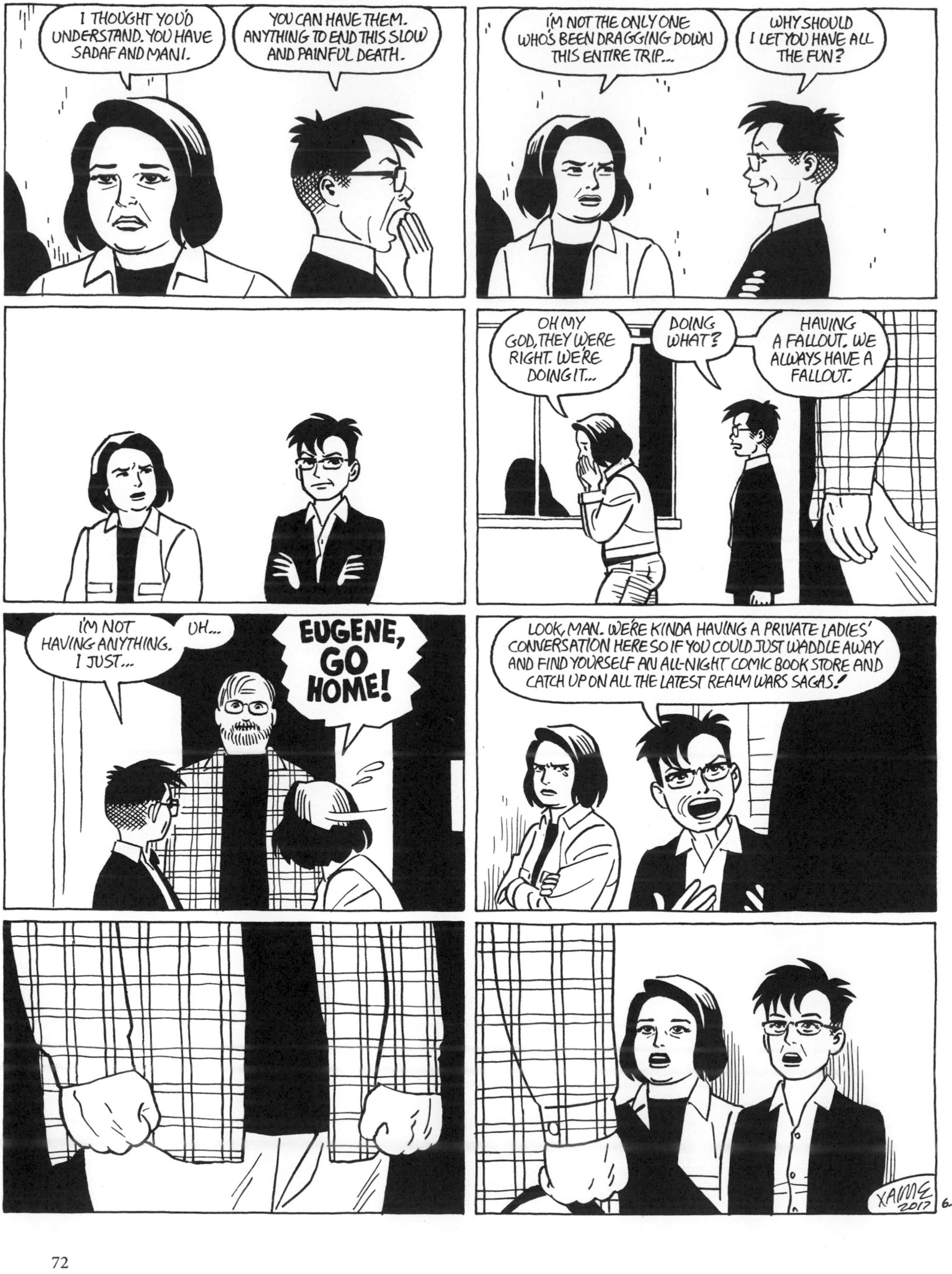
I THOUGHT YOU'D UNDERSTAND. YOU HAVE SADAF AND MANI.
YOU CAN HAVE THEM. ANYTHING TO END THIS SLOW AND PAINFUL DEATH.
I'M NOT THE ONLY ONE WHO'S BEEN DRAGGING DOWN THIS ENTIRE TRIP...
WHY SHOULD I LET YOU HAVE ALL THE FUN?
OH MY GOD, THEY WERE RIGHT. WE'RE DOING IT...
DOING WHAT?
HAVING A FALLOUT. WE ALWAYS HAVE A FALLOUT.
I'M NOT HAVING ANYTHING. I JUST...
UH...
EUGENE, GO HOME!
LOOK, MAN. WE'RE KINDA HAVING A PRIVATE LADIES' CONVERSATION HERE SO IF YOU COULD JUST WADDLE AWAY AND FIND YOURSELF AN ALL-NIGHT COMIC BOOK STORE AND CATCH UP ON ALL THE LATEST REALM WARS SAGAS!
XAIME 2017
6.

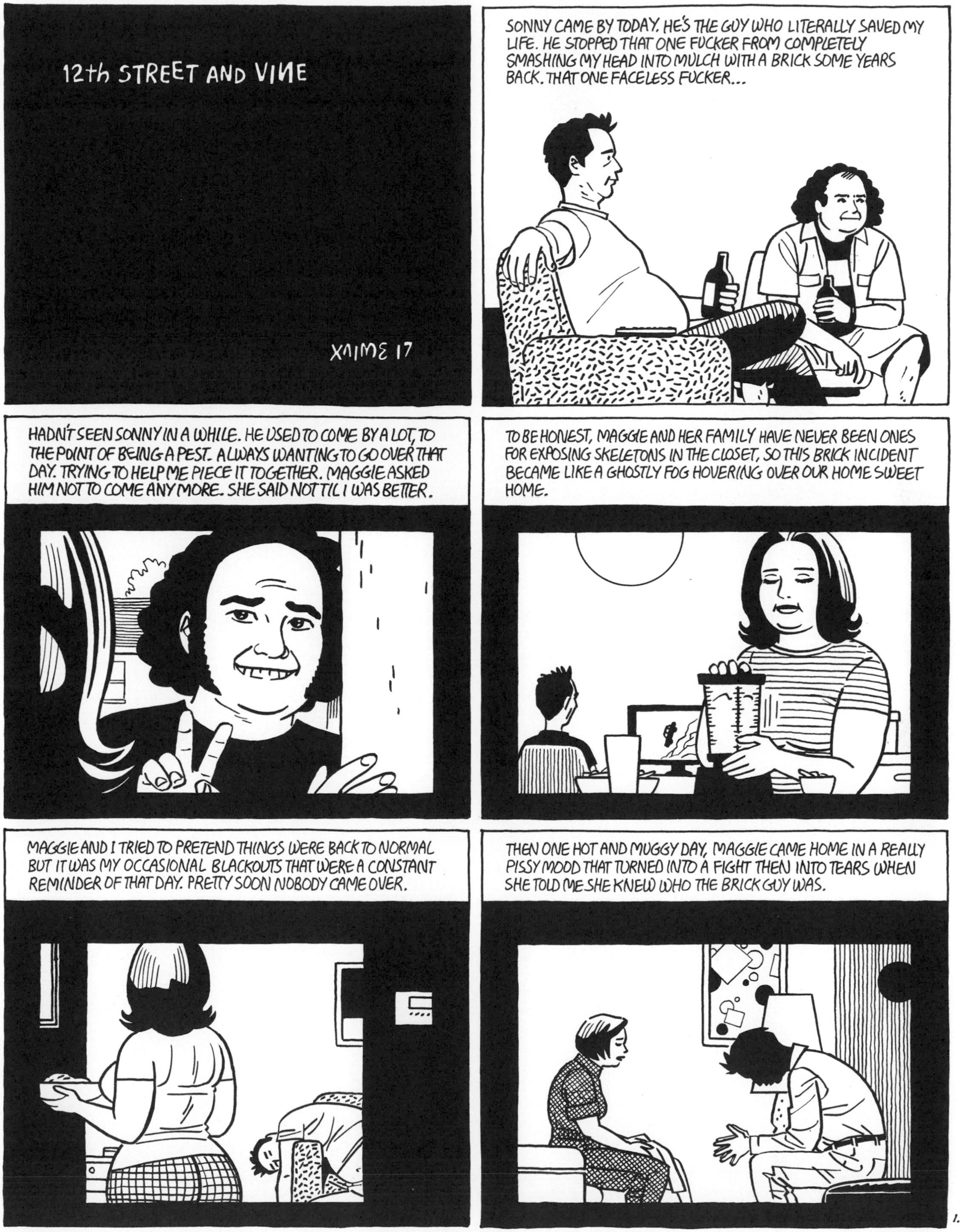
12th STREET AND VINE
SONNY CAME BY TODAY. HE'S THE GUY WHO LITERALLY SAVED MY LIFE. HE STOPPED THAT ONE FUCKER FROM COMPLETELY SMASHING MY HEAD INTO MULCH WITH A BRICK SOME YEARS BACK. THAT ONE FACELESS FUCKER...
HADN'T SEEN SONNY IN A WHILE. HE USED TO COME BY A LOT, TO THE POINT OF BEING A PEST. ALWAYS WANTING TO GO OVER THAT DAY. TRYING TO HELP ME PIECE IT TOGETHER. MAGGIE ASKED HIM NOT TO COME ANY MORE. SHE SAID NOT TIL I WAS BETTER.
TO BE HONEST, MAGGIE AND HER FAMILY HAVE NEVER BEEN ONES FOR EXPOSING SKELETONS IN THE CLOSET, SO THIS BRICK INCIDENT BECAME LIKE A GHOSTLY FOG HOVERING OVER OUR HOME SWEET HOME.
MAGGIE AND I TRIED TO PRETEND THINGS WERE BACK TO NORMAL BUT IT WAS MY OCCASIONAL BLACKOUTS THAT WERE A CONSTANT REMINDER OF THAT DAY. PRETTY SOON NOBODY CAME OVER.
THEN ONE HOT AND MUGGY DAY, MAGGIE CAME HOME IN A REALLY PISSY MOOD THAT TURNED INTO A FIGHT THEN INTO TEARS WHEN SHE TOLD ME SHE KNEW WHO THE BRICK GUY WAS.
1.

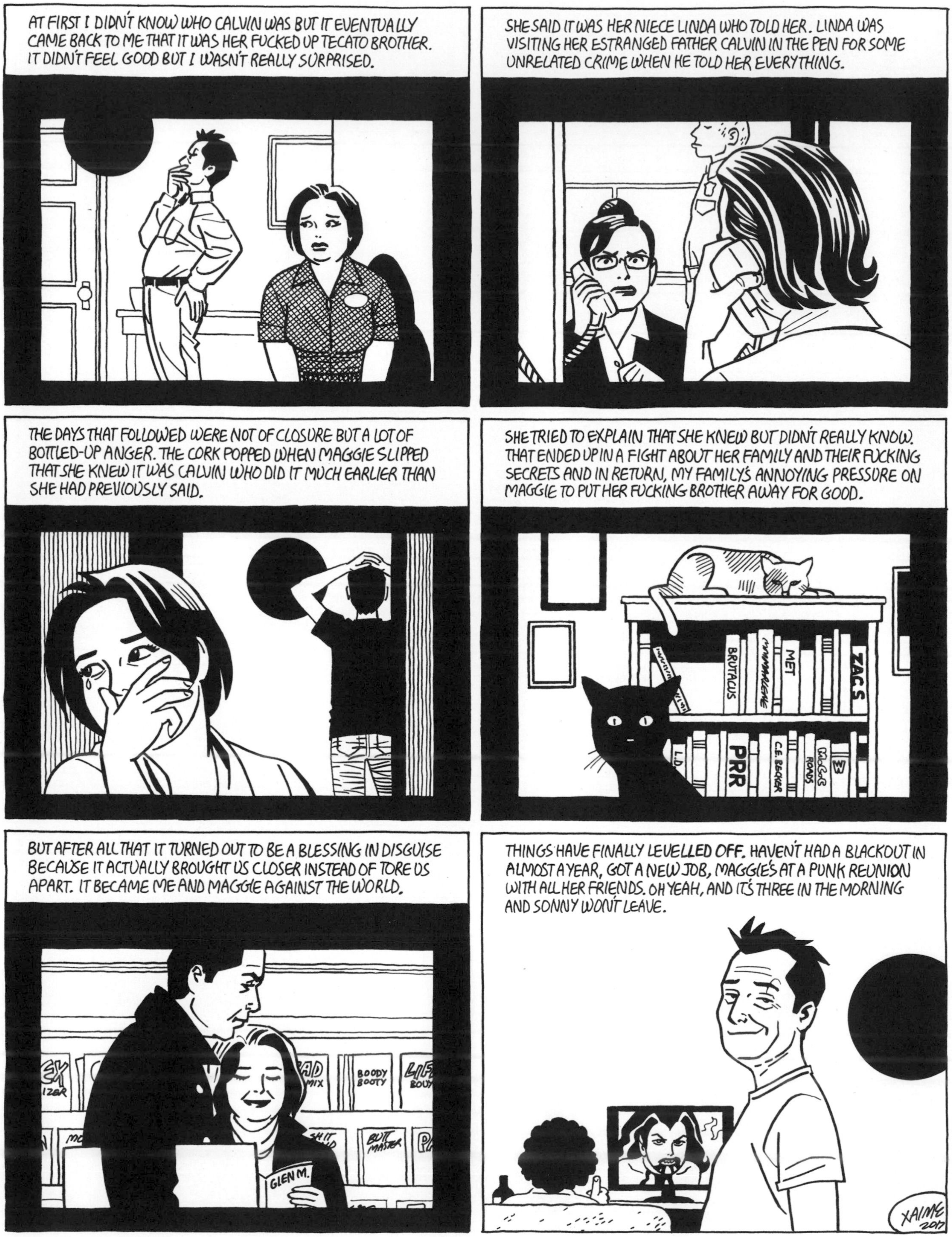
AT FIRST I DIDN'T KNOW WHO CALVIN WAS BUT IT EVENTUALLY CAME BACK TO ME THAT IT WAS HER FUCKED UP TECATO BROTHER. IT DIDN'T FEEL GOOD BUT I WASN'T REALLY SURPRISED.
SHE SAID IT WAS HER NIECE LINDA WHO TOLD HER. LINDA WAS VISITING HER ESTRANGED FATHER CALVIN IN THE PEN FOR SOME UNRELATED CRIME WHEN HE TOLD HER EVERYTHING.
THE DAYS THAT FOLLOWED WERE NOT OF CLOSURE BUT A LOT OF BOTTLED-UP ANGER. THE CORK POPPED WHEN MAGGIE SLIPPED THAT SHE KNEW IT WAS CALVIN WHO DID IT MUCH EARLIER THAN SHE HAD PREVIOUSLY SAID.
SHE TRIED TO EXPLAIN THAT SHE KNEW BUT DIDN'T REALLY KNOW. THAT ENDED UP IN A FIGHT ABOUT HER FAMILY AND THEIR FUCKING SECRETS AND IN RETURN, MY FAMILY'S ANNOYING PRESSURE ON MAGGIE TO PUT HER FUCKING BROTHER AWAY FOR GOOD.
BRUTACUS
MET
ZACS
PRR
C.E. BECKER
ROADS
W
BUT AFTER ALL THAT IT TURNED OUT TO BE A BLESSING IN DISGUISE BECAUSE IT ACTUALLY BROUGHT US CLOSER INSTEAD OF TORE US APART. IT BECAME ME AND MAGGIE AGAINST THE WORLD.
BOODY BOOTY
BUTT MASTER
GLEN M.
THINGS HAVE FINALLY LEVELLED OFF. HAVEN'T HAD A BLACKOUT IN ALMOST A YEAR, GOT A NEW JOB, MAGGIE'S AT A PUNK REUNION WITH ALL HER FRIENDS. OH YEAH, AND IT'S THREE IN THE MORNING AND SONNY WON'T LEAVE.
XAIME 2017
2.

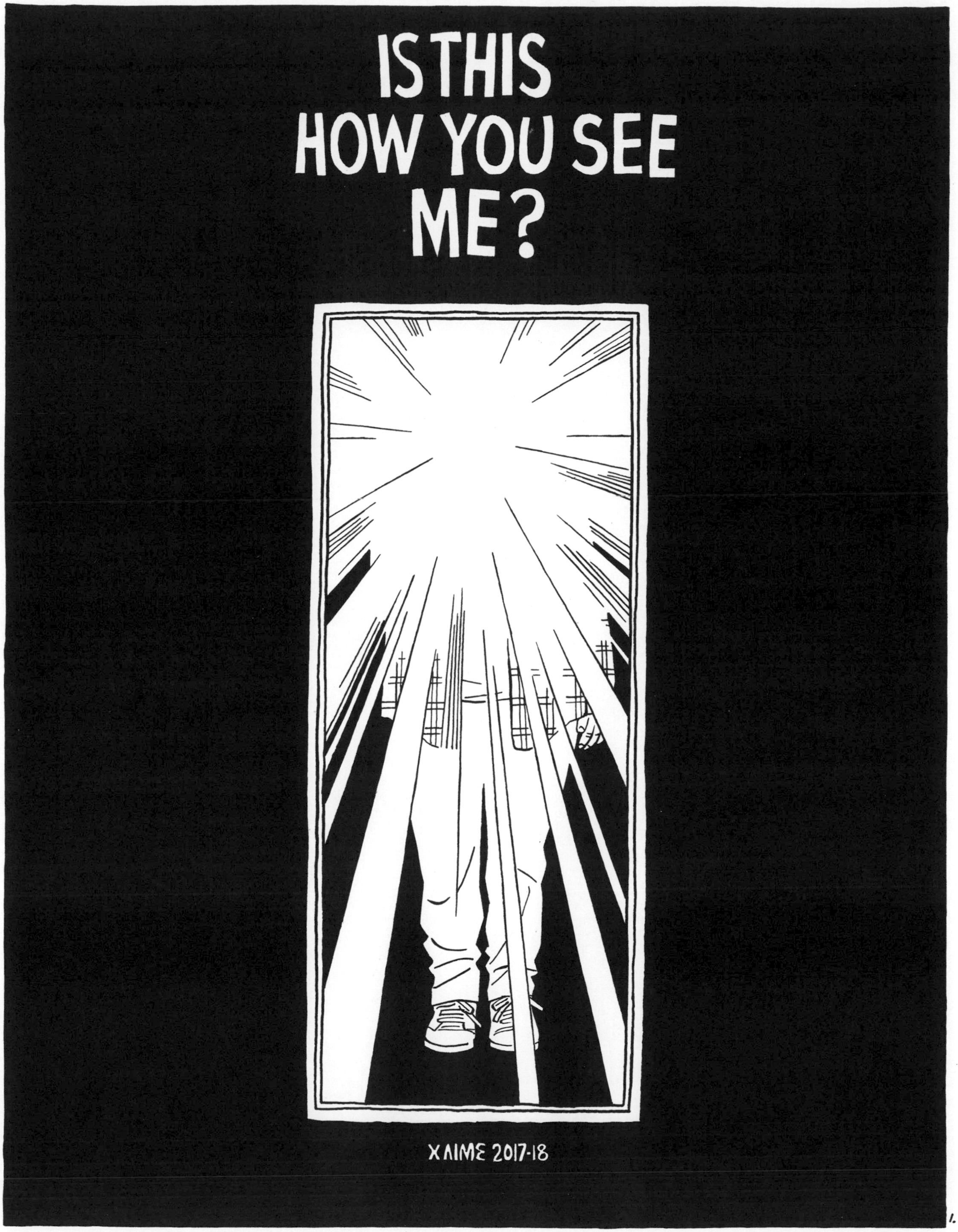
IS THIS
HOW YOU SEE
ME?
XAIME 2017-18

1.

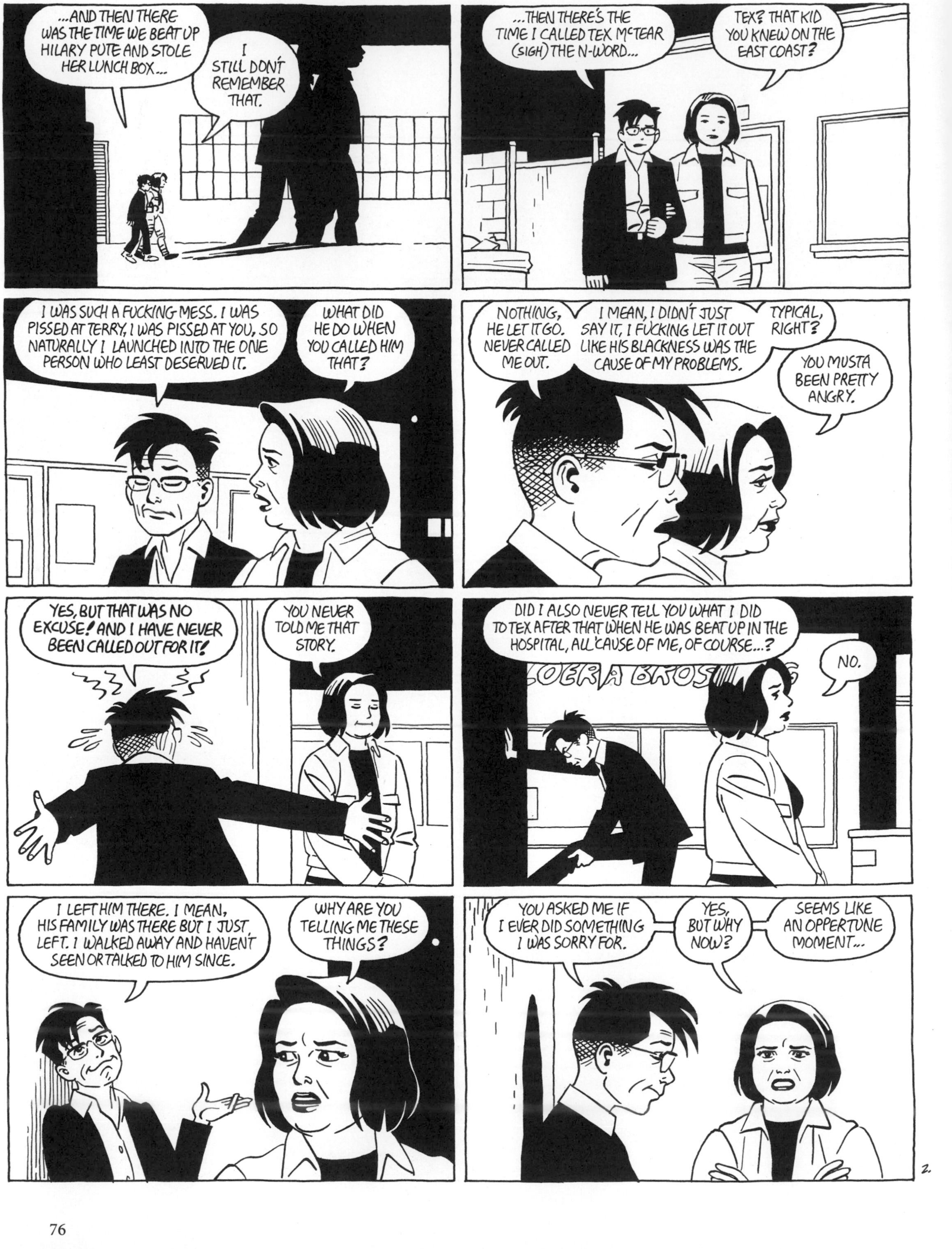
...AND THEN THERE WAS THE TIME WE BEAT UP HILARY PUTE AND STOLE HER LUNCH BOX...
I STILL DON'T REMEMBER THAT.
...THEN THERE'S THE TIME I CALLED TEX McTEAR (SIGH) THE N-WORD...
TEX? THAT KID YOU KNEW ON THE EAST COAST?
I WAS SUCH A FUCKING MESS. I WAS PISSED AT TERRY, I WAS PISSED AT YOU, SO NATURALLY I LAUNCHED INTO THE ONE PERSON WHO LEAST DESERVED IT.
WHAT DID HE DO WHEN YOU CALLED HIM THAT?
NOTHING, HE LET IT GO. NEVER CALLED ME OUT.
I MEAN, I DIDN'T JUST SAY IT, I FUCKING LET IT OUT LIKE HIS BLACKNESS WAS THE CAUSE OF MY PROBLEMS.
TYPICAL, RIGHT?
YOU MUSTA BEEN PRETTY ANGRY.
YES, BUT THAT WAS NO EXCUSE! AND I HAVE NEVER BEEN CALLED OUT FOR IT!
YOU NEVER TOLD ME THAT STORY.
DID I ALSO NEVER TELL YOU WHAT I DID TO TEX AFTER THAT WHEN HE WAS BEAT UP IN THE HOSPITAL, ALL 'CAUSE OF ME, OF COURSE...?
NO.
I LEFT HIM THERE. I MEAN, HIS FAMILY WAS THERE BUT I JUST LEFT. I WALKED AWAY AND HAVEN'T SEEN OR TALKED TO HIM SINCE.
WHY ARE YOU TELLING ME THESE THINGS?
YOU ASKED ME IF I EVER DID SOMETHING I WAS SORRY FOR.
YES, BUT WHY NOW?
SEEMS LIKE AN OPPERTUNE MOMENT...
2.

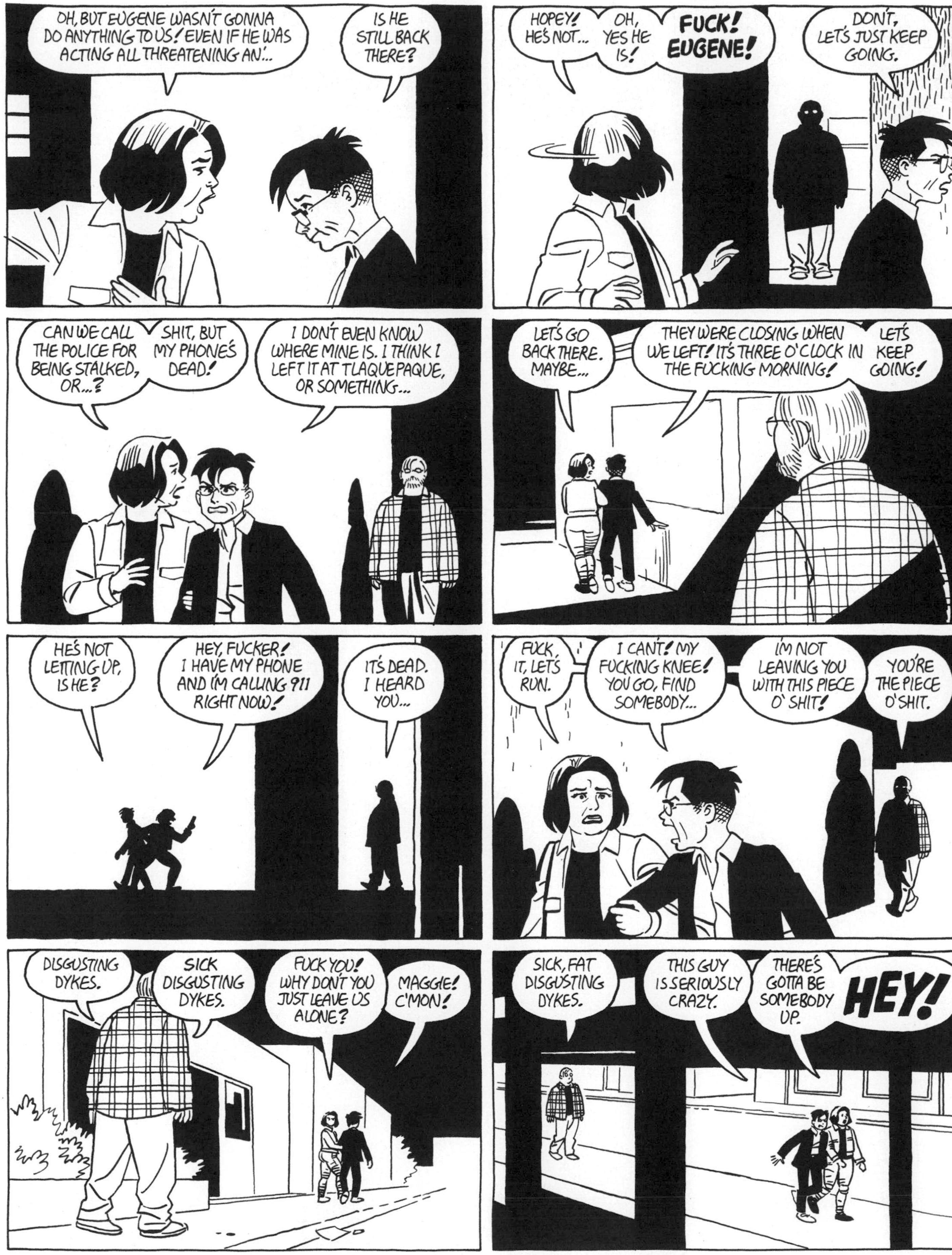
OH, BUT EUGENE WASN'T GONNA DO ANYTHING TO US! EVEN IF HE WAS ACTING ALL THREATENING AN'...
IS HE STILL BACK THERE?
HOPEY! HE'S NOT...
OH, YES HE IS!
FUCK! EUGENE!
DON'T, LET'S JUST KEEP GOING.
CAN WE CALL THE POLICE FOR BEING STALKED, OR...?
SHIT, BUT MY PHONE'S DEAD!
I DON'T EVEN KNOW WHERE MINE IS. I THINK I LEFT IT AT TLAQUEPAQUE, OR SOMETHING...
LET'S GO BACK THERE. MAYBE...
THEY WERE CLOSING WHEN WE LEFT! IT'S THREE O'CLOCK IN THE FUCKING MORNING!
LET'S KEEP GOING!
HE'S NOT LETTING UP, IS HE?
HEY, FUCKER! I HAVE MY PHONE AND I'M CALLING 911 RIGHT NOW!
IT'S DEAD. I HEARD YOU...
FUCK, IT, LET'S RUN.
I CAN'T! MY FUCKING KNEE! YOU GO, FIND SOMEBODY...
I'M NOT LEAVING YOU WITH THIS PIECE O' SHIT!
YOU'RE THE PIECE O' SHIT.
DISGUSTING DYKES.
SICK DISGUSTING DYKES.
FUCK YOU! WHY DON'T YOU JUST LEAVE US ALONE?
MAGGIE! C'MON!
SICK, FAT DISGUSTING DYKES.
THIS GUY IS SERIOUSLY CRAZY.
THERE'S GOTTA BE SOMEBODY UP.
HEY!
3.

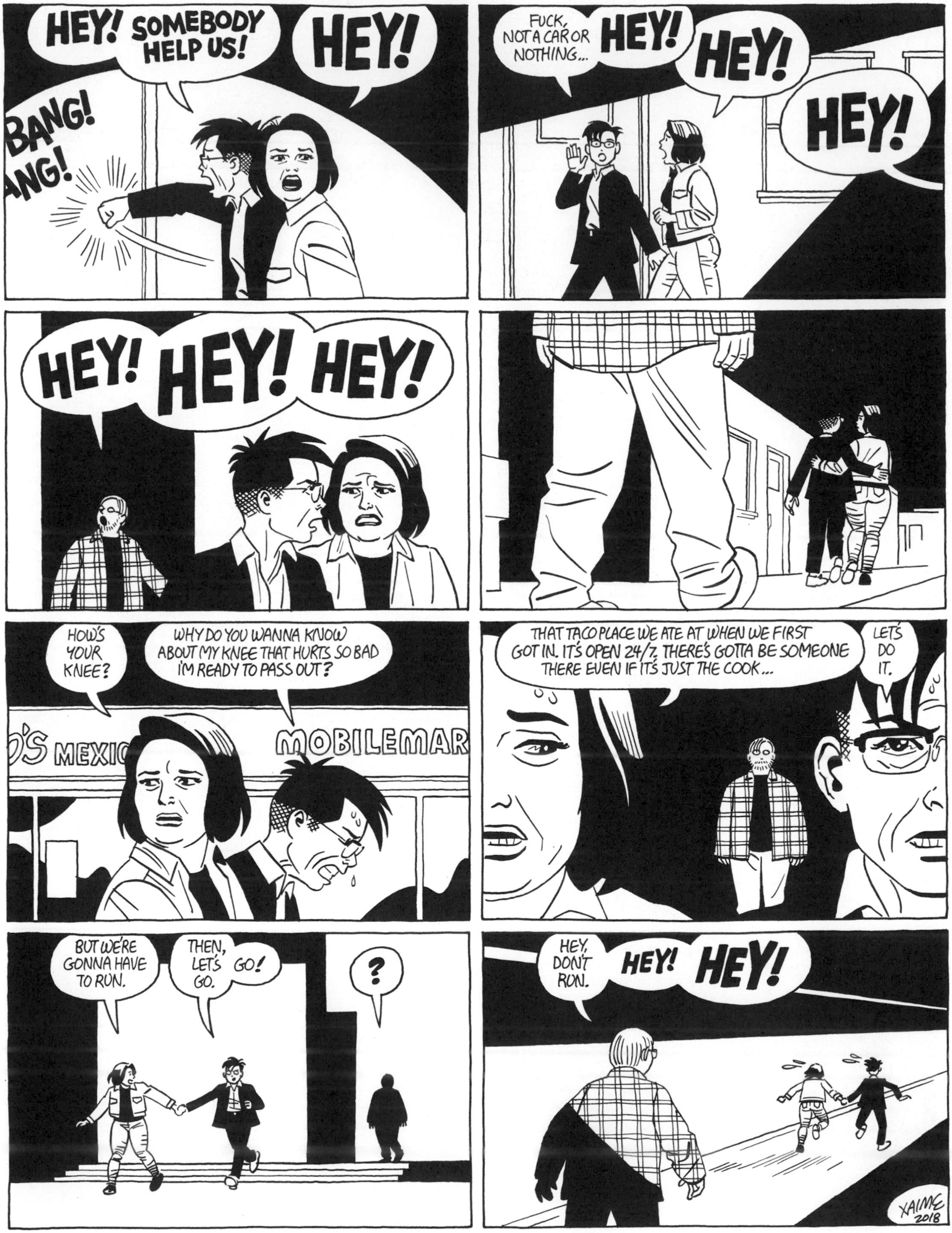
HEY! SOMEBODY HELP US!
HEY!
BANG!
ANG!
FUCK, NOT A CAR OR NOTHING...
HEY!
HEY!
HEY!
HEY! HEY! HEY!
HOW'S YOUR KNEE?
WHY DO YOU WANNA KNOW ABOUT MY KNEE THAT HURTS SO BAD I'M READY TO PASS OUT?
MOBILEMAR
THAT TACO PLACE WE ATE AT WHEN WE FIRST GOT IN. IT'S OPEN 24/7. THERE'S GOTTA BE SOMEONE THERE EVEN IF IT'S JUST THE COOK...
LET'S DO IT.
BUT WE'RE GONNA HAVE TO RUN.
THEN, LET'S GO.
GO!
?
HEY, DON'T RUN.
HEY! HEY!
XAIME 2018
4.

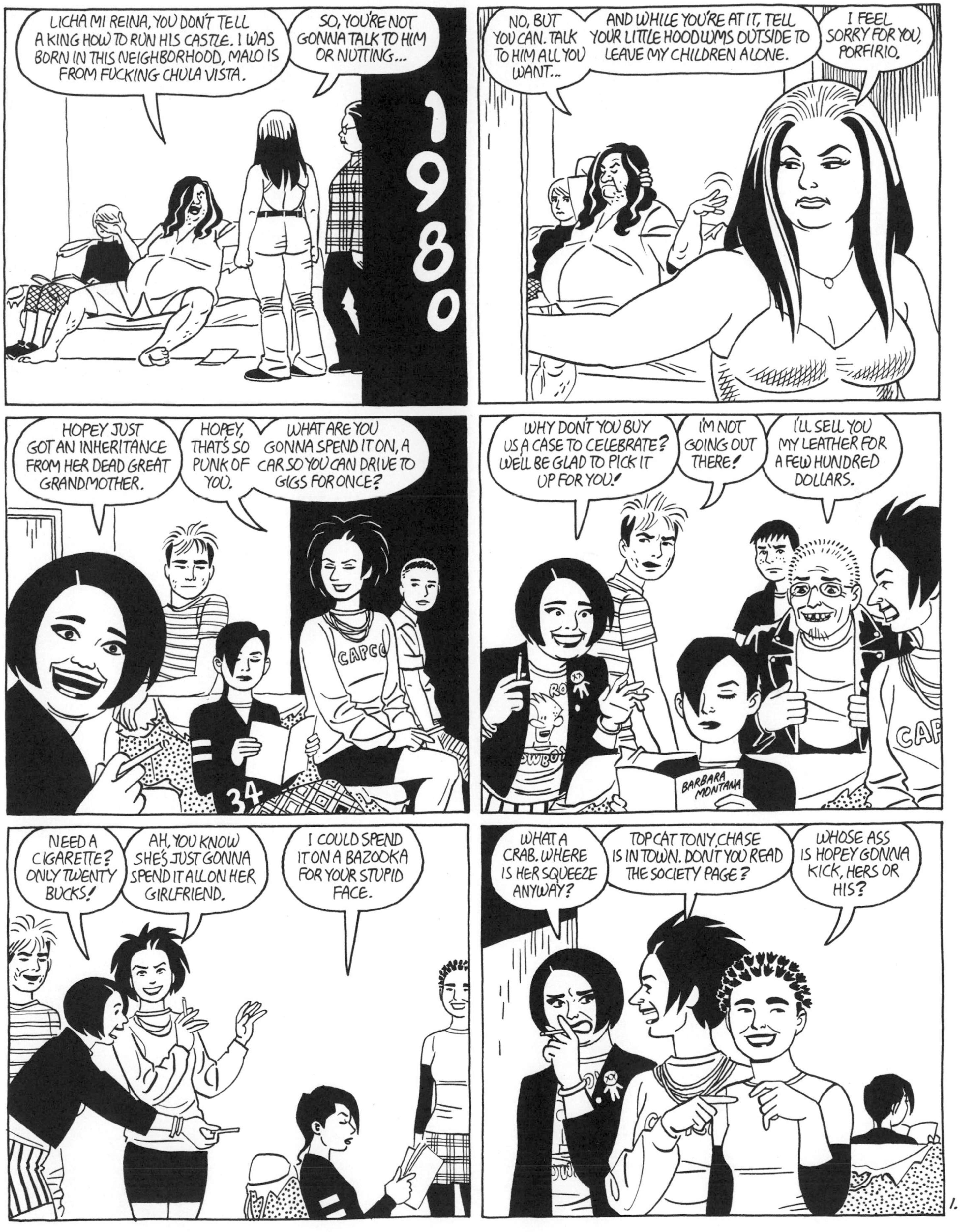
LICHA MI REINA, YOU DON'T TELL A KING HOW TO RUN HIS CASTLE. I WAS BORN IN THIS NEIGHBORHOOD, MALO IS FROM FUCKING CHULA VISTA.
SO, YOU'RE NOT GONNA TALK TO HIM OR NUTTING...
1980
NO, BUT YOU CAN. TALK TO HIM ALL YOU WANT...
AND WHILE YOU'RE AT IT, TELL YOUR LITTLE HOODLUMS OUTSIDE TO LEAVE MY CHILDREN ALONE.
I FEEL SORRY FOR YOU, PORFIRIO.
HOPEY JUST GOT AN INHERITANCE FROM HER DEAD GREAT GRANDMOTHER.
HOPEY, THAT'S SO PUNK OF YOU.
WHAT ARE YOU GONNA SPEND IT ON, A CAR SO YOU CAN DRIVE TO GIGS FOR ONCE?
WHY DON'T YOU BUY US A CASE TO CELEBRATE? WE'LL BE GLAD TO PICK IT UP FOR YOU!
I'M NOT GOING OUT THERE!
I'LL SELL YOU MY LEATHER FOR A FEW HUNDRED DOLLARS.
BARBARA MONTANA
NEED A CIGARETTE? ONLY TWENTY BUCKS!
AH, YOU KNOW SHE'S JUST GONNA SPEND IT ALL ON HER GIRLFRIEND.
I COULD SPEND IT ON A BAZOOKA FOR YOUR STUPID FACE.
WHAT A CRAB. WHERE IS HER SQUEEZE ANYWAY?
TOP CAT TONY CHASE IS IN TOWN. DON'T YOU READ THE SOCIETY PAGE?
WHOSE ASS IS HOPEY GONNA KICK, HERS OR HIS?
1.

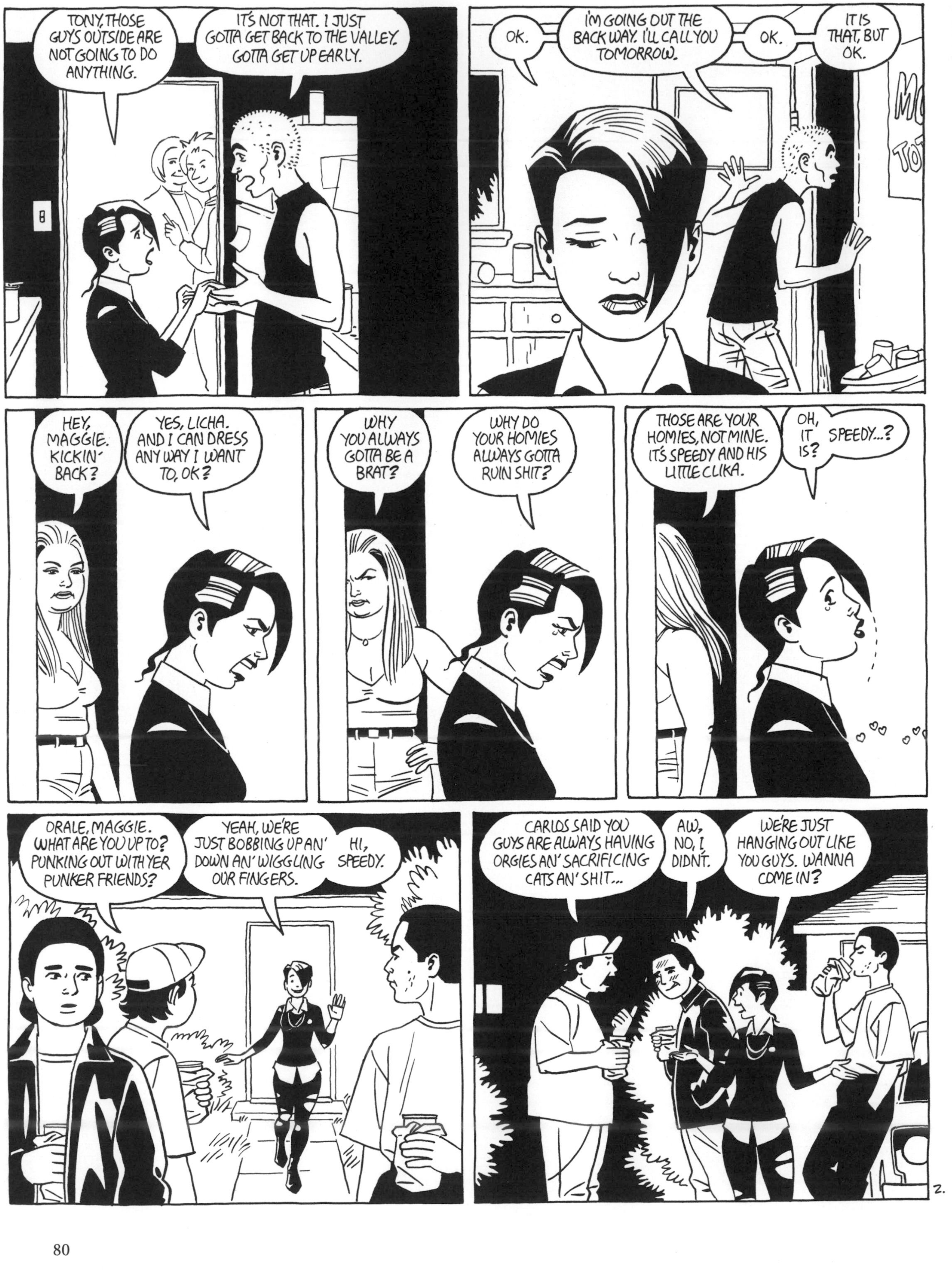
TONY, THOSE GUYS OUTSIDE ARE NOT GOING TO DO ANYTHING.
IT'S NOT THAT. I JUST GOTTA GET BACK TO THE VALLEY. GOTTA GET UP EARLY.
OK.
I'M GOING OUT THE BACK WAY. I'LL CALL YOU TOMORROW.
OK.
IT IS THAT, BUT OK.
HEY, MAGGIE. KICKIN' BACK?
YES, LICHA. AND I CAN DRESS ANY WAY I WANT TO, OK?
WHY YOU ALWAYS GOTTA BE A BRAT?
WHY DO YOUR HOMIES ALWAYS GOTTA RUIN SHIT?
THOSE ARE YOUR HOMIES, NOT MINE. IT'S SPEEDY AND HIS LITTLE CLIKA.
OH, IT IS?
SPEEDY...?
ORALE, MAGGIE. WHAT ARE YOU UP TO? PUNKING OUT WITH YER PUNKER FRIENDS?
YEAH, WE'RE JUST BOBBING UP AN' DOWN AN' WIGGLING OUR FINGERS.
HI, SPEEDY.
CARLOS SAID YOU GUYS ARE ALWAYS HAVING ORGIES AN' SACRIFICING CATS AN' SHIT...
AW, NO, I DIDN'T.
WE'RE JUST HANGING OUT LIKE YOU GUYS. WANNA COME IN?
2.

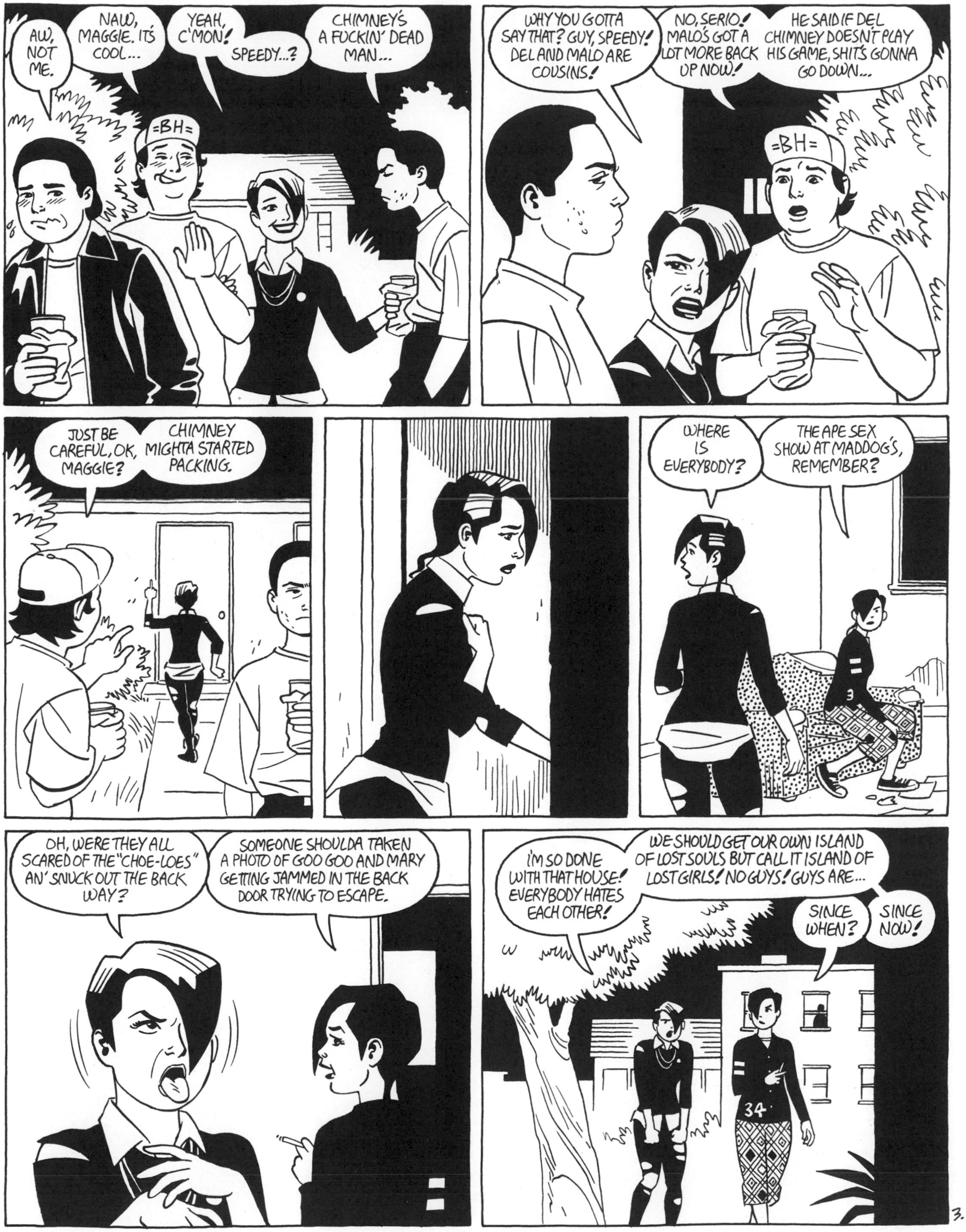
AW, NOT ME.
NAW, MAGGIE. IT'S COOL...
YEAH, C'MON!
SPEEDY...?
CHIMNEY'S A FUCKIN' DEAD MAN...
=BH=
WHY YOU GOTTA SAY THAT? GUY, SPEEDY! DEL AND MALO ARE COUSINS!
NO, SERIO! MALO'S GOT A LOT MORE BACK UP NOW!
HE SAID IF DEL CHIMNEY DOESN'T PLAY HIS GAME, SHIT'S GONNA GO DOWN...
=BH=
JUST BE CAREFUL, OK, MAGGIE?
CHIMNEY MIGHTA STARTED PACKING.
WHERE IS EVERYBODY?
THE APE SEX SHOW AT MADDOG'S, REMEMBER?
OH, WERE THEY ALL SCARED OF THE "CHOE-LOES" AN' SNUCK OUT THE BACK WAY?
SOMEONE SHOULDA TAKEN A PHOTO OF GOO GOO AND MARY GETTING JAMMED IN THE BACK DOOR TRYING TO ESCAPE.
I'M SO DONE WITH THAT HOUSE! EVERYBODY HATES EACH OTHER!
WE SHOULD GET OUR OWN ISLAND OF LOST SOULS BUT CALL IT ISLAND OF LOST GIRLS! NO GUYS! GUYS ARE...
SINCE WHEN?
SINCE NOW!
34
3.

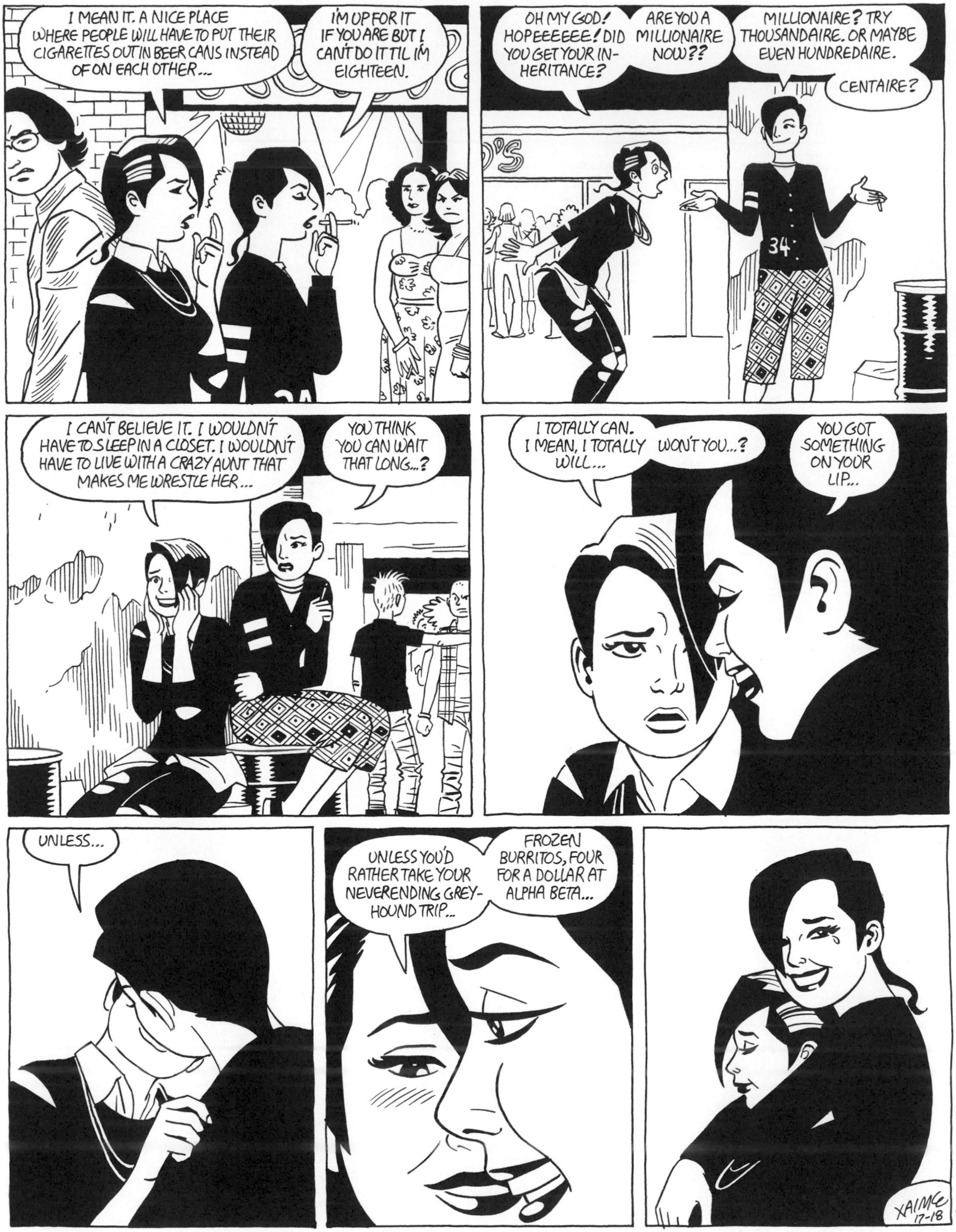
I MEAN IT. A NICE PLACE WHERE PEOPLE WILL HAVE TO PUT THEIR CIGARETTES OUT IN BEER CANS INSTEAD OF ON EACH OTHER...
I'M UP FOR IT IF YOU ARE BUT I CAN'T DO IT TIL I'M EIGHTEEN.
OH MY GOD! HOPEEEEEE! DID YOU GET YOUR INHERITANCE?
ARE YOU A MILLIONAIRE NOW??
MILLIONAIRE? TRY THOUSANDAIRE. OR MAYBE EVEN HUNDREDAIRE.
CENTAIRE?
34
I CAN'T BELIEVE IT. I WOULDN'T HAVE TO SLEEP IN A CLOSET. I WOULDN'T HAVE TO LIVE WITH A CRAZY AUNT THAT MAKES ME WRESTLE HER...
YOU THINK YOU CAN WAIT THAT LONG...?
I TOTALLY CAN. I MEAN, I TOTALLY WILL...
WON'T YOU...?
YOU GOT SOMETHING ON YOUR LIP...
UNLESS...
UNLESS YOU'D RATHER TAKE YOUR NEVERENDING GREYHOUND TRIP...
FROZEN BURRITOS, FOUR FOR A DOLLAR AT ALPHA BETA...
XAIME 17-18
4.

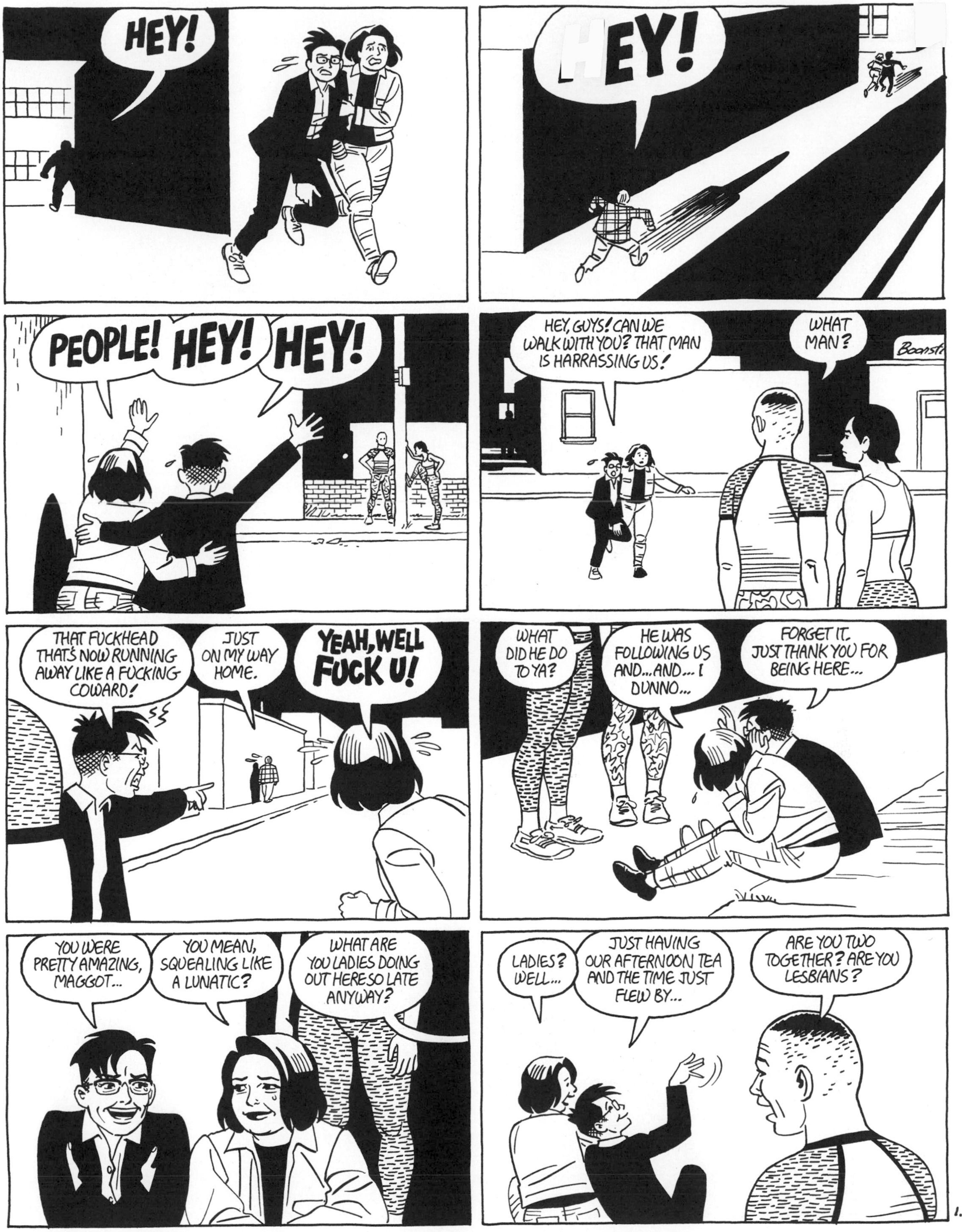
HEY!
HEY!
PEOPLE! HEY! HEY!
HEY, GUYS! CAN WE WALK WITH YOU? THAT MAN IS HARRASSING US!
WHAT MAN?
THAT FUCKHEAD THAT'S NOW RUNNING AWAY LIKE A FUCKING COWARD!
JUST ON MY WAY HOME.
YEAH, WELL FUCK U!
WHAT DID HE DO TO YA?
HE WAS FOLLOWING US AND... AND... I DUNNO...
FORGET IT. JUST THANK YOU FOR BEING HERE...
YOU WERE PRETTY AMAZING, MAGGOT...
YOU MEAN, SQUEALING LIKE A LUNATIC?
WHAT ARE YOU LADIES DOING OUT HERE SO LATE ANYWAY?
LADIES? WELL...
JUST HAVING OUR AFTERNOON TEA AND THE TIME JUST FLEW BY...
ARE YOU TWO TOGETHER? ARE YOU LESBIANS?
1.

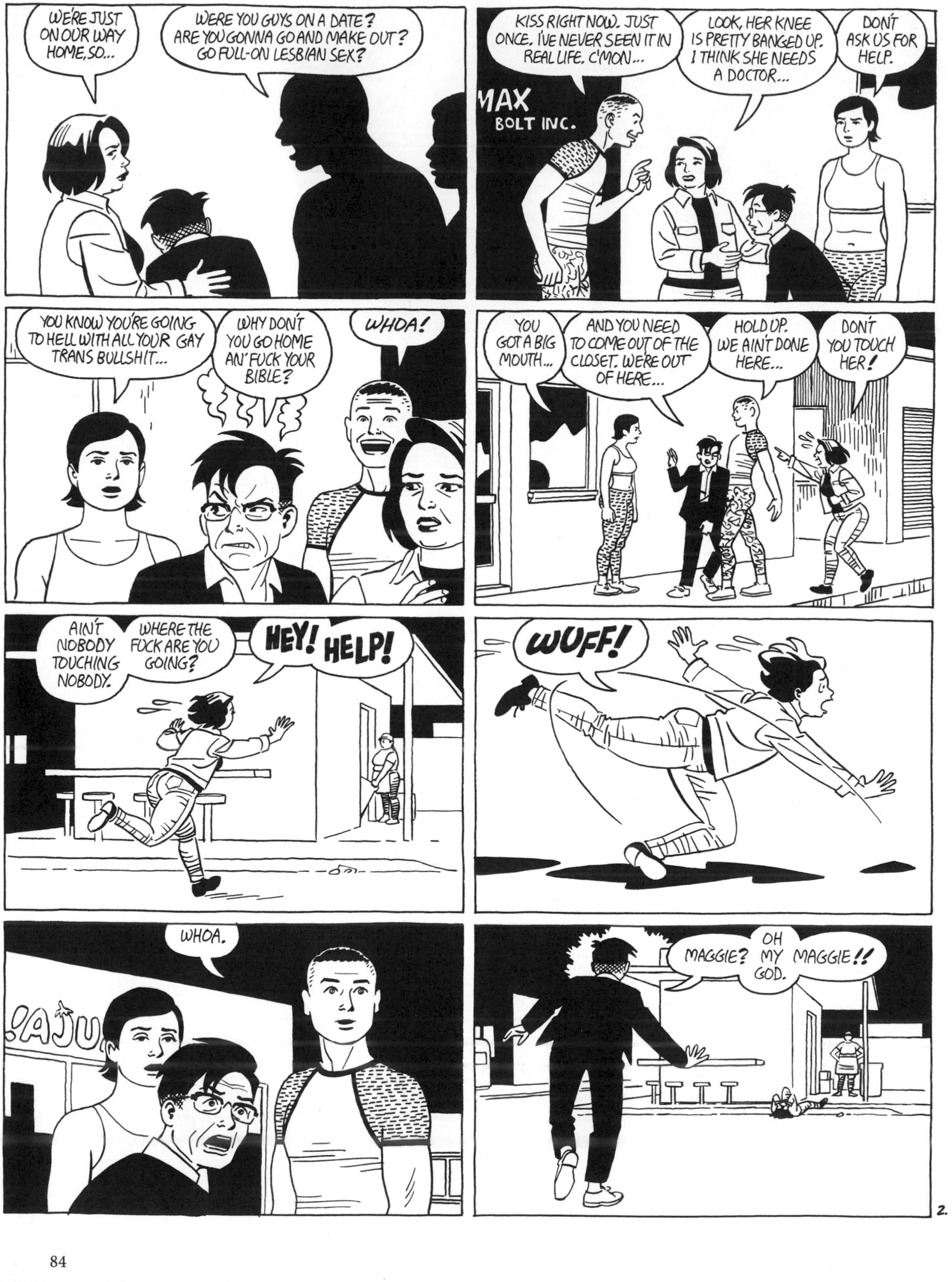
WE'RE JUST ON OUR WAY HOME, SO...
WERE YOU GUYS ON A DATE? ARE YOU GONNA GO AND MAKE OUT? GO FULL-ON LESBIAN SEX?
KISS RIGHT NOW. JUST ONCE. I'VE NEVER SEEN IT IN REAL LIFE. C'MON...
LOOK, HER KNEE IS PRETTY BANGED UP. I THINK SHE NEEDS A DOCTOR...
DON'T ASK US FOR HELP.
MAX
BOLT INC.
YOU KNOW YOU'RE GOING TO HELL WITH ALL YOUR GAY TRANS BULLSHIT...
WHY DON'T YOU GO HOME AN' FUCK YOUR BIBLE?
WHOA!
YOU GOT A BIG MOUTH...
AND YOU NEED TO COME OUT OF THE CLOSET. WE'RE OUT OF HERE...
HOLD UP. WE AIN'T DONE HERE...
DON'T YOU TOUCH HER!
AIN'T NOBODY TOUCHING NOBODY.
WHERE THE FUCK ARE YOU GOING?
HEY! HELP!
WUFF!
WHOA.
MAGGIE?
OH MY GOD.
MAGGIE!!
2.

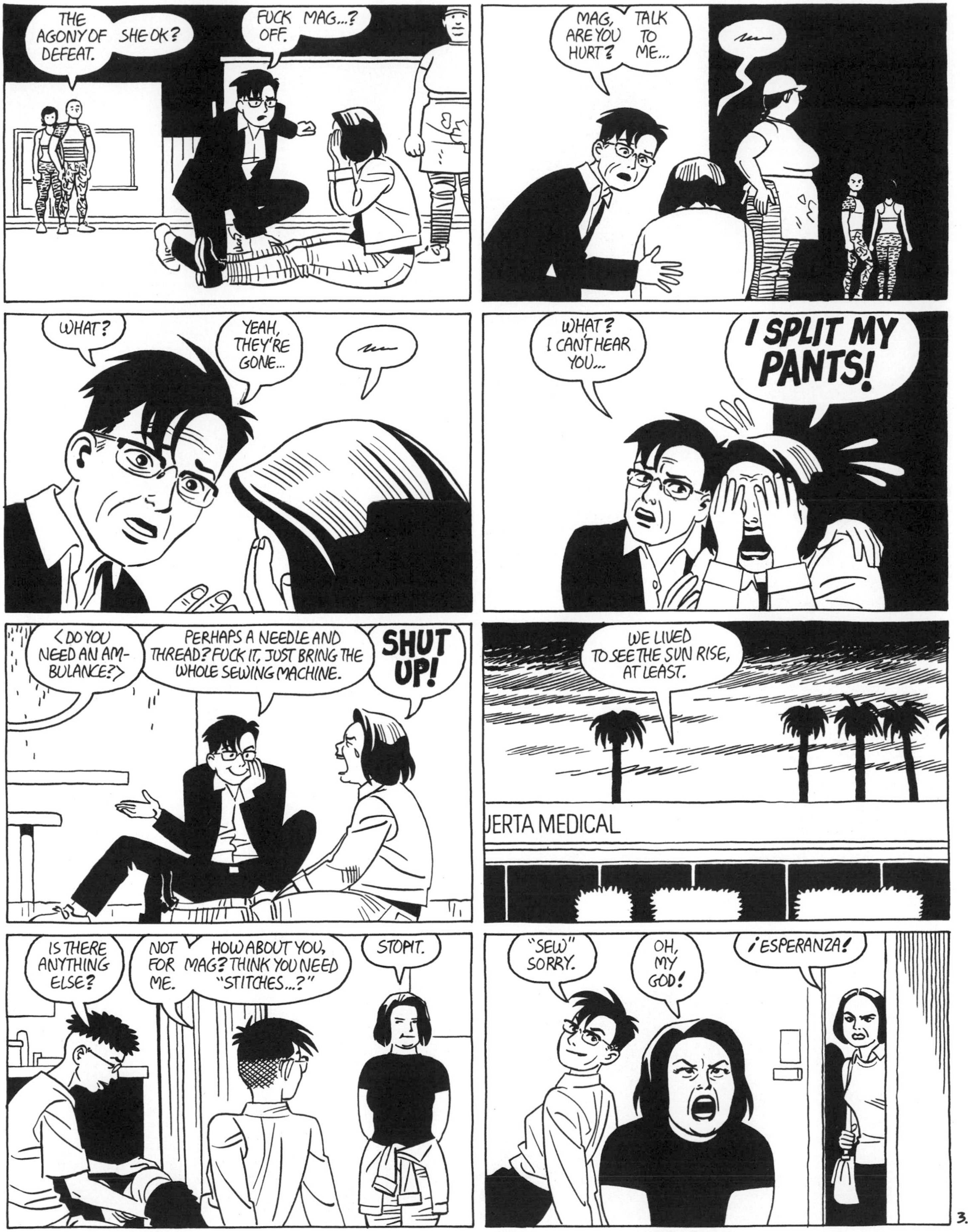
THE AGONY OF DEFEAT.
SHE OK?
FUCK OFF.
MAG...?
MAG, ARE YOU HURT?
TALK TO ME...
WHAT?
YEAH, THEY'RE GONE...
WHAT? I CAN'T HEAR YOU...
I SPLIT MY PANTS!
<DO YOU NEED AN AMBULANCE?>
PERHAPS A NEEDLE AND THREAD? FUCK IT, JUST BRING THE WHOLE SEWING MACHINE.
SHUT UP!
WE LIVED TO SEE THE SUN RISE, AT LEAST.
JERTA MEDICAL
IS THERE ANYTHING ELSE?
NOT FOR ME.
HOW ABOUT YOU, MAG? THINK YOU NEED "STITCHES...?"
STOP IT.
"SEW" SORRY.
OH, MY GOD!
¡ESPERANZA!
3.

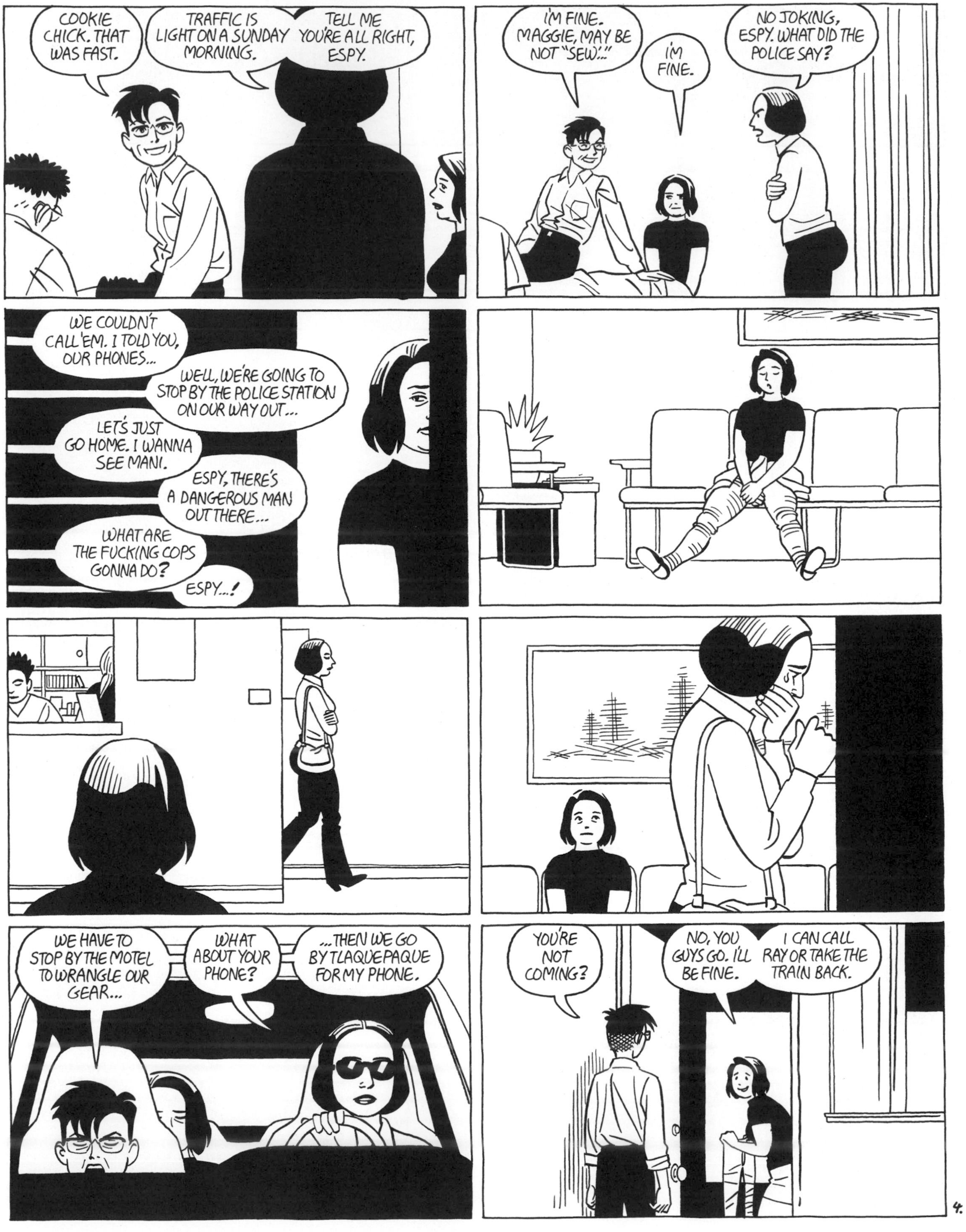
COOKIE CHICK. THAT WAS FAST.
TRAFFIC IS LIGHT ON A SUNDAY MORNING.
TELL ME YOU'RE ALL RIGHT, ESPY.
I'M FINE. MAGGIE, MAYBE NOT "SEW"...
I'M FINE.
NO JOKING, ESPY. WHAT DID THE POLICE SAY?
WE COULDN'T CALL 'EM. I TOLD YOU, OUR PHONES...
WELL, WE'RE GOING TO STOP BY THE POLICE STATION ON OUR WAY OUT...
LET'S JUST GO HOME. I WANNA SEE MANI.
ESPY, THERE'S A DANGEROUS MAN OUT THERE...
WHAT ARE THE FUCKING COPS GONNA DO?
ESPY...!
WE HAVE TO STOP BY THE MOTEL TO WRANGLE OUR GEAR...
WHAT ABOUT YOUR PHONE?
...THEN WE GO BY TLAQUEPAQUE FOR MY PHONE.
YOU'RE NOT COMING?
NO, YOU GUYS GO. I'LL BE FINE.
I CAN CALL RAY OR TAKE THE TRAIN BACK.
4.

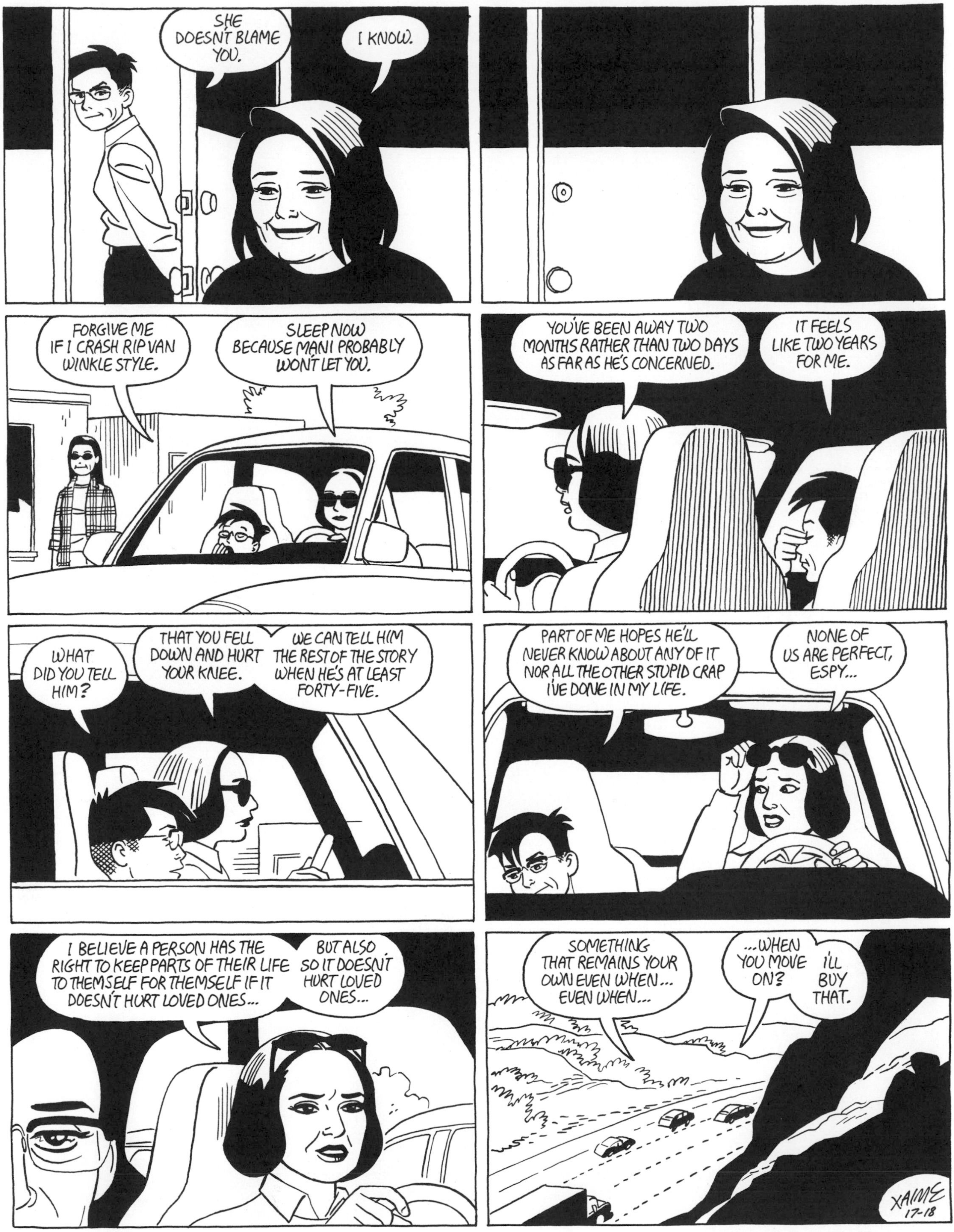
SHE DOESN'T BLAME YOU.
I KNOW.
FORGIVE ME IF I CRASH RIP VAN WINKLE STYLE.
SLEEP NOW BECAUSE MANI PROBABLY WON'T LET YOU.
YOU'VE BEEN AWAY TWO MONTHS RATHER THAN TWO DAYS AS FAR AS HE'S CONCERNED.
IT FEELS LIKE TWO YEARS FOR ME.
WHAT DID YOU TELL HIM?
THAT YOU FELL DOWN AND HURT YOUR KNEE.
WE CAN TELL HIM THE REST OF THE STORY WHEN HE'S AT LEAST FORTY-FIVE.
PART OF ME HOPES HE'LL NEVER KNOW ABOUT ANY OF IT NOR ALL THE OTHER STUPID CRAP I'VE DONE IN MY LIFE.
NONE OF US ARE PERFECT, ESPY...
I BELIEVE A PERSON HAS THE RIGHT TO KEEP PARTS OF THEIR LIFE TO THEMSELF FOR THEMSELF IF IT DOESN'T HURT LOVED ONES...
BUT ALSO SO IT DOESN'T HURT LOVED ONES...
SOMETHING THAT REMAINS YOUR OWN EVEN WHEN... EVEN WHEN...
...WHEN YOU MOVE ON?
I'LL BUY THAT.
XAIME 17-18
S.

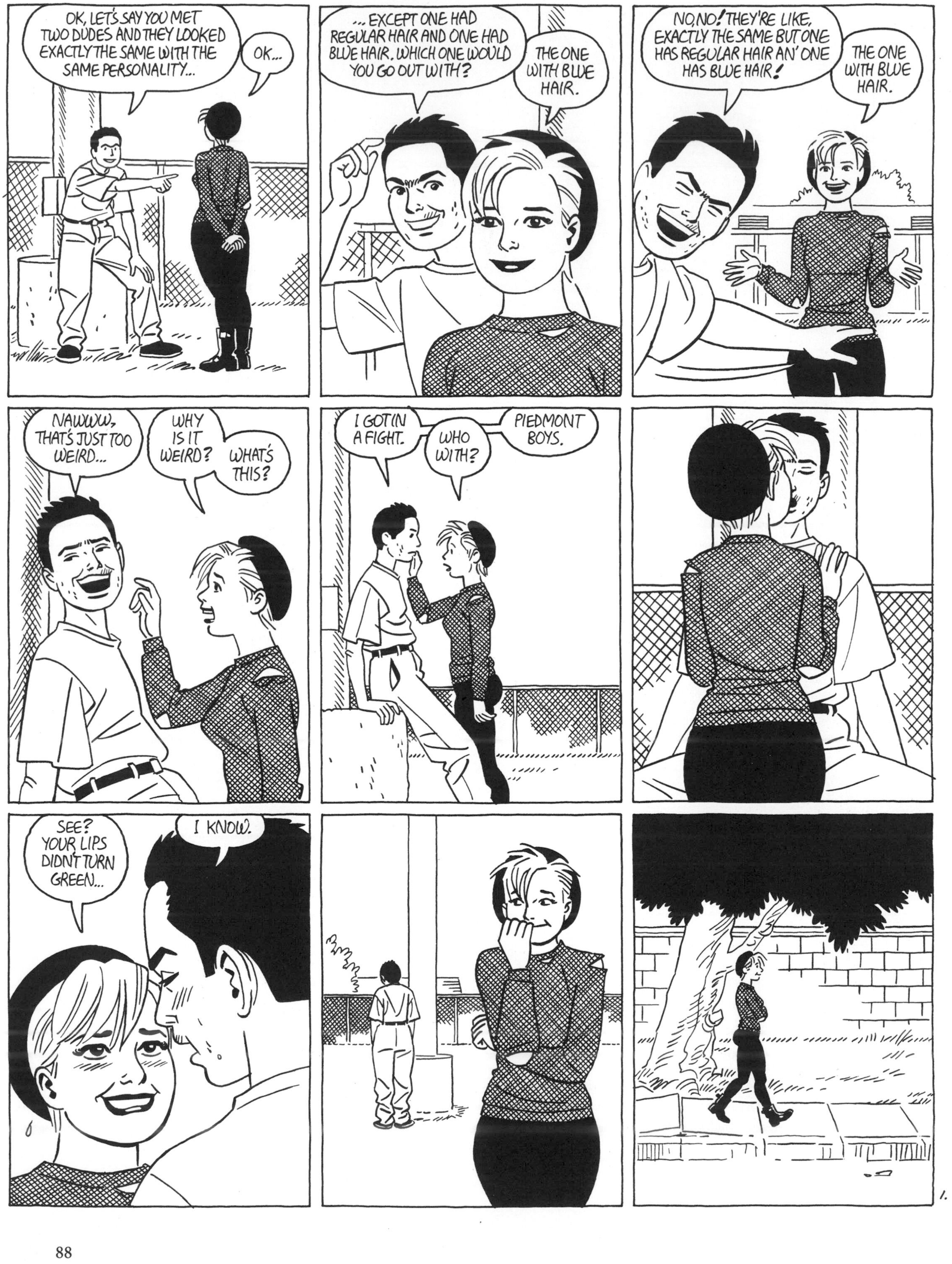
OK, LET'S SAY YOU MET TWO DUDES AND THEY LOOKED EXACTLY THE SAME WITH THE SAME PERSONALITY...
OK...
...EXCEPT ONE HAD REGULAR HAIR AND ONE HAD BLUE HAIR. WHICH ONE WOULD YOU GO OUT WITH?
THE ONE WITH BLUE HAIR.
NO, NO! THEY'RE LIKE, EXACTLY THE SAME BUT ONE HAS REGULAR HAIR AN' ONE HAS BLUE HAIR!
THE ONE WITH BLUE HAIR.
NAWWW, THAT'S JUST TOO WEIRD...
WHY IS IT WEIRD?
WHAT'S THIS?
I GOT IN A FIGHT.
WHO WITH?
PIEDMONT BOYS.
SEE? YOUR LIPS DIDN'T TURN GREEN...
I KNOW.
1.

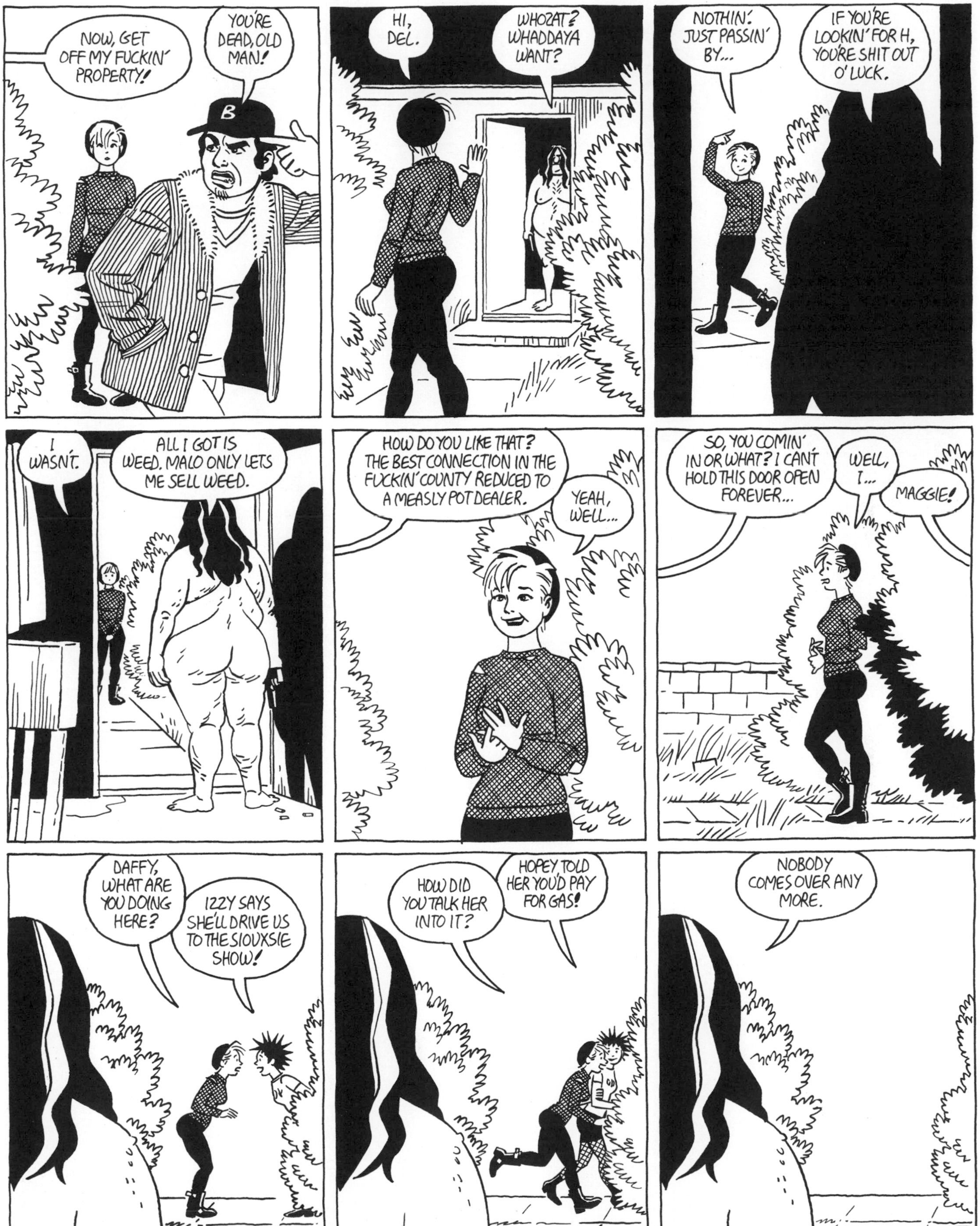
NOW, GET OFF MY FUCKIN' PROPERTY!
YOU'RE DEAD, OLD MAN!
HI, DEL.
WHOZAT? WHADDAYA WANT?
NOTHIN'. JUST PASSIN' BY...
IF YOU'RE LOOKIN' FOR H, YOU'RE SHIT OUT O' LUCK.
I WASN'T.
ALL I GOT IS WEED. MALO ONLY LETS ME SELL WEED.
HOW DO YOU LIKE THAT? THE BEST CONNECTION IN THE FUCKIN' COUNTY REDUCED TO A MEASLY POT DEALER.
YEAH, WELL...
SO, YOU COMIN' IN OR WHAT? I CAN'T HOLD THIS DOOR OPEN FOREVER...
WELL, I...
MAGGIE!
DAFFY, WHAT ARE YOU DOING HERE?
IZZY SAYS SHE'LL DRIVE US TO THE SIOUXSIE SHOW!
HOW DID YOU TALK HER INTO IT?
HOPEY, TOLD HER YOU'D PAY FOR GAS!
NOBODY COMES OVER ANY MORE.
XAIME
2.

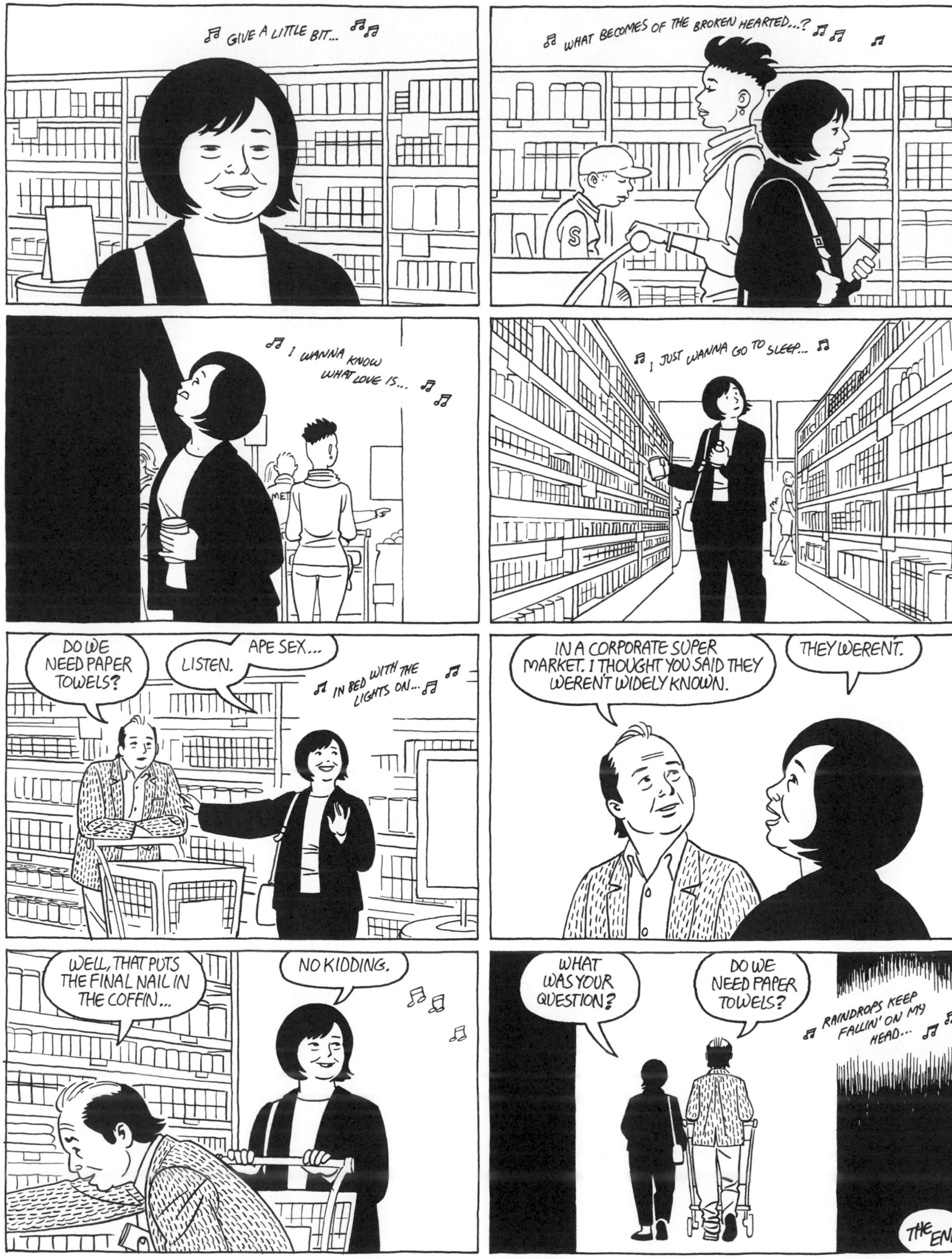
GIVE A LITTLE BIT...
WHAT BECOMES OF THE BROKEN HEARTED...?
I WANNA KNOW WHAT LOVE IS...
I JUST WANNA GO TO SLEEP...
DO WE NEED PAPER TOWELS?
LISTEN.
APE SEX...
IN BED WITH THE LIGHTS ON...
IN A CORPORATE SUPER MARKET. I THOUGHT YOU SAID THEY WEREN'T WIDELY KNOWN.
THEY WEREN'T.
WELL, THAT PUTS THE FINAL NAIL IN THE COFFIN...
NO KIDDING.
WHAT WAS YOUR QUESTION?
DO WE NEED PAPER TOWELS?
RAINDROPS KEEP FALLIN' ON MY HEAD...
THE END
1.

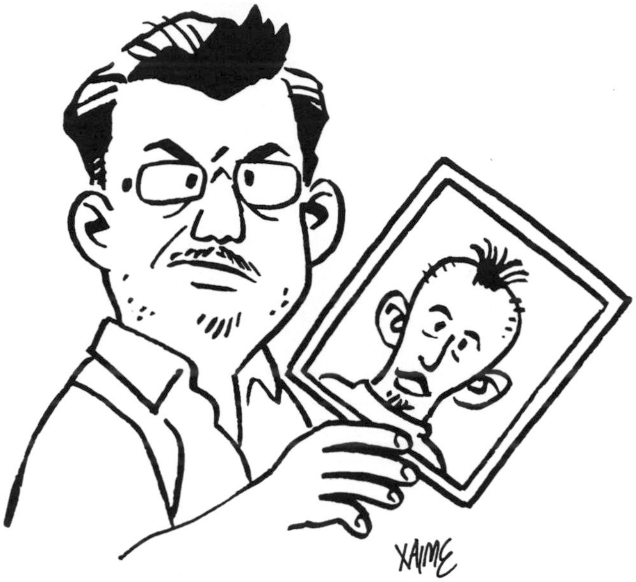
XAIME

JAIME HERNANDEZ was one of six siblings born and raised in Oxnard, California. His mother passed down a love of comics, which for Jaime became a passion rivaled only by his interest in the burgeoning punk rock scene of 1970s Southern California. Together with his brothers Gilbert and Mario, Jaime cocreated the ongoing comic book series *Love and Rockets* in 1981, which Gilbert and Jaime continue to this day. Jaime's work began as a perfect (if unlikely) synthesis of the anarchistic, do-it-yourself aesthetic of the punk scene and an elegant cartooning style that recalled masters such as Charles M. Schulz and Alex Toth. *Love and Rockets* has since evolved into one of the great bodies of American literary fiction, spanning four decades and countless high-water marks in the medium's history. In 2017, Jaime (along with Gilbert) was inducted into the Will Eisner Comic Book Hall of Fame, and, in 2018, he released his first children's book, the Aesop Book Prize-winning *The Dragon Slayer: Folktales from Latin America*. He lives in Altadena, California, with his wife, Meg.